Enthusiastic reviews for Lior Samson's novels –

Bashert (The Homeland Connection)

"Perfect! . . . a page turner that spins a good story."
–Peter Gordon, publisher

"Samson writes with a crisp elegance like John Le Carré and weaves his plot magically, sustaining suspense throughout the novel. The ending is a satisfying and surprising climax."
–James A. Anderson, author

"An ambitious novel, . . . yet succinct and readable, moving with the speed of light between interconnected events, three continents, and a group of unique and memorable characters. I recommend it."
Avraham Azrieli, author

"Samson keeps the pages turning in this retro-techno-thriller."
–Brett James, author, film producer

"An engaging thriller. . . . The characters are vividly drawn, with well-crafted dialogue that brings them to life and keeps you flipping the pages."
–Karl Wiegers, author, consultant

"I sped through this book, and then I re-read it, even though I knew how it would end. For a suspense-action novel, that's the highest praise."
–Johanna Rothman, author, consultant

The Dome (The Homeland Connection)

"Suspenseful and timely, . . . I cannot say enough good things about this novel."
–Alan Caruba, critic, BookViews

"An excellent read, and very highly recommended."
–Midwest Book Review

"Crisp, sardonic, sometimes amusing, and highly entertaining. [Samson is] a real story teller."
–James A. Anderson, author

"Showcases his talent for melding thought-provoking intrigue with non-stop action."
–Peter Gordon, publisher

Web Games (The Homeland Connection)

"This extraordinary author has the ability to anticipate events in ways that enhance his novels, and *Web Games*, his latest, is no exception. . . . You will not put it down."

–Alan Caruba, critic, BookViews

"An outstanding tech thriller—better than Tom Clancy. . . . This ranks up there as one of the best [thrillers] I've read in 2011." *– James A. Anderson, author*

"For readers who want their brain to be well-fed while enjoying the thrill-ride of action suspense. . . . I couldn't put this book down."

–Dawn Jones, teacher

"The story swiftly pulls the reader into a stream of events, . . . [and] the characters instantly come to life, as if you've known them for years."

–Jos P. van Leeuwen, university professor

The Rosen Singularity

"The plotting is ingenious and the characters come through strongly. It succeeds marvelously on the thriller level, but it also delivers a substantial intellectual and emotional kick."

–Rebecca Goldstein, MacArthur Fellow, author

"Vibrant and distinctive characters, and thoughtful, yet engaging narratives and conversations, . . . an exciting, pulse-pounding story.

–Laurie Jenkins, book blogger

"A highly entertaining thriller that weaves threads from cutting-edge medicine and biology, international intrigue, and cyber security."

–Bob Binder, consultant

Chipset

Also by Lior Samson, from Gesher Press

Bashert

The Dome

Web Games

The Rosen Singularity

Requisite Variety: Collected Short Fiction

Available from www.liorsamson.com
and from Amazon.com and other retailers.

The HOMELAND CONNECTION

chipset

a novel by Lior Samson

GESHER PRESS

Gesher Press is an imprint of Ampersand Press
Rowley, Massachusetts

Gesher Press | Ampersand Press
58 Kathleen Circle
Rowley, MA 01969
Author site: www.liorsamson.com

Gesher Press and the bridge logo are trademarks of Ampersand Press.

Printed in the United States of America.
5 4 3 2 1

ISBN 978-0-9843772-8-2

Cover and book design: Larry Constantine.
Text set in Gentium and Gentium Book, title and chapter titles in Nesbitt, folios and running heads in Antique Olive.

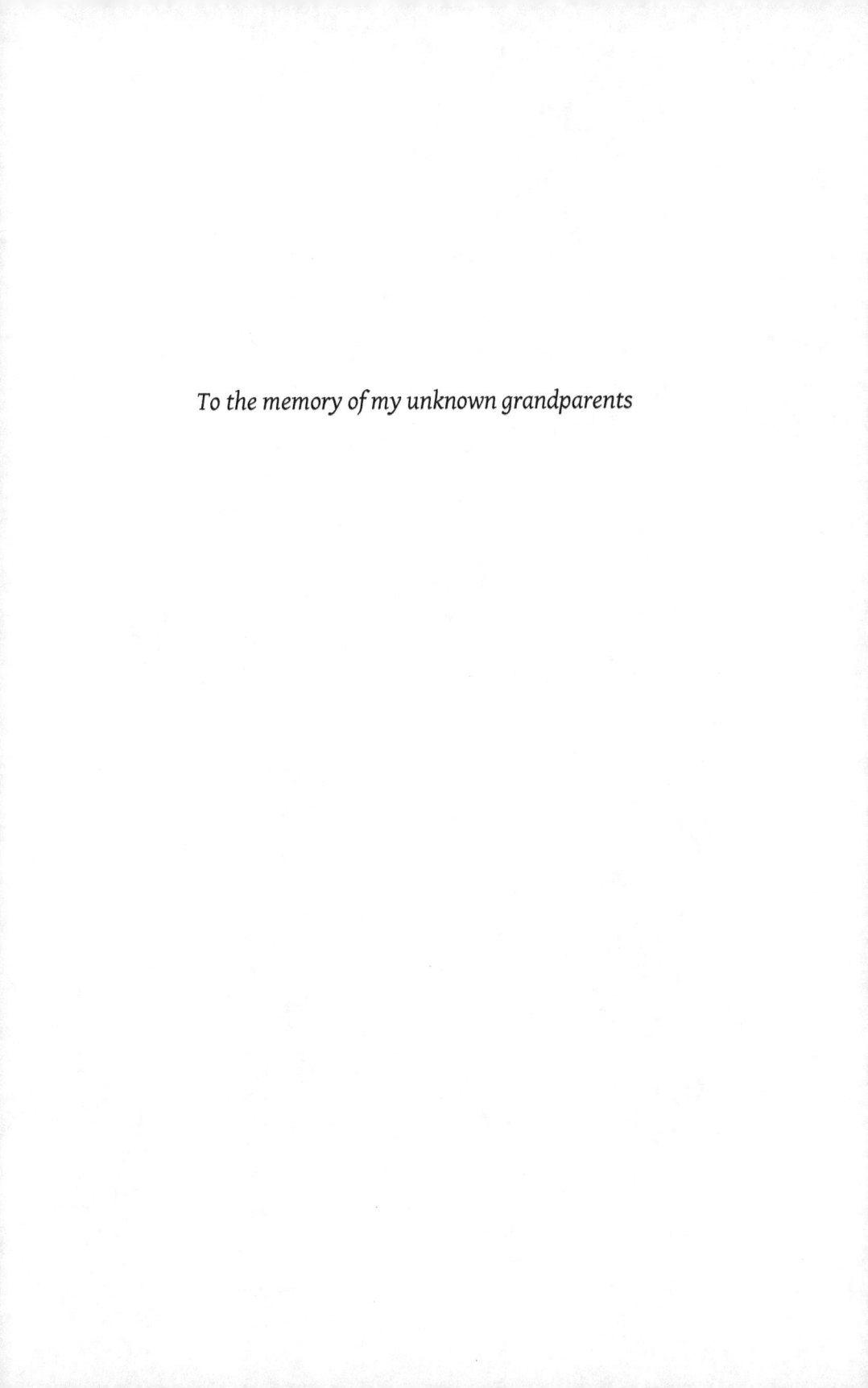

To the memory of my unknown grandparents

Author's Note

■ A word of explanation is in order. I have, from an early age, had this tendency to edge my way into things through side entrances and back gates. Today's new novelists seem to prefer to dash headlong up the front steps, often debuting as writers with the hubristic declaration of the first volume in some epic, umpteen-part Chronicles of Whatever.

My first full-length fiction was *Bashert*, a self-contained novel, which I wrote with no grand ambitions beyond telling well a good story—inspired by real events and real people but an imagined projection of both. I certainly had no fantasies about creating an enduring literary franchise. Perhaps this lack of grandiosity owes in part to a lifetime of progressive myopia, but, whether for real or metaphorical nearsightedness, I began without any clear vision of a fabulous factitious future.

A strange thing happened on the path from inspiration to publication. In the process of writing, I came to know some of my characters particularly well and to realize that they had further tales to tell. With the encouragement of my son, I brought them back to assume starring roles in another adventure. The result was *The Dome*, my second novel and the beginning of an accidental series that now includes four books.

With the current volume, the series has acquired a name, and a thematic thread has been revealed. This novel is, then, part of The Homeland Connection. The connection was there all along, and astute readers no doubt figured it out even before I did. As I wrote *Chipset*, I became conscious of clues, numerous and scattered, and of subtle foreshadowing in the previous three novels that pointed the way to, if not a conclusion, then at least a confluence of events and elements. This story, like the earlier volumes in The Homeland Connection, can be read on its own, yet it is also part of a saga spanning continents and decades. I do hope readers who start here will seek out and read the other stories that connect these characters to homelands.

As always, there are people who helped me get to this point. I'll start by thanking colleagues at the University of Madeira who helped with specifics: Ko-Hsun Huang, Yoram Chisik, and Roberto Sousa. Next, I want to acknowledge Roy Berger and the team at MedjetAssist, an organization providing air ambulance evacuation for injured and ill travelers worldwide. John Gobbels, their COO, not only spent hours talking by teleconference, but also provided feedback on the manuscript. As a part-time resident of Madeira, I am comforted that such a group exists.

The pilots and aviation specialists who reviewed and provided expert feedback on critical parts of the manuscript were a wonderful group who took me in hand and showed me the way through. They included Fred Abrams, William Babis, Roland Desjardins, Alan Hoffberg, Chris Johnson, and Cliff Noble. For engineering questions, I had help from Erik Christofferson at Raisbeck Engineering and Larry Franke at Avcon Industries. Larry was my go-to guy for technical questions about small jets and after-market performance modifications, and I thank him also for reviewing the manuscript. If there remain technical slips in the aviation scenes, it is no one's fault but mine.

Special thanks of a different kind go to Peter Gordon and Helmut Windl, who gave feedback and helpful suggestions on graphic design.

For this and the earlier volumes, many fellow writers have provided, through their work and their words, both inspiration and encouragement. Among them I want to single out a few for special appreciation at this time: Avi Azrieli, Steven Cherry (who has written a screenplay for Bashert), Rebecca Goldstein, Brian Levine, William Marantz, Talbot Simons, and Richard Zimler. The thriving online communities of fellow authors at LinkedIn and Amazon have also been great sources of inspiration, intelligent conversation, and the occasionally necessary dose of distraction from the loneliness of the long-distance writer. There are far too many individuals to identify by name here, but you know who you are. Thanks!

My peerless editor, Janet Lemnah, continues to protect me from myself by catching the attention lapses, misspellings, and malapropisms that everyone else who read my manuscript missed. Thank you.

My deepest appreciation goes to my hardest working reader and favorite critic: my wife, Lucy. A writer in her own right, she provides the pointed criticism, razor-sharp insight, and generous suggestions that have become an indispensable part of my writing process. She stays up late to read and mark up my drafts and then tells me in the morning where I went wrong. How lucky I am.

Chipset

Prologue

■ The cold white dot on the palm of Wáng Lĕi's hand grew into a small circle as a blue line crept slowly across the battlefield map on his computer monitor. Lĕi leaned over the keyboard, dripping cold sweat as he squinted and strained to bring the crisscrossing traces on the display into focus. His heart triple-timed as he reached to tighten the makeshift tourniquet on his left arm. Struggling to remember what his next move was supposed to be, he picked up the drawing stylus again from where it rested in its cradle.

A few more minutes was all he needed. He bit his lip against the frigid fire spreading slowly up his arm as he fought to slow his breathing and to steady his right hand on the graphical input tablet. Edging the stylus across the dull gray surface of the tablet, he nudged the blue line into its proper place in his battle plan. He was, by turns, clear-headed and determined, then dizzy and delirious. At moments he imagined himself as an ancient Chinese warrior in leather battle dress, except that his armor was nothing more than the motorcycle jacket he had not taken the time to remove when he entered the office, and his battlefield was a computer-aided design drawing painted on the monitor screen. In his right hand, his weapon: the stylus that he slid carefully over the graphics tablet in the ellipse of light cast by his anglepoise task lamp.

Lĕi looked down at his useless left hand where the pale circle kept growing and the numbers on his digital watch kept turning over. Not enough time.

They had come too soon. He had thought there would be days, maybe weeks in which to finish his work methodically before they came for him, but they had somehow gotten into the secured clean-room facilities of computer-chip giant Tenido Industries. They must have discovered what he was doing, and now they had delivered their message to him ahead of time. It could have been Kuo Han-Wei, left-handed Han-Wei, who had high-fived him on his way into the office. The pale image of that chemical congratulations for the completion of a new chip design was now spreading over his hand. He had no idea what it was, but he had no doubt that it was deadly. There would be no return to the mainland for him. He would not see his lovely Xiao-Lu again, or run with his son, Yuan, in the memorial park. He would not stand and lecture another class of software engineering students at Dalian Maritime University or argue with colleagues in the department over the future of automatic logic verification in computer-aided-design software.

He would finish the job, though, the work for which he would be well paid. Once his corrections were completed and submitted, the fee would be waiting in a Hong Kong bank and would ensure the welfare of his family even when he could not.

He tapped one of the function pads on the tablet to tell the computer to find an optimal rerouting for his newly drawn circuit path, then forced through a validity check on the test program and saved off the image. One more layer and the job would be done. He brought up another unrecognizable image resembling a nightmare cross between Jackson Pollack and Piet Mondrian paintings—a polychrome aerial view of a monstrous mega-metropolis, a complex urban landscape of endlessly intricate lines and lanes representing connections and components. The map, which made immediate sense only to Wáng Lěi and a handful of his most gifted chip-designing colleagues, loomed large on his screen, though the entire visible expanse was only centimeters across. He zoomed in to a scale that made features only microns wide look like broad avenues.

Instead of making easily noticed changes in the high-level design language typically used to describe such hardware, he was working directly on the layout for the microchip. He started moving what might be taken for buildings and parks and harbor-side jetties. He redirected streets and rearranged alleys. He dropped a grid of buildings into a newly cleared area and used a program override to force through another validity check, ordering the software to accept his word that what he was doing was correct. He was taking chances, betting that he had not misremembered the layout or the new interconnections, but there was no time for a real test that would have required hours of number-crunching, even on the company's powerful computers. The analysis had already been done ahead of time, piecemeal, in jobs submitted under forged login credentials and substitute billing codes. Lěi had been thorough and careful up until now, but now there was no choice except to plunge ahead.

He worked quickly, with long-practiced moves, even as his grip on reality and focus on the task that he needed to complete were slipping.

■ ■ ■

The computer was chirping away in protest when the night watchman found Wáng Lěi slumped over, his head on the desk and his right arm pinned beneath him, angled across the keyboard. The guard lifted him gently and shifted him against the back of the chair. At this, the computer stopped complaining and offered up a dialog with a green progress bar just resuming its crawl toward 100%. Without thinking, the guard watched and waited obediently for the final confirmation message to appear before reaching for the radio handset on his belt.

Chapter One

■ Karl was used to flying solo. Over the years, business trips had been honed to a formula. This was different. He knew how to deal with consulting clients; university students were another species. He could pack for a week in Frankfurt or Cape Town in ten minutes and have everything he needed. Ten days in Madeira with Shira didn't fit the template, and it felt like there was not enough time.

As always. Karl Lustig, conscientious traveler and consummate caretaker, had tried to allow a wide margin for getting them to the airport, but the margin kept being eaten away by the complications of abandoning the kids. Trying not to appear anxious, Karl stole a glance at his watch as he held the door of the taxi open for his wife. A wash of air-conditioned wind pushed ineffectually against the soggy Miami heat. Shira slid into the backseat, then swiveled toward him and smiled gamely as tears melted into the corners of her eyes.

"You're not going to cry, are you?" he said, trying his best to sound solicitous rather than impatient. "Shoshi will be fine."

"But she's only four." Shira flicked at a lock of her curly silver-and-black hair in an unsuccessful attempt to disguise that she was wiping the corner of her eye.

"Yes, she's only four, and she didn't cry. Look, Shoshi is with her Bubbe and her big brother, and she adores them both. She was even too busy playing doll family with your mother to say goodbye to us. Does that sound like a little girl who is unhappy?"

"But what if she misses me? She's never really been away from me, not for any period of time."

Karl was thinking about who would be missing whom, and the cabby was glancing from his mirror to the dashboard meter and back again as if to say, "Are we leaving anytime this week?" Shira scooted over to make room for Karl, who got in, closed the door, and put his arm around her. He opened his mouth as if to say something, but long experience had taught him that these were the times when it was best merely to listen and to wait.

There was a rap on the window behind him. Binyamin was holding Shoshi, who was cantilevered in his arms, straining, reaching out toward them with both chubby hands.

"Well, look who's here," Karl said, as he rolled down the window and threaded her through and into his lap. "Hey, my Shoshana-Banana, what are you doing here?"

"I'm doing goodbye to you and Ima," she said, scrambling over Karl and into her mother's arms. She curled up with her head on Shira's shoulder and ceremoniously plunged her left thumb into her mouth, a stubborn habit that had become more a declarative gesture to her audience of the moment than true self-comforting. Karl steeled himself for what could become a protracted extraction process, but Shoshi suddenly sat up again and climbed back into his lap, put her arms around his neck, and planted a loud kiss on his cheek, just above the margin of his neatly trimmed beard, the line that fringed his jaw like sparse dirty snow. The thinning hair on his head had been white for years, but his whiskers still remain specked with the umber of his youth.

"Okay," Shoshi announced, "now you can go to the air-oh-plane."

Karl climbed out of the cab with Shoshi, handed her back to her big brother, and gave him a grave pat on the shoulder. Now it was Karl's turn to fight to keep the tears away.

"Chill, Abba," Binyamin said, his customary amused grin spreading into a wide smile. "It's only ten days. She'll be fine; we'll be fine. You and Ima deserve this time away from us. You never really had a honeymoon. So don't worry about us. I'll take care of Shoshi. And Bubbe."

"I know you will, son, I know you will." Binyamin, who had just turned seventeen, was putting on years right before Karl's eyes. Bini, as he was known to them, had skipped the gangly teen stage and gone straight into being a solid young man with a sweet face, an easy temperament, and a tough body. In a year, he would start his military service in Israel, and he was already plotting his course for military intelligence, carrying on a family tradition of a sort by following in the footsteps of his late father. Migdal had been with Israel's elite intelligence agency, Mossad, before resigning to start a controversial Israeli-Palestinian cooperative trade initiative. Karl, who had had his own unconventional entanglement with Mossad, discounted his influence on his stepson.

Shoshi leaned back in her brother's arms and took his face in both her chubby hands. "Let's go, Bini. We were playing a game, remember?" Shoshi, who was tiny for her age, had the commanding presence and intelligence of a young Shirley Temple with chocolate curls. No visitor to the family ever failed to note who the ruling princess of the household was. Both Karl and Bini were like play-dough in her hands; only Shira was not completely at her daughter's mercy.

Shoshi, bouncing with impatience, gave her big brother a peck on his chin before adding, "Come on, I said!"

"Shoshi, *rega, rega.* Just wait." He shifted Shoshi to one hip and awkwardly fished something out of one of the lower pockets in his cargo pants. "This just arrived by DHL courier for you." He handed Karl a small padded envelope papered with an address label and a customs declaration that indicated its contents were dummy samples with only nominal declared value. "I thought it might have to do with your work."

"Thanks, Bini. It probably does." He took the envelope, noting that it had been opened and resealed by U.S. Customs and Border Protection. "Love you, Bini," he said. "We'll see you in a couple of weeks. Be good. Behave." Behind him, Shira was sending air-kisses but was too choked up to say anything.

Bini shook his head at them in disbelief and feigned disapproval as he backed away towards the condo building. He shifted Shoshi up onto his shoulders, turned, and broke into a trot that brought squeals of delight and protest from his baby sister.

"He's going to be a great father someday," Karl said, watching in wistful admiration.

"He's had a good role model."

"I mean, how many teenage boys do you know who can be so mature and responsible?"

Shira didn't answer. She was thinking of Karl as the young man she had never known, trying to picture him as a teenager. Even for an artist whose mental life was ruled by images and shapes, it was hard for her. Karl was already approaching sixty when they had met and married, and now, though he was as vigorous and engaged as men ten or twenty years his junior, she could see the years piling on and feel the reminders of the decades that separated them accumulating their effect with ever greater speed.

Karl, whose attention tended to shift quickly, was already occupied with opening the DHL packet. Inside was a plastic anti-static envelope with two large computer chips and several smaller ones visible through the cross-hatching of black lines. He held the envelope up near the window and tilted his head to look through the bottom of his glasses in order to check the markings on the top of one of the two-inch black squares: 27U466-CS.

"I sure hope those Customs clowns didn't mess these up." The geek in Karl was excited by their arrival—he had helped design them, and it was the first time he had actually held the finished chips in his hands—but he was also puzzled. They were supposed to have been forwarded to him in Madeira from German colleagues in Dresden, thereby remaining within the European Union and avoiding extra customs scrutiny. Somehow they had arrived at the wrong address at the wrong time. "Do you know what these things are worth, Honey?"

Shira turned away to hide the tears that had returned, pretending to be checking her handbag as she quietly said, "No, I have no idea. I don't even know what they are."

"It's a computer chipset based on the advanced avionics microprocessor I helped design. These are commercial-grade sample versions of the military chips which cost the U.S. government nearly $26,000 a set. Of course, we get them for much less, since we designed them." By 'we' he meant Israel and his consulting client, Israel Tactical Systems in Rehovot. The Weizmann Institute, which had close ties with IsTac, had rewarded Karl for his contributions to their industrial security projects by arranging for him to be a guest lecturer at MIRI, the Madeira Intelligent Robotics Institute. The computer chips for which Karl was now serving as delivery boy were destined to beef up the intelligence of the next generation of Semi-Autonomous Underwater Vehicles or SAUVs, free-roaming submarines used in oceanographic research but with potential military applications as well.

Karl held up the envelope. "Do you realize what these chips are to us? This is our all-expenses-paid ticket to a dream gig: three lectures over ten days on beautiful Madeira. This is our escape from the oppressive heat of Haifa to mid-70s weather, cloud-speckled skies, and brisk ocean breezes in Madeira."

Karl was not completely sure whose idea it was to leave the kids with Shira's mother in Florida, but the more he thought about it, the more he looked forward to teaching, hiking around the island with Shira, and sampling the joys of Portuguese wines. In the meantime, Shoshi would get to see Disneyworld, her grandmother would see enough of her and her brother to stop pestering Karl and Shira to "bring them over," and Bini would get to feel like he was not only free of his parents but also enjoying the status of being the man of the condo. And if the burden of approximated adult responsibilities got too much for him, he could always turn to his uncle Barry, Shira's brother, who lived in the area with Mark, his partner of many years.

There was no simple direct way to get from Miami to Madeira, as Karl had learned when planning the trip. Almost every route to the island required multiple stops and changes of planes. They had considered going through Boston, Karl's home base before he had moved to Israel and married Shira. From there they could take the Azorean airline, SATA, directly to Madeira with only a few hours stopover in Ponta Delgada in the Azores, but Karl, who schlepped to Boston several times a year on business, pleaded for something fresh. It had been many years since Shira had returned to England, where she was born and raised, and the two of them had never been to London together, so they had opted for Miami to Heathrow with a few days layover in London before heading on down to Funchal, capital of Madeira.

Both Karl and Shira had their own genealogical agendas for the trip. Shira's mother had distant roots among the Sephardim, Jews who had left Portugal for Amsterdam in the fifteenth century, then sailed for the New World, ultimately ending up in New York by way of South America. In her mother's eyes, their trip was a pilgrimage to Portugal, even though there was no known family connection to Madeira itself and the only thing Sephardic about Shira was her thick, black hair that only recently had acquired its silver-gray highlights.

Karl had another agenda. He, too, had roots in England, although they were as murky as a foggy evening in London. Karl knew that his parents had met in London near the end of World War II, that his mother was a "war bride," and that he had been born about the time his parents had married, implying an impulsiveness to their relationship that he had never witnessed himself. Beyond that, he knew little of their history. His taciturn parents, both civil engineers, had not been people to talk much about themselves. Dinner-table conversation when Karl was growing up in Upper Peninsula Michigan was more likely to center on strategies for stiffening suspension bridges than on family history. From them, Karl had gotten the message that reason trumped emotion and today eclipsed yesterday. He had absorbed an outlook that rarely if ever peered into the past. Until now.

With his seventies looming on the horizon and a nearly grown stepson full of questions, Karl had started digging. As a technology journalist, he was adept at online research and at tracing connections and contacts to fill in the blanks. His amateur genealogy, though, had led to little, so he had retained a professional, one Filomena Worthington, head of Bridges Genealogy Limited. She was now doing the digging for him, and they were to meet during his stopover in London.

Shira was looking expectantly at Karl as he snapped out of his reverie. "Okay," he said to the driver, "at last we can head to the airport. I imagine you probably have to deal with a lot of this kind of family departure drama in your work." Shira gave him a gentle nudge telling him to shut up, so he left it at that. They rode to the airport in unaccustomed silence—Shira preoccupied with worry over the children but determined not to show it any further, and Karl already anxiously rehearsing his first presentation for the students and faculty at the University of Madeira.

Chapter Two

■ Tourists with tots in collapsible strollers and travel pros with briefcases and Tumi roll-aboards paraded dutifully back and forth through the maze of moveable post-and-webbing barriers marking the snaking lines for the security checkpoint at Miami International. Even before he and Shira reached the podium where a bored security guard was flashing his UV penlight at boarding passes and checking identifications, Karl, a black-belt frequent flyer, had opened the side zip on his backpack, removed his jacket, and loosened his shoes.

Micro-managing as a way to cope with her own anxiety, Shira mother-henned them both through separating their computers, loading the plastic trays, and negotiating the metal detector. On the other side, the tray with Shira's netbook was followed by one heaped with her pack and handbag, but then the conveyor belt for the x-ray stopped and reversed. A hand signal from an inspector leaning toward the display screen brought another agent to the other side of the conveyor, precipitating an intense but hush-voiced dialogue. As passengers backed up in the queue waiting for their zapped carry-ons to re-emerge, Karl inched his way around the end of the belt to get a glimpse of what the holdup was. A TSA agent with a supervisor badge was holding a plastic bag crisscrossed with black lines and comparing it to the false-color x-ray display. Karl groaned and turned back to Shira.

"What is it? What's wrong?" she said.

"Do you want to say goodbye to your husband now or wait until they haul him away under armed escort?"

"What on earth are you talking about?"

"My jacket. I forgot about what was in it."

She gave him a look that mixed confusion with deep disapproval.

He lowered his voice. "Look, I'll explain later. Right now, just play along and stay cool. I'm going to have to think fast and try to remember what it was like working with Lev and Anat at Mossad."

The supervisor, a shaven-headed wrestler with a soup-strainer moustache, started toward them carrying Karl's tray just as another TSA person took off at a trot on some mission. Finally, the conveyor belt started moving again.

"Are these yours?" the supervisor asked, holding out the tray toward Karl.

"Yes. Is there a problem?"

"Could you just step aside and follow me?"

"What about my laptop and my backpack?" Karl said, pointing toward two more trays being shunted along by other passengers retrieving their belongings.

The wrestler nodded to yet another agent now approaching. "They'll be taken care of. Please just come with me."

Karl watched as his backpack and computer were carried over to a station where an operator stood ready to swab them down with a pad held in a pair of tongs. Still following the well-trodden footpath of feigned ignorance, Karl addressed the supervisor's back, "Can you tell me what this is about?" No answer. The supervising wrestler turned and gave Karl a look that said "I'm waiting" and stepped away.

Shira, who had been following everything with concerned curiosity, shouldered her purse and backpack and started to follow Karl, but the agent took a little jog, blocking her path, and directed her toward a bench along the wall. "You can wait over there, ma'am," he said.

At an unmarked door, Karl's escort waved an ID badge in front of a keypad, then punched in a code. The dull thunk of an electronic latch sounded, followed by a sharp be-be-beep when the man opened the door and waved Karl in. The room was windowless and bare save for four vinyl-and-metal chairs and a shallow metal table against one wall. Surveillance cameras near the ceiling winked from opposite corners. The door closed behind them.

The TSA supervisor set the tray he was carrying on the table, retrieved Karl's passport from it, and flipped through the pages as he waited in silence. The door be-be-beep again, and an armed federal marshal entered and stood to one side.

"You travel a lot, Mr. Lustig," the supervisor said, placing the passport back in the tray. "Can you tell me what you were carrying in your pocket?" he added, holding up Karl's jacket.

Karl ran his tongue along his molars, mulling over his choices, trying to guess what tactic would most likely get him out of the room and onto his flight with Shira. As he was weighing his words, a third man entered the small room and handed a clipboard to the supervisor. "Here's that list you wanted, Ed. Should I stay?"

"Not necessary, Julio. Thanks." The door slammed behind the dismissed Julio, and Ed the Wrestler set the list aside without looking at it. He pulled the anti-static bag from the jacket pocket and held it out toward Karl. "Anything to say?"

"They're computer chips."

"And?"

"And nothing."

"Would you explain what you are doing with them?"

"Carrying them, obviously. I was on my way to deliver a talk about them at a university in Portugal."

"Do you have an export license?"

"Should I? They are not being exported. In fact they were just imported and cleared by U.S. Customs without any problem."

"Is that something you can prove?"

"Sure, the original shipping packet is still in my jacket. Here, I'll show you." Karl reached toward his sports jacket.

"I'll get it for you. Is this what you mean?" He unfolded and held up the opened DHL packet.

"Yes, check the documentation. Everything is kosher. I'm just taking them back with me."

"That's called exporting. There are restrictions on exporting dual-use technology like computer chips."

"What about my laptop? I travel back and forth with that all the time, and it's got similar chips in it. No one ever asked me for an export license before. And what about all those other passengers with computer chips in their laptops? What's this really about?"

"It's about this list," he said, holding up the clipboard. He lifted his glasses and squinted at the chips in the poly bag, then started scanning down the top sheet on the clipboard. "And, bingo, there you are." he tapped a line on the paper. "27U466-TA"

"Sir, with all due respect, I suggest you double-check. I don't think the part numbers match."

"Looks the same to me."

"The difference is the last letters. I think if you check again, you'll find the part number on the chips from my jacket end in CS, not TA. It's a different chip."

"Do you care to explain what the difference is?"

"Yeah, I'm carrying commercial-grade samples; you're looking for military-grade chips used in tactical avionics."

The man glanced back and forth between the chips in the bag and the list on his clipboard. "How do you know about what these codes mean?"

Karl, deciding to risk being more aggressive, switched tactics. "It's my business to know." He reached toward his jacket draped over the tray but was stopped again by the supervisor. The marshal at the door took a half step forward. "I just want to get my wallet and show you my identification," Karl said.

Ed the Wrestler fished around in the tray, then handed Karl his wallet. Risking a bluff, Karl pulled out his IsTac security card and slapped it on the table. The official-looking plastic card, with "Israel Tactical Systems" across the top and the rest of its text in Hebrew, reflected rainbows from its authenticating hologram.

"I'm a U.S. consultant on industrial security with top clearance from the government of Israel. I helped design those chips, and I'm delivering them to government researchers in Portugal. A couple of phone calls can confirm all of this."

There was a long pause as the supervisor kept looking at his list and bobbing his head. "Wait here. I need to do some checking." He tossed the poly bag and clipboard into the plastic tray, picked up the identification card and Karl's wallet, and stuffed Karl's dangling jacket back in. He signaled to the guard to open the door and left carrying the tray.

Karl glanced at his watch: nearly four o'clock. Their British Air flight left for London at 5:25. It was a long and anxious fifteen minutes before Ed the Wrestler reappeared. "Here are your things, Mr. Lustig. Have a nice flight." He handed over the tray with Karl's belongings in it. "Your wife is waiting with the rest of your carry-on luggage."

"Can you tell me just what this is about?"

"No. Have a nice flight." He held the door open for Karl.

Karl, who was not ready to let it go, did not move to leave. "Was this an Interpol alert?" he asked. "Is the TSA tracking me over long-finished business? Is this connected with my work for IsTac? Have chips of this sort been stolen? Maybe it's because of my writing on cyber-terrorism." He watched the man's face carefully as he recited the list.

"I couldn't say, Mr. Lustig. You are free to go unless you want to file a report now. But I suspect that if you do, well, then you might not make your flight."

"I see. And thanks for confirming what this was about." Karl pushed past the guard without giving the Ed the Wrestler a chance to respond.

■ ■ ■

At the premier lounge, Shira finally confronted him. "Okay, what was that all about?"

"Nothing. Could be just random or could be that we are being tracked. It's probably because of my work. Once you get on some list, they hassle you endlessly. I know an author from Boston whose only crime is that he writes thrillers about international terrorists. He gets searched wherever he goes. It's American tax dollars at work, the post-9/11 plan for fuller employment in a down economy. If you can't get a job doing anything useful, you can work the lines at an airport."

"Are we going to get this treatment at every airport?"

"No, no. Just a pat-down and pawing through our carry-on stuff, most likely. That's how it usually goes."

"Usually?"

"Well, that writer once protested about being pulled aside for a second search just before boarding the plane, made some crack about his Montblanc pen being a dangerous weapon, since it was mightier than a sword. Those TSA guys have no sense of humor. They strip-searched him and took their time going through everything in his carry-ons. Made him miss the flight. He wrote to his congressman but got nowhere, of course. Still, it worked out—he got even."

"How?"

"He based a group of incompetent security goons in his next novel on the crew that held him up. The verbal portraits were pointed, recognizable, and quite funny. The guy doing the body cavity search snaps off his surgical glove after the anal check, sending a dab of do into the face of his buddy, and . . ."

"And that's supposed to be funny?"

"Well, not hysterical funny, but . . ."

Shira was giving him her lopsided squint, a signal to change subjects. "What are you up to, Karl Lustig. Please tell me you are not playing espionage games again."

"Okay, I'll tell you I am not playing espionage games again."

"Not what I meant, Mister."

"I know. I'm not working with Mossad, if that is what you are asking. But that does not mean Mossad might not be involved with me. Somebody is looking for the very microchips that I happen to be carrying to Madeira, or at least their close cousins."

"I still don't get it.

"In my surprise over getting the chips before we left—what with the kids and all—I forgot how serious it is that they were sent here. They were supposed to have been couriered directly from Dresden to the University of Madeira. I am guessing that the mix-up is because of a copy of our itinerary sent to my editor at iTech Weekly, which I also CC'd to my colleague in Germany, a researcher who consulted on that last project. He sent the chips to the wrong address. And I should have transferred them to my checked bags."

"What's the problem? They already went through customs without any hassle. They're not weapons or contraband, are they? What is the problem?"

"The problem is that it's a trade trapdoor. It may be okay for them to enter the country, but to take them out of the country without prior approval and a pile of paperwork is a felony. These may not be weapons, but they are classified as military technology. Export of this kind of stuff is tightly controlled in this country. So, when they took me aside for questioning, I just channeled Lev."

Shira's frown deepened. "Lev Novakov, I remind you, is retired from Mossad. He doesn't do derring-do anymore, and if you are going to think like him, maybe you should consider a similar career change."

"Don't start. You know that retirement is not in the cards for me, at least not now. Besides, Anat is still steering Technical Services at Mossad. So maybe from now on I'll just try to channel her. And I will tell you this. Whomever I channel, this old dog still knows how to sniff out the piss on the ground."

Shira gave him a sidelong glance of disapproval. "Just so the old dog doesn't return to old habits of howling at the moon or running with the pack."

"Don't worry. I don't do that kind of running around anymore. I'm just a consultant and writer. That's all."

"Right. And whom do you consult with? Defense contractors. And what do you write about? Industrial security. It does not sound like you have moved very far from your already well-marked territory, old dog."

"Look, all I want is some easy down-time with you, Darling, a holiday on the Isle of the Wood." Shira raised one eyebrow, but Karl, knowing there was no point in pursuing some resolution, let the matter drop. With their flight still an hour off, he headed for the bar to get them a couple of glasses of wine. There was plenty of time.

Chapter Three

■ The steamy air at Yi-Lin's on the edge of Ximending, Taipei's renowned pedestrian shopping area, was heavy with the smell of hot oil, star anise, and garlic. The early lunchtime crowd had already arrived at the tiny café, but there was still one place open at the counter. It was, of course, the only seat that mattered to Kuo Han-Wei. He sat down and placed his order. Then, as if speaking to a ghost hovering in the air straight in front of him, he began to address the customer seated to his right: a man he knew as Monchu but whose name was almost certainly assumed, a man of unclear ethnicity who could pass for Chinese or even one of Taiwan's aboriginals, but imperfectly. "The business cards" Han-Wei said to the air, "went to press five weeks ago. The proofs were perfect, no visible flaws."

He waited for a response. The man next to him, a head taller and a decade older than Han-Wei, only nodded as he continued to eat his noodles. He ate like an ex-pat foreigner, steadily but awkwardly, as if he had practiced much to cover up the fact that he had learned how to eat with chopsticks as a young man rather than as a young child.

Han-Wei felt compelled to continue. "The cards were delivered and the press has been thoroughly cleaned."

The man finally spoke without turning. "Yes, of course. We already know." His accent was Taiwanese, but like his handling of the chopsticks, it was practiced rather than innate. "But you moved in haste. It was too close and not as we had planned."

"But my invoice, Monchu, you will honor it?"

Now the man turned and smiled, a tilted smile that brought deep lines to his sun-leathered face. He could have been a simple farmer were it not for the cruelty that flashed in his dark eyes. "Honor?" he said. "What a strange word coming from your lips."

Han-Wei's lips parted slightly in unspoken protest.

"You will be paid. Promptly," the man said. "The briefcase at my feet is yours, I believe. Enjoy it while you can." As the man rose to leave, he put his hand lightly on Han-Wei's shoulder. "The people appreciate your work," he confided, "but your services will no longer be needed." He swiveled and joined in with the exiting crowd being buffeted by the next wave of diners pushing to enter the café. Outside, at the corner, he crossed the busy street, dodging motor scooters and the wash of pedestrians. He pushed into the revolving doors of a one-star hotel, nodded to one of the guests as he walked through the lobby, and exited directly out a side door.

In Yi-Lin's, Kuo Han-Wei could not resist checking the briefcase. He wanted to see for himself the orange fifty-euro notes bound in neat packets, the cash for which he had risked his life. He reached down with his left hand to feel for the case at the foot of his stool and apologized to the young woman on his left who was finishing her pork-ball soup. Lifting the cordovan leather case to the counter, he once more apologized to her. The case looked brand new, its two combination latches still set to triple zero. He snapped them open and lifted the lid for a peek.

Han-Wei and the young woman next to him, along with the server bringing him his noodles, were among those to die that day when the small bomb, hidden in the briefcase, exploded. The Taipei police, tracing the purchase of the briefcase to Kuo Han-Wei's credit card, treated the matter as a suicidal protest, without clear motive. It did not take them long to move on to other concerns. In that, they had their own motives and incentives.

▪ ▪ ▪

Yitzak Shuva rattled his fingers on the blue-and-beige half-wall of his boss's open office. "Got a minute?" he said. Even here at company headquarters near the Weizmann Institute in Rehovot, IsTac was an informal and radically egalitarian organization. Everyone lower than the President worked in cubicles. The company had a pedigree that went all the way back to the 1940s when it had been founded as Levitz Radio Works by refugees from Nazi Germany. As Israel Tactical Systems, IsTac, it had become, along with its less publicity-shy cousin, ElBit Systems up in Haifa, the axis of Israel's defense technologies industry. The innovative, roll-your-own electronics and complex systems both companies churned out were an important ingredient in the recipe that gave Israel and its defense forces an edge over competitors and enemies. Building on Levitz Radio's pioneering work in transistors and its early lead in semiconductor technology, IsTac had become an innovator in microchip design and fabrication. Its components powered many of the advanced avionics and weapons control systems that helped make the Israeli Air Force the best in the region. Versions of their electronics were also sold to other countries that wanted a similar combat edge, including the United States and its European allies.

Ari Fassbender waved Yitzak into his cubicle but didn't turn from the computer screen that he was studying intently, head tilted back and sweeping slowly back and forth several inches from the monitor, like a giant, bald scanner in bifocals. Ari was an old-school engineer-turned-manager. He didn't micro-manage his people, but he did keep a close eye on everything the group did. "Okay," he said at last. "What's up, Yitzak?"

"I have a request here from one of our consultants, Karl Lustig, who helped with the design of the new 460 series avionics chipset. He's giving a lecture at some university and wants some artwork for his PowerPoint deck."

"What's the problem? Why are you involved? Customer Relations can send him nice studio shots of some of our chips."

"He wants to show the insides, the architecture."

"Hang on. Is this guy okay? We are talking about the 460 series, right? Those are double-damn secret."

"He's legitimate. Came with clearance and recommendation from contacts at Mossad. And he was worth what we paid him, one of those guys who really can think outside the box. He contributed a couple of concepts that we translated into game-changing security features.

"Anyway, he seems to know how this business works, and I am not worried about him talking out of turn or posting pics on Flickr. His email makes clear he just wants a photo to throw up on the screen that somehow conveys something of the complexity of the CPU chip, which was his baby."

Ari took off his bifocals and chewed on one of the earpieces for several seconds. "I've got it. Send him one of those x-rays we got from the researchers in Germany, the, what are they called?"

"Ptychographs, x-ray ptychographs. You're talking about the computer-enhanced x-ray images, right? From our collaboration with the Technical University of Dresden?"

"Yeah, that's what I'm talking about. They have this new way of imaging microchips without opening them up and wrecking them."

Yitzak shook his head in disapproval. "Have you seen the images?" he said. "They resolve fine detail, yes, but pretty fuzzy, still, and they have yet to work out the tomography, so you can't visually separate the layers. It's all jumbled up. The technique is promising but not prime-time, not yet."

"Exactly. It will have the impact this guy wants, but without giving anything away. And the art has already been cleared for journal publication. Just pull one of the approved-for-publication images off the server, crop it down to one of the quadrants so it's incomplete, and send it off. My authority. I'll confirm it by email."

Yitzak started to leave, but Ari called him back. "What's up with the field test of that new chipset? Any word from ElBit or the IAF?"

"You know how tight-lipped the Israeli Air Force is? We aren't going to get squat from them until long after the systems are operational—unless something goes wrong. Then we will hear the screams all the way from Ramon in mere minutes."

"Okay, then let's hope we don't hear anything for a long time. What about ElBit? They are basing the next generation of drone avionics on our chipset."

"I've pinged my contact there, but they aren't saying anything either. I'll keep you posted."

Yitzak left and Ari returned to the charts he had been studying, part of an inspection report on a subcontractor, a chip fabricator in Taiwan. One of his engineers had just returned from a weeklong visit to the plant looking into the rising defect rate in some of the microchips turned out by the factory. The report was a piece of engineering detective work, a so-called root-cause analysis. The manufacturer had been experiencing a higher than expected reject rate on-site, and a tiny but worrying percent of the microchips actually delivered were failing the more stringent extended burn-in tests run by IsTac after receipt. These tests over-clocked the chips, running them faster than normal and at elevated temperatures for hundreds of hours. Military grade chips like these were expected to operate without error for the full test period. The engineer's report claimed to have found and corrected the cause, a single worker whose attention tended to wander. She had been transferred to another facility, and the chip failures had already dropped back below the statistical threshold that had alerted Ari.

Ari had never been comfortable with outsourcing the fabrication, although he understood the economic arguments. He trusted Israelis and no one else in the world—and not all Israelis, at that. He knew his own company like he knew his wife and friends. To him, everyone else was an outsider. Deciding to play it safe, Ari sent a note to Quality Assurance recommending a series of supplemental tests for all components coming from the plant in Taiwan.

Chapter Four

■ The best part of London was Sheffield, and the best part of Sheffield was the bogs. That is what Karl told Shira on their third and last day in England as he fingered the smooth wood of his newfound talisman.

Karl, for some reason, had always experienced London as stuffy, unfriendly, and crowded—and confusing. The early morning of their arrival had been spent trying to locate Bridges Genealogy of London to meet with Filomena Wentworth. When they called to get directions, the receptionist, who answered the phone, told them that the office was in Cheltenham Chambers "not more than a quarter-hour distant from your hotel." An hour later, when Karl finally admitted that he was thoroughly lost, they hailed one of the signature black London taxicabs, whose driver happily took them a few blocks and then hinted that a big tip would be in order for the inconvenience caused him by their ineptitude.

Filomena Wentworth turned out to be a large woman with blue-gray hair who spoke too loudly but with such a pleasant English accent that it was hard to get too fussed about the aural assault. Although she seemed to know what she was talking about as she rattled off the records and databases that had been consulted, she had come up empty handed.

"You did say her maiden name was Ryesdale, did you not? Well, I could find no birth record for a Julianna Ryesdale, and I looked from 1915 to 1935—with variant spellings, of course. Yes, I know you said you were sure she was born in 1925, but memory is imperfect, and, frankly, women have been known to stretch the truth when it comes to their birthdates, as might suit the purposes at hand. For that matter, neither could I find a birth record for you. No Karl, no

Karlfred, and no Fred either, not under Ryesdale or Lustig anytime around the 1945 date you gave me. Odd, wouldn't you say. That is, unless you're mistaken about some of your ancestry—names, dates, whatnot. I mean, we must have a starting point, mustn't we?" Besides being loud, Filomena had a tendency to rattle on without pause for response.

"Of course," she continued, "1945 was right at the end of the war and matters were sometimes raveled in the records department around that time. Rather disheveled, I might say, as one who has had to rummage through what some agencies passed off as paperwork during that era. You would think that wartime would make for careful documentation and close attention to official detail, but such was not always the case, I can assure you. Children were sent off to families in the country with no more than a slip of paper and two changes of clothes, parents perished in the Blitz, and aunts and uncles—sometimes mere friends or acquaintances—took on children as their own. Adoption by adsorption, one might say were one being clever with words."

"Wait a minute, adoption." Karl spoke quickly in order to squeeze the words in before she continued with her monologue.

"You didn't say anything about adoption, now did you, Mr. Lustig. That is rather a different matter altogether, wouldn't you say? Of whom are we talking? When was this hitherto unmentioned adoption? You understand, of course, that you are raising new issues here involving completely different records than the ones I was consulting. Based on the information that was supplied to me. By you."

Karl nodded, "I really should have mentioned it. I don't know for certain if anyone was adopted, but I have long had some vague notion that my mother was or that maybe I was. I just remember a conversation once. My parents were talking, and I overheard the word 'adopted.' Lots of kids imagine that they were adopted, especially ones that feel out of place in their families. That was me. People were always saying that I didn't look like either my mother or father. I once asked my parents to tell me the truth, was I their son? I must have been ten or eleven. They looked me straight in the eye and told me that I was their son, and they had the papers to prove it. Then I remember them looking at each other and nodding.

"That's it. At the time I didn't think too much about it, but now that I look back, it strikes me as a bit off. But maybe that is just my memory doing its thing."

"Well, now Mr. Lustig, seeing as how the researches have so far come to naught, perhaps we should look into this. Adoption makes the investigation a touch more difficult. This is not the United States of America with all its rights of the adopted and rights of that group and the other and with all the files accessible over the World Wide Web. But if you will permit me a little more time—at the same rates, of course—I would be glad to put my skills at your disposal."

At that point Karl looked to Shira for her opinion or approval. She shrugged. "I know my ancestors on both sides," she said. "This is your family. I'd say go for it."

With most of the day still open and Karl not terribly taken with London proper, Shira suggested they decamp northward. Having been with Karl to Boston on multiple occasions, she argued that, as long as they were digging into the past, it was time for Karl to see where she grew up. Although Karl pointed out that he was neither born nor raised in Boston, she dismissed it as irrelevant to her proposed excursion.

"This time of day Sheffield is only a couple hours by train from King's Cross," she told him. "Let's go."

So, on impulse, which had always been a core feature of Shira's temperament, they took the train to spend the afternoon in Sheffield, where they trudged up winding streets that intersected at odd angles and changed names every hundred meters until they reached the low, gray stone fence and the tall, gray stone house in which Shira had grown up. Shira stood at the weathered wooden gate that spanned between carved pillars, studying the house but seeing it not as it was but as it once was, with her and her brother playing in the back garden and their mother discovering the two of them hiding behind the potting shed, exchanging underwear. She was seeing her father, in his great wingback chair, with the sweet-dusty scent of his pipe filling the parlor, telling her that he wanted grandchildren, that she should settle in and give up on her silly notions of becoming an artist. She was hearing her brother casually sandwiching his coming-out declaration between "Please pass the salt cellar," and "Your pot roast is excellent, as always, Mum."

Now, Shira stood at the gate, staring into the past, while Karl patiently waited at her side. Then Margaret Farnham popped up from where she was weeding the flower beds just inside the fence and said, "Right, then. Is there something I can do for you?"

The house had long ago changed hands, but the Farnhams, the retired couple who now owned it, greeted them warmly and insisted they have a look around and then stay for a spot of tea. When Shira mentioned hiking on Hathersage Moor and Ringinglow Bog as a girl, the Farnhams' faces lit up. "Then we must do a bit of bog trotting, mustn't we," Margaret insisted. "Surely your husband should come to know the beauty of the moorlands before you leave," she added. With that, she turned from gray-maned retiree into the tour organizer she had once been, sweeping up Karl and Shira into her instant itinerary.

The afternoon proved pleasantly strenuous. As the four of them made their way up the climb to Birchinlee pastures, Karl had become fascinated by the deeply eroded gullies known as peat hags, black slashes that sliced into the landscape. Over protests from Shira, he had scrambled into one scar so deep that it reached down to the solid ground beneath the accumulations of peat. There he unearthed a thumb-sized branch preserved under the heath, a small remnant of an ancient wood that had once stood where now was only treeless uplands.

"Look at this," he said, holding it up for Shira's inspection. "I could drill out the center for the scroll, carve a *shin* on it, and turn it into a beautiful mezuzah with a built-in heritage from your homeland. This is amazing. Feel how smooth the wood is, polished by the centuries."

"More than centuries. It's been four thousand years, give or take a few centuries, since there were trees here," Meg Farnham told them. "That's a fossil you're holding there. A relic of a distant past, a piece of the wood that was."

"And you're a lovely fossil, my Meg, you are," said Chester Farnham, his first and last words of the day. His Meg smiled indulgently at him for a wink, then returned to her role as tour guide.

It was dark before Shira and Karl were able to excuse themselves. The Farnhams insisted on driving them to the station, where they caught a late train back to London. At King's Cross they emerged into a light drizzle that was just enough to be called rain but not enough to stop them from walking back to their hotel. Karl, exhausted from the excursion and still recovering from the five-hour time shift, flopped down on the bed and fell asleep while Shira called home for a long chat with her mother, Bini, and Shoshi.

Despite protests from Karl, after a slow start to the next day and a mid-morning brunch, Shira insisted on a walking tour of some of her favorite un-touristy spots. A basement museum of Celtic jewelry was followed by visits to a succession of art dealers, an antiquarian book shop, and, finally, one of the lesser but still imposing cathedrals that Karl endured with polite indifference. Following a long walk along the Thames, they finished the day footsore and even more worn than the day before. Karl wanted to call room service for a light dinner, but Shira reminded him of how much she hated hotel food and declared that they absolutely could not leave town without eating at what she claimed to be London's best curry parlor, Siddhartha.

Siddhartha turned out to be an unimpressive walk-down eatery with nine tables for four and a menu in the form of a simple matrix of selections—choice of lamb, chicken, duck, beef, pork, or "seafood"—versus curry style—madras, korma, dopazi, tandoori, tikki, balti, jalfrezi, vindaloo, rhogan josh, and regions and variants that Karl had never heard of before.

"There must be fifty ways to cook your curry," Karl crooned to the Paul Simon tune.

Shira groaned. "Your math is even worse than your singing; I make it 72."

"But that doesn't scan."

"Well, then scan the menu and pick what you want."

"Ah, but how do I love thee, oh curry. Let me count the ways."

Shira groaned again, then made her choice—beef korma—by closing her eyes and pointing a finger at the chalkboard menu. Karl went for his customary lamb vindaloo, the dish that he ordered on his first visit to any Indian restaurant, from Boston to Mumbai. It was his personal litmus test of Indian cooking.

On their way back to the hotel after a leisurely two-hour meal accompanied by multiple tumblers of India pale ale, Karl admitted that it was the best lamb vindaloo he had ever tasted.

"I don't understand your thing about vindaloo," Shira said, "I love curries, but the Indians go too far with vindaloo. Much too hot."

"It's actually the Portuguese, you know, with vindaloo, that is."

"Really?"

"Well, from Portuguese Goa. The name is a corruption of the Portuguese *vinho d'alho*, from the words for wine and garlic. See, everything is interconnected. Not just people, but things, places, ideas are all part of a web. Six degrees of separation. Right? I wonder what the Portuguese call vindaloo. Maybe vindaloo?"

They finished off the evening with a glass of Bordeaux in the lobby bar back at their hotel, then collapsed in their room in each other's arms without bothering to undress. In the morning, they had, by Karl's timetable, enough time for quick showers, a hurried repacking of their bags, and a perfunctory checkout.

Just as their taxi for the airport was pulling away from the kerb, Karl's cell phone played the opening vamp from Dave Brubeck's "Take Five."

"It's Filomena," the voice on the phone said, "from Bridges Genealogy. I have been following up with the Adoption Registry."

"Great! Were you able to get the records?"

"No, sorry about that, but I did learn something. I was wondering if you might call this morning. There's someone on her way here whom I surmise you would wish to meet. She also has something that I think you might find of some interest."

"My wife and I are, at this very moment, on our way to Heathrow to catch our flight to Madeira. Can you tell me what this is about?"

"Well, yes, of course. I've located your mother's sister, and she is on her way to our chambers with a packet of letters. She claims they were written by your mother."

Karl's heart started racing. He muted the phone and turned to Shira. "Do you think we have time for a stop on the way to the airport? They've found something of my mother's."

Shira glanced at her watch and shook her head. "It's going to be close, or at least closer than you prefer."

Karl hesitated a moment before tapping his phone and returning it to his ear. "We'll be there in ten. I don't mean to be rude, but it will have to be take-away style: just in and right back out again."

The woman said it would be acceptable and then disconnected. Shira gave Karl her what-am-I-going-to-do-with-you look as he gave the new address to the driver. The driver shrugged and said, "It's your bob."

At Cheltenham Chambers, Karl told Shira to wait with the cab while he ran in to meet Filomena. She was standing outside her office and smiled as Karl stepped off the lift. "I wouldn't bother you with this knowing that you are on your way to holidays, but I was quite sure you would regard it as important. Please, come in and meet Helen Ryesdale."

Helen was a handsome woman who looked to be in her late seventies. She had once been tall, but now was bent like a storm-ravaged tree. She stood and held out her hand to Karl. Her skin felt like limp lettuce against Karl's hand, but her brief grip was strong, and she smiled up at him warmly before sitting down again, folding herself back into the chair.

"I don't understand," said Karl.

Filomena gestured toward another chair. "Please, have a seat, just a moment, and I'll endeavor to enlighten you. As I told you, the Adoption Registry does not support online search, so I went yesterday to the offices to see what I might accomplish in person. I mentioned that I was researching the Ryesdale family, and an elderly volunteer who was making photocopies overheard. Ryesdale is not a terribly common family name, and she perked up at the mention. Seems that one Thomas Ryesdale was a social worker with whom she had once been employed at a private agency, the Bishops' Adoption Office, during the Forties. I consulted directory services, which is where I suppose I should have started instead of digging right into genealogical and adoption records. Sometimes I wonder where my head is. I rang up Helen here, and, well, it is her story to tell."

Helen Rysdale smiled and looked down at a beribboned package in her lap. "These were given to me by my older sister, Julianna. My parents adopted her at the end of the war. I only knew her for a year or so—I was ten and she was nearly grown—but I so looked up to her. My parents took her in during the war. She was a war orphan whose arrival in England was undocumented, and she had no papers. It was such chaos then and in the first years after the war, with so many orphans, so many children living apart from their families, so many people unaccounted for or without proper papers. My father, through his work at the BAO, was able to adopt her and shuffle enough paper and pound enough stamps to make it all proper, proper enough at least to get new passports for her and her son, Karl. Then the American came along and took her away. Or maybe I should say, she took him away. She told me when she first moved in with us, that she wanted to go to America, that she would marry an American. And so she did."

She paused when Karl raised his finger. "You said Julianna," he interjected, "and her son, Karl, right?"

"Yes, he was just a baby when she lived with us. For a while, she sent me letters telling me about her life and how fast Karl was growing and what he was learning. But the letters slowed and my replies fell behind, and then I married and started my own family. I always wondered what became of the boy."

"He became an engineer and a computer programmer and a writer who now lives in Israel," Karl said quietly.

The woman's voice dropped and her expression flattened. "Yes, of course, he did." It was unclear whether she understood who the man now talking with her was. Then her smile broadened. "These are for you," she said. "Julianna, your mother, gave them to me before she and her new husband boarded that ship for America. She told me to keep them until she returned, but she never did, and I don't think she ever intended to. She had a way of looking forward, never back, of moving, always onward toward something else. I don't know if that makes sense to you."

"Oh, it does, it does. I am much the same, ever peeking around the next turn, letting go of one ring as I grab for the next."

"These, then, are yours." She held out an inch-thick stack of fat envelopes tied into a neat packet with a faded blue satin ribbon.

Karl accepted the packet. "Thank you," he said. "I do apologize, but I really must be off. We should keep in touch, though. You are family." He tucked the packet under his arm and reached into his jacket pocket. "Here is my business card. You can email me."

Helen looked anxiously toward Filomena and then back at Karl, a pained expression spreading on her face. "I don't have email, but this woman has my details if you want to write or ring me." She stood to take Karl's hand again, this time holding onto it as she spoke. "Your mother was very dear to me, Karl, and a mystery also. She spoke little of her past or how she came to be in London, but I knew she had been through much."

"That was like my mother. My parents were two of a kind, neither one dwelled on the past. Like me, they were always too busy looking ahead." He held up the packet of letters. "Perhaps these will answer some of the questions I should have asked when they were alive. Thank you again."

▪ ▪ ▪

Shira made a show of looking at her watch as Karl approached the taxi. "Well?" she said as he got in and signaled the driver to take off. Karl set the packet on the seat beside her. "Letters? Aren't you going to look at them?" she asked.

Karl nodded, then very slowly tugged at the faded ribbon, which remained creased and pinched, retaining the imprint of the neat bowknot even after he slipped it from the packet of letters. The top envelope, a slightly different shape than the others, was blank, but the ones beneath were addressed, in German, the first few to "*Meine liebes Schwesterle*"—my dear little sister. As he riffled through the stack, Karl saw that some were marked "Liebe Hannah" or simply "Hannah." The bottom few were marked "Liebe Chana," a variant spelling of the same name. Shira, looking over his shoulder, asked, "So who is this Hannah? And who wrote these letters? It looks as if they were never sent."

"I thought they were my mother's letters, or letters to her, but my mother's name was Julianna. Her sister, Helen, I just met for the first time."

He untucked the flap of the topmost envelope and slid out the folded, time-darkened sheets within. "It does look like my mother's handwriting, including the flourish she always put on the tails of some letters. But, it's in German," he said. "I can read some of it. 'Dear Hannah,' it starts. 'It has been such a long time since I wrote to you and so much happened . . . has happened. I have met the most wonderful man, an American, where I work. He is with the Corps of Engineers,'—that's in English—'and they are here for now helping with . . .' It says *Wiederaufbau*, which is, something to do with building, construction, only *wieder*, again, ah, yes, reconstruction, perhaps. I do love the way Germans build big words out of strings of smaller ones. Anyway, going on: 'He speaks German but with a very funny accent. He . . .' I don't know some of these next words and . . . no, it doesn't make sense. I'll have to wait until I can get someone to translate these for me. I just don't know enough German."

"Maybe while we're in Madeira?" Shira said. "Didn't your friend say that a lot of Germans visit the island?"

"Right, we'll go down to the Marina and grab some tourist coming off one of the German cruise ships. *Entschuldigung, können Sie diese Briefe für mich übersetzen?* Excuse me sir, can you translate these letters for me? Yes, that ought to work."

Shira snorted in impatient derision. "Don't get sarcastic with me. We'll find a way. This is interesting stuff."

Karl nodded as he slipped the ribbon around the packet again and tucked it into his backpack. He was already shifting gears, thinking of the interesting stuff he would soon be talking about in Madeira.

Chapter Five

■ In the near dark, Lieutenant Rina Safam crossed the tarmac, her short-cropped, jet-black hair tousled by the faint desert breeze, her boots crunching on the pavement in the pre-dawn stillness as she strode toward her F-16i "*Shufa.*" She thought of the jet as hers, her "storm," as it was nicknamed in Hebrew, even though she was not the pilot but only the "wizo," the Weapons Systems Officer who sat in the rear seat and served as navigator and bombardier. Despite her country's vaunted commitment to gender equality, Rina had needed to work hard to make it in the Israeli Air Force, to reach the point where she was one of the small cadre of women who flew combat aircraft. She knew that her father, a veteran of Israel's ragtag air defense immediately after independence, would have been proud to see his little girl flying for Israel, his adopted country.

The ground crew were just finishing their last-minute ministrations, fitting extra armaments and completing the filling of the CFTs bulging along the upper sides of the fuselage. The streamlined Conformal Fuel Tanks provided an extended range for the heavily modified fighter-bomber. The maximum range was a matter of speculation outside Israel, but Rina knew it was long enough for today's daring, long-distance mission. In addition to the Israeli-designed avionics pod with its advanced radar and imaging systems mounted on the centerline below the aircraft, the loadout included two of Israel's newest weapons, enormous bunker-busting guided bombs that hung from hardpoints, the weapons mounting fixtures under each wing.

After the U.S. had failed to make good on its promise to deliver its most powerful ground-penetrating bombs, the 5000-pound GBU-

28, Israel had developed its own Guided Bomb Units. The long, slender GBUs now suspended below the F-16i were not the modest MP-500 that had been tested and publicized in March of 2012 in a piece of carefully timed political theater; these were its ultra-secret big brother, with deeper penetration than anything the Americans had yet deployed. Known as "*Maccabee*" or "hammer," the new GBUs had been designed with one particular target in mind: the deeply buried, hardened nuclear facilities of Iran. With its rocket-assisted approach, the GBU would hit the ground at nearly three times the speed of sound. Its hardened nose would take it drilling through earth and concrete, and sophisticated electronics would detonate its explosives precisely at the instant it reached the buried void of a targeted laboratory or command center.

This morning's flight was an exercise. It was always an exercise, it seemed, but Rina knew that any exercise could become the real thing, that practice and drill were part of what gave the IAF its enviable record of success on daring missions. All their weapons and munitions were the real thing, and for the first part of the mission they would follow the exact procedure that would be used on an actual attack run. The mission, if ever enacted, would be a bold and desperate move for Israel, an unsanctioned and unsupported first strike to put an end to Iran's nuclear weapons program before Iran finished the work in their preparation for finishing Israel.

Rina's pilot, Eitan Dantzig, a combat-hardened veteran with round cheeks, buzz-cut red hair, and an adolescent sense of humor, was in his seat running through his pre-flight checks as she climbed into her place behind him and then lowered the clear canopy. The first of their squadron already had engines ignited and were lined up for takeoff. It was a complex exercise, with twenty F-16i aircraft configured for bombing runs supported by a dozen F-15i fighters and six enhanced aerial refueling tankers.

Takeoff and the first minutes afterwards were routine. The squadron rendezvoused with their fighter support and settled into low altitude flight that would keep them below regular radar. Then Rina's displays lit up.

"Eitan, we are being painted."

"Too early for Jordanian radar. What is it?"

"Not X-band," she said. "Modulated Ku band. Odd. Now it's gone."

"Wolf Leader. This is Cub Alef. We've been painted. Anyone else?" They were using scrambled communications; had it been a real mission, they would have maintained radio silence until approaching the target area.

"This is Wolf Leader. Anyone painted with radar, report in." There were no responses. "Must have been a fluke. Carry on."

The flight continued for a couple more minutes as Rina watched her instruments closely and tracked their position. "Eitan," she said over the intercom, "we are approaching coordinates one-gimmel-one, our fail-safe point."

"I know. Got that, Rina. Hold your breakfast." Eitan flexed his wrist on the side-stick for a smooth roll and climbing turn. The plane continued on course. He waggled the stick side-to-side as a test. The plane stayed level.

"Eitan, we're nearly at the fail-safe. What are you doing? We have to turn back."

"I'm turning. I'm turning. Something is wrong with the flight-control system."

"Autopilot?"

"No, never engaged. I'm switching to backup, the old system." He reached with his left hand to flip up the cover on a newly installed control at the edge of the cockpit panel, then pressed and held the button to switch over to the backup computer system. He expected to see the displays blink, but everything remained steady. He pulled on the side-stick with some force, but there was still no response as they roared on toward the border.

Rina's voice on the intercom was fast and clipped. "We're nearing Jordanian airspace, we have to head back. This is just an exercise."

The radio barked in her ear. "This is Wolf Leader. What are you doing, Cub Alef. Turn back."

Eitan spoke firmly. "Rina, take control. Turn us around."

Rina's heart sped up as she twisted the lever that would switch the controls and make her the pilot. The F-16i could be completely controlled from either the forward or rear seats. She had flown in training but never since on a mission or exercise. She flexed her hand in preparation and took hold of the side-stick, gently rocking and twisting it to begin a turning climb. The aircraft continued, straight and level, on course for Jordan and on to Iran.

"Rina, what's wrong. Bring us around." The urgency in his voice doubled.

"I'm locked out, too. Nothing is responding. All displays are nominal, but none of the controls respond." Rina flipped switches and twisted knobs, but the array of screens before her remained stubbornly stable.

With neither manual backup nor override for the "fly-by-wire" computer-operated flight controls, they were helpless passengers. Eitan called Wolf Leader. "This is Cub Alef. We have completely lost control of the aircraft. No response to any input. Given the mission profile, we can't let this thing crash on foreign soil. Requesting permission to activate self-destruct on IFF and avionics pod."

There was a brief silence on the radio, then: "Permission granted. Better do it now."

Eitan ran through the sequence of switches to trigger the self-destruct on the Identify Friend or Foe, but the activation indicator didn't light. "Self-destruct is locked out, too, Wolf Leader. Destruct failed. Shoot us down. Let us know when you have missile lock."

Again, there was a pause that seemed to stretch on. In the lead F-15i, Captain Aharon Jacobi dropped back, swiveled his head to center the heads-up indicator in his helmet on the run-away F-16i, then squeezed the button on his side-stick. "We have missile lock. Bail."

"As soon as you fire, we'll bail."

"Too close."

"No time. Take us out now. We'll bail."

Captain Jacobi knew there was no time to hesitate; his duty was clear. He swallowed hard as he flipped the lid atop his side-stick and pressed down on the trigger, releasing the air-to-air missile at his own wing-mate.

In their F-16i, Eitan and Rina both pulled hard on their ejection levers.

Chapter Six

■ The Airbus 319 rounded the tip of the east end of the island and banked to circle for the approach into runway 05 at Funchal airport. Shira looked out her window and groaned. "That's where we're going to land?"

"Yes, isn't it beautiful? See all those pillars?" His voice shifted subtly as Karl dropped into what Shira always thought of as his lecture mode. "In order to have room to land full-size modern jetliners they had to build that section there. About a third of the runway is a bridge out over the ocean perched on concrete pylons. See? Those things are more than 200 feet tall. It's an engineering marvel."

The geeky admiration in Karl's voice was familiar to Shira, but she didn't share his enthusiasm, particularly while their plane was banking hard and she was wondering how they could possibly turn in time and land in an airport that, to her, looked like little more than an overgrown strip mall with a parking garage.

Karl, oblivious to her discomfort, continued his monologue. "Do you realize, with the mountains on one side and the sea on the other, and only one approach often cursed by wicked crosswinds, pilots have to be specially certified to land here?"

Shira turned from the window. "And this is intended to make me feel better?"

Karl, duly chastised, quickly concluded that discussions of the marvels of Portuguese civil engineering could wait for a better moment. He was a self-confessed propeller head, a born and bred geek who often had to hold his technical enthusiasm in check, particularly around his wife. She was an artist at heart who designed jewelry for a living, a living that until recently had made up for Karl's meager success as a technology journalist and sometime consultant. But her contracts with European fashion stores had been drying up while Karl's growing reputation had landed him several lucrative consulting jobs. He had been in the right place and time with a series of online articles on new approaches to industrial security. Now, he was in demand as an expert in a world of growing digital anxiety.

He liked playing the role of guru but was beginning to feel his age when it came to the pace of the consulting life. As a design consultant, he was paid well but was correspondingly expected to perform well, which often meant pulling technological rabbits out of scruffy hats on short notice. Since his consulting career had started to take off again, he had not yet tripped up, but there had been a few stumbles where the rabbit didn't want to come out or was none too lively when it did. Karl had always been good on his feet, and could usually tap-dance long enough to distract the audience while he came up with another idea. As a young man, these close calls had been exciting, now they made him anxious.

▪ ▪ ▪

The Airbus slalomed toward the runway in the gusty cross-winds, but the pilot found the right groove at the last moment, angled in slightly crabwise, and touched down with neither a bounce nor a skid. A few of the older passengers toward the rear of the plane applauded as the nose dipped in the hard braking maneuver needed to bring it to a stop before it passed the turnoff for the low terminal building.

After acres of controlled cacophony at London's Heathrow, Karl was unprepared for the modest size and marked informality of Madeira International Airport. He and Shira grabbed their carry-ons and waited behind the flight attendants as an open stairway was rolled up to the side of the plane. They exited into bright sun and a brisk but warm wind. At the bottom of the stairs, a uniformed woman in a fluorescent green safety vest stood and waved the passengers across the tarmac toward the terminal building a dozen meters away. Another woman directed them along the open walkway leading past a wall of murals depicting early settlers on the island rendered in the characteristic blue ceramic tiles known as *azulejo.* Inside, passengers drifted, following other passengers who seemed to know where they were going. Two flights of escalators carried them down past ads for Funchal's casinos and gaudy tile mosaics depicting a giant creature that neither Karl nor Shira could decipher. "Is that a chicken or an orange sea-serpent?" Shira asked. Karl shrugged in response.

At the bottom of the escalators, passengers milled around in uncertainty until a display above one of the three baggage carousels finally announced their flight from London just before bags began to tumble off the conveyer belt feeding the carousel. Near the exit, two bored customs officers leaned against the wall, but no one was stopped or questioned, and no luggage was inspected. Outside, in the small arrivals hall, they were met by a smiling middle-aged man with a mustache; his hand-lettered sign carried the single word "Lustig."

"*Bem vindo á Madeira,* welcome to Madeira. I am Luis. I drive you for your apartment. I apologized on my English."

"No apology is necessary. *Desculpe, não falo bem português,*" Karl responded, trying out some of his recent learning. "Sorry, I don't speak Portuguese very well, either," he repeated in English, for good measure.

"*Não é verdade. O senhor professor fala bem português.* Not true, your Portuguese is good, better than is my English, but I need to practice. Please, follow with me. I take your bags, Senhora."

Luis led them outside and toward a half empty parking lot and a cream-colored van with the blue-and-black *Universidade da Madeira* logo painted on its side. He loaded their luggage in the back, then opened the sliding door for them.

Leaving the airport, they were welcomed by a waving field of giant drooping phalluses, the three-meter flower stalks of agave plants nearly covering the embankment. As the van accelerated toward the first tunnel, Luis started a running narrative in mixed Portuguese and English about the many tunnels that threaded the island. The trip from the airport into Funchal, the capital on the south side of the island, would take only 15 minutes, he proudly explained, where once it would have taken an hour on winding roads. "But I am always the fast driver, you can see," he added. As they swung around a slow moving truck and accelerated into another tunnel, Shira gave Karl a look that said she wished Luis was not quite such a fast driver.

In the stretches between tunnels, the *via rápida* into town gave views of a glassine sea on their left and glimpses into small communities nestled in deep green valleys to the right. Defying the endless plane of the sea, the land was one of verticals: high bridges over steep canyons, houses climbing impossible slopes, terraces carving out narrow strips of land from the hillsides, plantings of crops and exotics stair-stepping toward the clouds.

Eventually, a view ahead revealed the natural bowl that was Funchal proper. On a smaller, steeper scale, the plan of the city and harbor triggered thoughts of Haifa. Here the terra-cotta roofs of densely packed houses peppered the landscape and reached far up into the hills, ending in a sharp line where Norfolk Island pines and scattered palm trees gave way to dense native laurasilva and the stately skeletons of the invasive eucalypts that together crusted the mountaintops. And over it all, the Cap, the cloud that hovered on the peaks, the loving fog that nurtured the trees and fed the springs of the island.

Once off the highway, wide lanes were replaced by narrow, winding streets that made sharp angles and climbed steeply up the side of the mountain. White and yellow stucco houses abutted the streets and perched on overhangs at cliff edges, stacked like storage boxes, crowding their neighbors. Everywhere, forest-green shutters covered the windows, and orange tiles covered the roofs. A glance down or up could bring vertigo, as Luis zigged and zagged on a route that seemed calculated to make them lose track of direction. Karl remarked that it must be confusing to drive in Funchal, and Luis answered, "It is easy to navigate in Funchal: east, west, up, and down, the four points of the compass. Your apartment is only twenty minutes from downtown and the waterfront; just walk downhill on the narrow street behind your building. Twenty minutes down and thirty minutes back, uphill. Simple. The University is just . . . but Professor Duarte will come to get you later and show you. At 15 hours."

The apartment, in a modern, five-story building on a quiet side street only blocks from the University, was small and dark. Shira surveyed the rooms, shaking her head in disapproval, then immediately set about to make it her own by opening the green shutters on all the windows and pulling back the curtains. She finally smiled again after opening the floor-to-ceiling drapes in the main room. A sliding glass door opened onto a small balcony that gave views of the stippled blue-gray ocean in one direction and a densely packed jungle of bananas growing in a small *quinta*, an urban farm just over a low wall on the other side. Flooded by bright light, the apartment's small rooms with their white walls and dark woodwork, suddenly expanded, and Shira was home.

She unpacked with the usual immediate efficiency with which she approached all transitions, made another quick call to check in with her mother, then sprawled out for a nap in the larger of the two bedrooms. Karl was too anxious about his upcoming lecture to nap. He had intended to use the long flight from Miami to work on his first lecture, but good intentions had fled immediately after the in-flight dinner and after-dinner glass of port. In London, he had clicked through the slides for his presentation and concluded that there were too many words, not enough pictures, and little action. He had to hope that the demonstration he planned would liven things up.

Karl retrieved his laptop from his backpack, carried it out onto the balcony, and opened it on the small table in the corner. While it booted up, he leaned on the hand-rail and looked out over orange rooftops and black-and-white church steeples toward the marina far below, where a large cruise ship with a giant cartoon eye decorating its bow could be seen steaming out of the harbor.

Karl logged in on his computer and found a Wi-Fi signal from someplace in the building on which to piggy-back. At the top of the stack of email that he retrieved was a message from Yitzhak Shuva at IsTac. He opened the attachment, a photo, then pulled up his

PowerPoint file, paged down to an appropriate point, and dragged the photo onto a new slide. Returning to his email, he scanned an item from one of his news feeds, a story about unconfirmed reports of the crash of an Israeli military jet in the Negev desert, denied by the IAF but attested to by both eyewitnesses and unnamed sources in the government. One witness, a Bedouin herder, claimed to have seen a missile strike the plane. Karl wanted to do more research on the story, but checked his watch first and decided to do the responsible thing and make one more pass through his PowerPoint deck. The rest of the several dozen accumulated messages would have to sit.

Chapter Seven

■ After finishing his review and correcting a couple of typos, Karl changed into his sports jacket. He gently awakened Shira, who complained that he hadn't left her enough time to get ready. "I was just trying to be nice," he said, "letting you nap a little longer."

Despite the protests from Shira, they were ready and waiting outside the apartment building ten minutes early. At twenty past the appointed hour, Duarte Camacho, Karl's contact and host at the University, finally showed up in a metallic-lime Peugeot. He apologized for being late, but added, "It is the Portuguese way, you know. Our clocks are set to Greenwich time, but we operate on Madeira time, which is twelve or twenty or even twenty-five minutes slower. You will soon become accustomed."

Duarte explained that he would be driving the route that Karl would follow walking to and from the University. "And then, we turn left here and down the hill and there it is. You walk down the steps over there and you are at the main entrance. To the left, is the University of Madeira and to the right is Madeira Tecnopolo, which is a sort of a research center and, I think you would say, business incubator, where our Institute, MIRI, has its headquarters. And there is also a center for conferences and expositions, but it is not too much used. The convention of the Portuguese Communist Party, auto shows, an occasional folk-rock concert that keeps the neighbors awake in the summer, that's about it."

The University, a single, sprawling white building, rose several stories and stretched down the ravine below. A bare, open plaza spread between it and Madeira Tecnopolo. Students milled outside the main university entrance smoking and talking, and scattered groups sat on the steps leading from the street or in small circles on the concrete tiles that paved the plaza.

"So, that is where you will enter, Doctor Karl, but we will have to drive around to get a parking place, which is a problem in the middle of the day because we have over 3,000 students and far too many of them have cars. A lowly researcher like me cannot get a space in the garage."

They ended up on the far side of the building where Duarte steered the car up onto the sidewalk and into a narrow space between other cars similarly placed. They entered through a bare metal door that opened into a wide, brightly lit stairwell. "We are here on floor minus three and must to go up to the floor plus two, so let's go around to the elevators. There is no time now for a tour, so I will take you directly to the lecture room. Oh, and we have the printer you requested. Professor Rui will be bringing it for you, but it is an old one, I hope it will be all right."

"It will be all right. That's what I wanted. I confirmed the model with Professor Delgado."

The second floor was brightly lit by skylights above a central atrium that sliced like a rectilinear Grand Canyon down through the entire building, flooding it with natural light. Duarte led Karl, pushing his way through crowds of students moving between classes and queued to enter lecture halls.

Karl worried over whether he would have time to set up properly, but, as Duarte had warned, nothing started at the appointed time in Madeira, and Karl wasn't introduced to start his talk until a quarter past the hour. People continued to drift in for another fifteen minutes or so during the first part of Karl's presentation.

▪ ▪ ▪

Karl strained his neck to check whether his PowerPoint slide was projecting correctly on the wall screen high above him. The tiered rows of chairs and narrow tables in Antifeatro 9, the lecture hall, were about half full, which Duarte had told him was very good. The students and faculty were listening politely, although Karl was beginning to wonder how much they understood, not because of the language—most everyone he had met so far seemed quite comfortable in English—but because of the highly technical and rather specialized nature of his talk.

"So," Karl said, "that covers the taxonomy of vulnerabilities in industrial control systems and also the exploits that can breach them. The take-home lesson is that any software-hardware system that is networked can be breached, and these days, almost everything is—or soon will be—networked. Trains, planes, and automobiles, televisions, stereo systems, and even refrigerators are getting Wi-Fi capability.

"With the automotive industry pushing for full-time Internet connectivity in new models, this is worrying. Police are adding to the worry by asking for the built-in capability of remotely disabling a vehicle. The smarter the car"—he advanced the slide to an image of a SmartCar, a two-seater popular on the island—"and the more its functions are under direct computer control, the more it is an open invitation to hacking and the injection of malicious code."

He looked out at the mixture of expressions in the audience, some already glazed and distant, some strained in fierce concentration. It was time for a demonstration.

"Let me shift gears here and draw your attention to that desktop laser printer over there that my colleague, Professor Rui Delgado, has just set up for me." He pointed toward a small utility cart just inside the door to the hallway. "You will note that it is plugged in, but otherwise not connected with anything else. Now, please note, this is a standard model, familiar to many of you, because it is the same cheap, obsolete printer that they put in many of the student computer labs." There was a quiet wave of half-suppressed, half-forced laughter. "In fact, this actually is one of the cheap printers that I had stolen from one of your labs." Another ripple of laughter.

"Professor Delgado, would you please come back up here and help me?" Rui Delgado rose reluctantly and looked around, unsure of himself. "Please, I just want your testimony on this," Karl said. The Professor stepped down from his seat in the front row and stood, smiling, beside Karl. "Tell me, Professor, do you recognize that printer? Can you verify that it is the same printer that you just brought at my request from, er, *Laboratório Dois?*" Somewhat embarrassed, the Professor walked across the room and made a show of inspecting the printer. He nodded. "Very good," Karl said, "and can you confirm that it has not been out of your sight since you brought it here and that I have not touched it?"

A somewhat anxious look began to spread over the Professor's face as he said, "Yes, that I can confirm, maybe. I think." The Professor's graduate students, all seated in the first row, were grinning.

"Okay, now watch this magic." Karl advanced to the next slide, which displayed a grid of labeled buttons. "This is my hacker control panel. I'll start here." He positioned the mouse pointer over a big button on the projected slide that was labeled "Connect." A light on the printer blinked for a few seconds, but otherwise nothing seemed to happen. "Not very interesting. Let's try another one." Karl clicked on a button marked "Print." The printer whirred into life, then began slowly spewing out a page, all black. At Karl's request the Professor reached for the page and held it up for the audience to see. "Voila! Magic!" Karl declared. The group laughed politely. "Right. And you all"—he gestured to the audience—"are thinking, 'Big deal!' All I'm doing is printing over Wi-Fi. Any twelve-year-old can do that." Many in the room were now smiling and nodding. Karl turned to the Professor. "And why are you holding that sheet of blackened A4 paper so gingerly, Professor?"

"It's hot."

"Well, of course, it's hot off the presses." No one laughed, so Karl continued. "Let's try this other button marked 'Fetch' and see what happens." The printer indicator lights blinked while an image of a printed page slowly painted on the projector screen overhead. It was in Portuguese and appeared to be part of a programming exercise. "Anyone recognize this? It's a copy of the last page previously printed by that printer, retrieved over the network from its internal memory. This particular printer only stores the last two sides printed, but some big networked office printer-copiers have huge hard disk drives that can store everything printed or copied over many months. Think of yourself as a corporate spy with access to this technology.

"Still not impressed? Okay, how about some real magic?" Some of the students sporting the biggest grins now nodded enthusiastically. "Okay." Karl positioned the mouse pointer over another button labeled "Fire." This time the printer started to print almost immediately, another all-black sheet, but then pulled the paper back in to print the other side. The sheet re-emerged, now all black on the reverse, but was instantly sucked back in. Out and in, out and in, only a few inches each time. The drive motors in the printer whined, and a stream of thin gray smoke started to rise from the back. Finally the paper was ejected completely onto the output tray, where it started to curl and smoldered for a few seconds before bursting into flame. The Professor jumped back and the audience erupted into cheers and applause. "Thank you, thank you," Karl said, bowing before tossing a wet towel over the now smoldering printer.

"So, what happened here? Who can tell me?"

"You trashed our printer!" cried one student, feigning indignation. Another called out, "You burned out the motors on the printer. So?"

"Well, actually not. All that whining and grinding was just for show. What I really did was remotely doctor the printer's embedded program so it over-heated the fuser, the hot little rod that melts the powdered toner ink onto the paper. I covered the paper with black to make it absorb heat more readily, then my malicious software spit it out at the right moment so that it would ignite when in the open."

One of the faculty near the back of the room was now demanding to be recognized. "But ," he began, "you must have cheated, because there is a thermal switch in all such printers that interrupts the power if the printer gets too hot. The thermal switch is not under program control; it's just a bimetal strip, a simple spring and an electrical contact."

"Thank you, Professor. You are absolutely right about the thermal switch, wrong that I cheated. I didn't overheat the printer, I overheated the paper and kicked it out just before the thermal breaker could trigger. And for those of you who are now worried and maybe angry at this crazed consultant who flies in and destroys perfectly good printers, I already had permission from the University to use a printer that was due for replacement anyway. So, you will get a brand new printer in your student lab."

"Yeah, and when will we get that replacement?" someone called out from the back of the room. "In another year, maybe two." The whole room erupted in laughter.

"All right, so now I think you understand that the vulnerability of programmed, networked equipment is real. I want to draw your attention to another button on my little control panel, the one labeled 'Burn All.' It launches a bot, a program that trawls the local network looking for printers of the same brand and then works the same black magic on every one it finds." He paused for effect. "No, I am just kidding. However, such a vicious piece of software would not be hard to write. With the right inside knowledge of the embedded program in the printer and the special commands to alter it, any of the grad students here could write that code. Which is why you will all be fingerprinted before leaving the room.

"After that little fun and excitement, let me turn to more serious considerations than office equipment and home appliances. Let's consider vulnerabilities and possible exploits in military install-lations and critical industrial infrastructure."

Karl told the group the now well-worn story about the Stuxnet worm, the malicious software uncovered in 2010 that had been developed by Israel and the United States to penetrate Iran's uranium enrichment facilities at Natanz. Stuxnet had targeted the industrial control systems that operated and monitored high-speed gas centrifuges at the plant. Once inside, it set about systematically and surreptitiously disabling them by abruptly speeding up, then slowing down the drive motors. Over a thousand centrifuges had been crippled before the plant operators caught on, because the Stuxnet code made it look to the technicians as if everything were running normally.

"That is known as a 'man-in-the-middle' attack." Karl told them. "The malicious code inserts itself between the operator panel and the equipment, making it look like everything is going well. It's like those heist movies where the thieves feed video recordings to the monitors so the guards don't see that the bank is being robbed.

"Techniques are being developed—I can't go into detail at this point—that protect against man-in-the-middle attacks by hard-wiring connections between equipment and the control panels for the human operators. The protection is built into the hardware and cannot be bypassed under program control.

"In truly critical systems, like the complex computer systems that help fly planes or run nuclear reactors, other new defensive tactics are being developed." Karl advanced to the next slide, a soft-focus, black-and-white image of a complicated lattice.

"This is an x-ray photo called a ptychograph. It shows part of the layout of a specialized computer chip, a ruggedized microprocessor designed for military avionics applications. This chip uses advanced multicore technology to pack more power into a smaller package. That package is part of a bundle of top-secret technology developed by Israel to make their avionics smarter, faster, and also signify-cantly less vulnerable to damage from EMP or electro-magnetic pulse.

"What is most significant for our discussion is the inclusion of hard-wired protection against malicious software. Built into the chip itself is circuitry and fixed programming that detects and blocks any program that could compromise the system. You might think of it as embedded anti-virus technology." He pointed toward a student in the third row who seemed to be busy surfing the Web on his open notebook computer. "It is like the anti-virus software that runs on your laptop. I can say nothing more about the details except that it is very clever and very effective. I know that, because I helped invent it working with my client, Israel Tactical Systems. More than that I cannot say or I would have to use my remote access skills to hack into the electronic locks of the University and seal you in this room forever." He paused for laughter that didn't come.

"Anyway, what you are looking at is a cropped x-ray scanning photomicrograph prepared for me by colleagues in Germany who have developed a highly sophisticated mathematical approach that uses"—he took a deep breath and spoke quickly—"wave-front reconstruction and collimated high-energy x-rays combining multiple long-exposure diffraction images into a single, ultra-high-resolution image." He stopped and took another noisy breath. "Or something like that, so I have been told. If you are interested, I can provide links to published papers.

"So, this slightly fuzzy graphic is a peek at the insides of our new chip with its embedded security technology." Karl stared at the screen of his laptop, then twisted to study the image projected behind him. He paused, puzzled, for several seconds. Something was not right. The x-ray diffraction image was not razor sharp, but there was enough detail for Karl to get a sense of the overall layout. He kept staring at the screen while some in the audience began to grow restless. He turned around, chagrined. "I'm sorry. I think I may have the wrong slide. But then"—the green dot from his laser pointer swirled over the intricate image above him—"it's probably not all that important, since, at this magnification, it's all just blurred lines and blobs anyway. If this is the right image, buried somewhere in there is the new technology I helped design."

Karl, thrown off by his confusion over the slide, was not in best form for the rest of the lecture, and the remaining minutes dragged. He took questions for the last five minutes. The questions were polite, and most seemed more intended to make a point than to get information. Karl finished up with a slide showing an image of the bright yellow experimental research submarine developed by MIRI.

"Here is the bottom line on security vulnerabilities in embedded systems. Just because the program is on a silicon chip and just because the chip is in your iPhone or SmartCar—or your semi-autonomous underwater vehicle like this SAUV designed by the Madeira Intelligent Robotics Institute—does not mean you have no security risks. If your system has connection with the outside world—any connection at all—it is vulnerable to penetration. If it is programmed—in any language in any medium—then it can be reprogrammed." He clicked his remote control, triggering animated bubbles to appear to be coming from the yellow SAUV, which tilted and then slid slowly off the bottom of the slide. The word "*Obrigado!*" replaced the submarine in the projection. "Obrigado. Thank you," Karl said above the quiet applause that followed. He glanced up toward where Shira was seated. She was smiling and giving him a thumbs-up.

Karl, still obsessing over the ptychograph of the computer chip, would have liked to have gone directly back to the apartment or to some office where he could study the x-ray picture. Either the layout wasn't right or his memory of the architecture was wrong. His hosts, however, had different plans for their honored guests. From the lecture, Karl and Shira were shuffled directly off to a reception at Tecnopolo and then to a dinner at Doca do Cavaca, a small seafood restaurant not far off the Avenido Monumental, a major avenue leading west out of central Funchal.

Rui guided them out onto the open upper deck of the restaurant and to a table with a "*Reservada*" sign on it. "This is my table. I ask for it especial when I come here. Please sit and enjoy the view back toward the Marina and up toward Câmara de Lobos. I will take you there also. Another time." When the waiter arrived carrying a large tray arrayed with several different whole fish, Rui reassured them. "This place, I think, has some of the best seafood in the area. If you haven't had it before, you should try the *espada preta*, black scabbard fish. It is a Madeira specialty, and they do it very nicely here, with banana."

"Which one is that?" Shira asked.

"The big one down the middle." He indicated what to Shira looked to be the ugliest creature ever to swim in the ocean. Black, with eyes the size of jar covers and a wide mouth filled with razor-sharp triangles, it looked like a fisherman's nightmare.

"Yes, I read that it's very good," she said. "And what is this pretty one?"

"Ah, that is *dourado*, what you would call sea bream, also very nice. I took the liberty of already ordering appetizers for us all, *lapas* and *atum*, and a wine for us to start, *vinho verde*, a light white wine, very traditional. But for the fish we will switch to a good *vinho tinto*, a red wine from the Douro region in the north of Portugal. We Portuguese drink red wine with fish or seafood, chicken, everything. But even better is a big red with *espatada*, a regional specialty, beef marinated in wine and garlic and grilled on a laurel stick. We will do that. Tomorrow. Or soon."

The appetizers arrived, a tuna and onion salad and limpets served in their ruffle-edged shells dressed with butter and garlic. Karl took one of the limpets and sent an inquiring smile Shira's way, who gave a small, quick shake of her head.

Rui passed the platter to her. "Do try one. They are delicious."

"Thank you but, no. I don't do shellfish. But the wine is wonderful."

Rui looked shocked. "No shellfish? But . . ."

Shira smiled broadly but said nothing.

Duarte jumped in. "Not everyone likes them, of course, and I have heard they can be a real problem for anyone with shellfish allergies."

Karl looked to Shira, wondering if she was going to say anything and trying to decide whether or not to offer an explanation of why a Jew wouldn't eat shellfish, but Rui was ready to move on.

"Your lecture was very good, Professor Karl, very entertaining. But do you really think the security threats are as serious as you try to make them sound?"

"You don't have to accept my word for it. Check with the experts: Kaspersky in Russia, Langner in Germany, Symantec in the U.S., or surf the Web. Parts of the Stuxnet code have already been recycled in new threats aimed at banks. The American defense people fend off thousands of attacks a day."

"That is the sort of thing I would expect from people who make money off of security threats."

Karl looked about to speak, but Shira, always at the ready to calm troubled seas, turned toward the harbor. "This is really a beautiful spot you picked, Rui. And this tuna salad is wonderful with the bread."

Lubricated by more wine, the conversation caromed from food to Karl's lecture and on to the wonders of Madeira as the dinner stretched out like the sea before them.

▪ ▪ ▪

It was late at night when Duarte dropped them off at their apartment. The food and wine, the hours of lively conversation about contemporary culture and timeworn tradition, had put all thoughts of computer chips out of Karl's mind. Standing on the veranda, looking out over the brightly lit slopes of Funchal and then toward the sea, Karl reached to put his arm around Shira's waist. "It's not all bad," he said, quoting the closing line from one of their favorite movies.

She tilted her head to lean on his shoulder. "No, not all bad," she said.

Chapter Eight

■ Rubbing his chronically reddened eyes, Heinrich Waldmeier turned from the monitor display on the desk in his tiny office at the Technical University of Dresden. A researcher who had led the Applied Radiation Physics group for most of its existence, his role now had been reduced to little more than administration and playing departmental politics. His name was on the door and still appeared on papers. He still spoke at conferences and offered occasional sound bites to the press, but it was the writing and research of others that he presented. His own research now fabricated budget spreadsheets and grant applications, his experiments were discussions with potential collaborators, and his analyses were devoted to explaining why samples that should be emerging from tests unharmed and still functional were instead ending up as scrap. He approached it all with dutiful resignation.

Heinrich turned back to the monitor screen and scanned down the columns summarizing the series of x-ray ptychography experiments, noting beam energy, exposure duration, angle of incidence, and all the parameters of each test run. Alongside ran frequent annotations: "sample destroyed," "sample scrapped," "discarded sample." It shouldn't be happening. He re-sorted the table and graphed its contents as plots over time to see if there were a trend. How odd, he thought, the steps in the bar chart showing the sample failures were evenly spaced in a seven-day cycle. Over recent months the lab had been transitioning from a pure research facility to one that also provided what amounted to a commercial service doing hard x-ray imaging for clients around the world. To keep up with both research and fee-for-service work, they now operated seven days a week using the weekends to catch up on what was euphemistically called sponsored research. It was this work that accounted for the bulk of the scrapped samples, most of them logged on Sundays. Were the technicians getting sloppy over the weekend? Could equipment fatigue be a factor? Was it particular research projects?

He generated a list of the projects accounting for the ruined samples. Tenido Industries in Taiwan was underwriting research on automated image analysis for quality assurance testing. That project accounted for the largest number of discards. Next in line was the tomography project working on 3D imaging in cooperation with IsTac, the Israeli defense technology company that had collaborated with the University on the original development of the ptychograph system.

He pulled up the sample disposition logs for those two partner clients. Both clients required strict accounting for samples, all of which had to be either returned or destroyed. All but a handful of the samples listed as destroyed were in a single family of microchips, the 460 series. Why did that series ring a bell for him? Of course, it was his colleague, the consultant from Haifa, who had requested two samples of the new 466 chips. The request had just been fulfilled at the direction of IsTac and the Israeli government. And now this. It seemed like an odd coincidence to him and prodded him into continuing.

He switched to the folder containing ptychographs from the Tenido-sponsored research and started flipping through images from recent experiments, beginning with the latest and working backwards. The high-resolution images had already been forwarded by encrypted email to Tenido for analysis. Something was wrong that he could not quite put his finger on. Each run produced a series of images; in recent weeks, they were all of the same chip from the 460 series, a large, multi-core microprocessor. To Heinrich, whose scientific training was in physics, the layouts on his screen made no more sense than the abstract modern art his wife preferred to hang in their apartment; all were just crisscrossing lines and irregularly spaced blobs. Why did this particular ptychograph stand out to him?

Suddenly it struck him: he had seen this image before. Not something like this image—they were all necessarily somewhat alike—but this exact image. He paged back through the other sets until he found what he thought was the match. He carefully aligned the images in the corner of his screen, then flipped back and forth between them. They were identical. As a scientist, however, he did not trust his eyes or any other form of subjective observation. Were they in fact identical or just extremely close? How could he check?

Heinrich called up a simple file comparison utility and scanned the two files. They were identical. They were not two different but very similar ptychographs from two runs; they were exact copies. Somebody had, on at least one occasion, faked the results, filing a copy of a ptychograph from an earlier experiment. What was going on? Maybe this was a cover up for a botched procedure. Maybe it was laziness on the part of one of the technicians. In any case, it was a serious breach of scientific protocol and of the contract with the sponsor.

He needed to figure out how widespread the problem was, but he couldn't just go browsing through many hundreds of images hoping to spot duplicates, then do byte-for-byte file compares on ones that might be replicated. Suddenly inspired, he copied all the images from the last six weeks into a single folder, then sorted them by file size. They fell into groups of four to six with the same number of bytes in the files, even though the files had different sequence numbers in their names. He sent pairs of files with the same reported length to the file comparison utility: 100% match, 100% match, 100% match. For weeks, at least, the technicians had been recycling results, shuffling and rearranging but actually sending off copies of earlier images. And Tenido hadn't complained. That was also strange. Were they not even looking at the results they paid so handsomely for?

Before he contacted Tenido or IsTac, their partners in Israel, he would need to have a talk with the technicians responsible. Weekends were not staffed by paid technicians but by post-doc researchers whose work activities did not fall under Germany's strict labor regulations. Heinrich typed an email and sent it to each of the group's three post-docs to make an appointment to see him in his office on Monday morning.

▪ ▪ ▪

At a campus north of Tel Aviv, a high-security site known to many Israelis as simply "The Hill," Anat Dorfman walked up the two flights to the small conference room, using the exertion to focus her mind. She did not know what the meeting was about, but being summoned by the Director marked it as important.

Anat, in her fourth year as Chief of Technical Services, was one of the highest ranking women in Israel's Institute for Intelligence and Special Operations, better known to the media and espionage aficionados as simply *HaMossad*, the Institute. Her small but elite crew of computer geeks and science-and-technology specialists was responsible for technology analysis and for technical support of Mossad operations around the world.

"Ah, good, TechServ is here." The new Director, an imposing figure with broad shoulders and wearing his signature military fatigues, stood at the end of the table and gestured toward a chair on the side facing the door. "You already know everyone, so let's get on with the briefing." He gave a sharp, throat-clearing cough, which he habitually did when he was displeased. "We have a serious and extremely sensitive matter developing. Dror, why don't you begin."

Dror Magen, who coordinated field operations in Asia, flashed a smile that lasted mere milliseconds, then opened the folder in front of him. He slipped something out of a side pocket, then reclosed the folder before Anat could get more than a glimpse of a first page topped with a passport-style photo. Without explanation, Dror sent a small, charcoal-gray object sliding across the table like a square air-hockey puck. Anat intercepted it with one hand as it sailed off the edge of the table. Without examining it, she announced, "A microprocessor."

"You can tell that without even looking it over?"

"It's my job to know, Dror, just like it's your job to know what's going on in East Asia." The Director squinted slightly and fixed his gaze on Anat for a few seconds before shifting to Dror, reminding them both of his disapproval of the recurring tension between the two. Anat fingered the chip and continued. "It's a no brainer. Size, shape." She turned it over in her hand. "Number of pin-outs arrayed on the underside." She righted it again and held it out at arm's length to read the markings. "One of ours, a new design, faster and more rugged than the 450 series it replaces, but plug compatible. Why?"

"Wrong question. The question to ask is where."

Anat tried not to let her annoyance at Dror's manipulation show. "Okay, Dror, I'll play. Where?"

"From Langley. The Americans. Shawn McCauliffe, to be precise." Dror, enjoying the drama, let another eye-blink smile escape. Between these tachistoscopic upturns, his mouth remained set in an inverted U that gave his perfectly round face an almost comical look. Behind his back, he was known as Smiley, not only an ironic commentary on his demeanor but a conscious nod among colleagues to David Cornwell, British master of espionage fiction.

"McCauliffe? That village idiot?"

"McCauliffe is no idiot. He only plays one on TV. Which is why I am skeptical about his motives for forwarding it to us."

"Are they returning it? Was it defective?" David Bulofsky, a recent transfer from Defense Intelligence, could be counted on to ask questions for which the answer was an obvious no. Hawk-nosed, with angular eyebrows like furry carets, he was both the youngest and most junior of the inner circle at the table. Perpetually unhappy, he carried the look of someone who had just caught scent of a garbage pail in need of emptying.

"Nothing of the kind," Dror answered. "This is not one of the evaluation units bought by the Americans; those all have traceable serial numbers both externally and embedded digitally. This one was sold to a CIA field agent working under deep cover—in China."

The Director twitched his hand toward Anat. "What's your assessment?"

"That doesn't make sense," Anat protested. "It must be a rebadged commercial grade chip. They are not cheap, but they can be had."

"What's the difference?" Another twitch from the Director.

"Nothing you can see. They are physically and functionally identical in all respects to the military components, except military chips are certified from -55 to +125° Celsius while the commercial ones fail at temperatures much above 85, operate at a quarter the speed, and lack certain undisclosed security features." She scanned the stares from around the table. "What? This is my job to know the small stuff. Like, for instance, the fact that the commercial versions are actually programmed to return small random errors on selected arithmetic functions, making them all but useless for demanding computations like real-time image analysis for target acquisition."

"This one is not rebadged." Dror responded with a tone of derision. "It passes all the tests and returns the correct handshaking code sequence when queried for security access. It's the real deal."

"Then how?"

The Director leaned forward, placing both hands on the table with index fingers extended as if they were twin pistols. "That's why we are here today. To find out—or to figure out how we are going to find out. This is obviously a serious breach of security. The scum who offered it to the American agent thought he was dealing with the Iranians. They, of course, haven't got the sophistication to reverse engineer it and then clone it on their own, but—"

"Where there is one, there can be more." Dror finished his sentence for him. "That, at least, is what the American was told. He asked whether the complete chipset was available and how many he could get. The dealer said, 'How many do you want?' As a matter of faith, the dealer promised to deliver twenty chipsets—the microprocessor and all the peripheral and support chips in the series—for an even million. That's dollars. Only fools are asking for euros anymore."

Bulofsky's thick eyebrows shot up. "The Americans aren't going to pay, are they?"

"Hardly. They are on this guy like fruit flies around a blackening banana. They want to track down his source, the source of our leak. For the Americans, even worse than the thought that the Iranians might get the technology is their near certainty that the Chinese already have it."

"They have proof?" Anat asked.

"No, just the certainty of context. The dealer who supplied the chip was Chinese. Well, Taiwanese."

Julian Savoy raised his chubby hand to speak, a pointless practice that no one else in the room ever observed. "The Taiwanese and the Chinese may play at rapprochement, but they still hate and distrust each other, direct flights between the island and the mainland aside." Julian was the group's other source of the obvious, but his simplistic declarations and baby-face features hid a field-sharpened mind that the Director had quickly come to count on to reach the right conclusions when the facts were obvious but the meanings were not.

"They may hate each other," the Director said, "but they both speak the same language—which these days is expressed not in pictographs but in dollar signs."

Anat's brow creased in concentration. "I'm wondering why the Americans sent this over and shared their intelligence with us. They must have a reason."

Bulofsky jumped in. "Because they are pissed as hell at us for losing control of critical military technology, and they want to rub our noses in it. And in this case, I wouldn't blame them."

Anat didn't buy it and, from the expression on his face, neither did the Director. "Since when did the Americans give us goods and information out of anger?" he snapped. "Or sympathy, for that matter. No, they give us information when it suits their purposes. They offer us help when their agenda is served. Something else is going on."

Anat bit her lip for a second, as if unsure whether to speak or not. "Maybe this time they want our help, but don't want to make an official request through channels."

The Director nodded approvingly. "That, at least, is plausible. Their efforts in China may be floundering, which they would not want to admit, so they want us to work it from the other end, which we had better do because this has the makings of a security disaster."

"And they know that, too," Julian tossed in, "so we do their scut work, which makes us into just another branch of the American intelligence services."

The Director stood up. "So be it," he said. "For now. But remember, as the branch is bent, so grows the tree. We'll bend, even as we are making the tree lean in a direction of our choosing. Dror, get our guy in China on this. You take the lead. Anat and the rest of you, give Dror whatever he needs, but no independent action. This has got to be focused, efficient, and quiet. I want answers and fast."

Chapter Nine

■ Anat's low heels rattled on the steps as she hurried back down to her office. She had no intention of dropping down on all fours to become Dror Magen's beast of burden. As she always had done, she would quietly start her own line of investigation, beginning with reviewing everything she could get her hands on about the 460 series chipsets. What made them worth fifty-thousand dollars each on the illegal arms market?

At her desk, she pulled out the microprocessor that she had casually pocketed back in the Director's office. It always amazed her how much you could get by with when surrounded by people who trust each other. The same move in the field somewhere would have been noticed in an instant; here at headquarters, the tradecraft that everyone learned in training was shelved and replaced with casual credulity.

The chip bore the logo of Israel's own IsTac Systems. The part number ending in TA marked it as military grade. There was a shiny area on the otherwise matte upper surface where an etched external serial number had been polished off. She wondered if one of her people might be able to somehow recover the serial number with the right chemicals or imaging techniques.

She was about to take a macro photo of it with the camera she kept in her desk drawer when her phone rang.

There was a sharp cough on the line.

Anat smiled to herself. "Director, so soon. Is there anything I can do for you?"

"Return the chip to me when you're done."

"What chip? I thought Dror had it."

Another staccato cough. "The hand may be quicker than the eye for Dror, who was too busy thinking ahead about leading this mission and what the payoff might be for his career if he succeeds or the cost if he fails, but, please, give me credit. I see all and know all. That's how I got this job. I may be new to the position, but I am no newbie. I got here the hard way, by noticing what others miss. Do what you need to with the chip, but just get it back to me."

"Right."

"And don't wreck it in the process."

"Right."

"Tell me what you come up with. Not Dror. And certainly not Bulofsky. Just me."

"Got it."

"Remember, you report to me. Support Dror as long as it doesn't compromise that."

"Thank you, sir."

"Yeah." The phone clicked off.

This was the way Anat liked to work, with a free rein, unencumbered by oversight, but with an implicit mandate. Dror Magen, who followed and believed in procedure, wouldn't know what to do with that sort of remit. It was unclear what the Director's full agenda was, but Anat seemed now to be part of it with both Magen and Bulofsky possibly under some suspicion.

She started with researching the technical details of the 460 series chipset with its exotic new microprocessor. She already knew that it was not functionally any major breakthrough. In fact, the whole idea of the project had been to maintain backwards compatibility by keeping the same pin-outs and instruction set, while turbo-charging the engine inside. It accomplished that by crowding more components into the same little box, including a multi-core architecture that allowed it to do as many as 16 tasks in parallel supported by innovative logic that enabled it to extract latent opportunities for concurrent calculation without requiring any new programming. Coupled with its much faster clock rate and tolerance for higher temperature operation, it was considered a major step forward in military computing technology. Defense contractors like

ElBit, IsTac, and others were already using it at the heart of complete new systems with enhanced features and capability made possible by the powerful microprocessor. Because of the pin-for-pin and instruction-for-instruction compatibility, its adoption for high-end applications had been remarkably fast, despite its high single-unit price and carefully controlled availability.

After reviewing the technical dossier, Anat turned to the people side of the picture, searching through internal files, news stories, and field intelligence for names of people and organizations associated with the design, development, and deployment of the new chips. Among the handful of usual suspects and a bunch of new names and faces, one in particular leapt out at her. The same name was found to be associated with two intent-to-file applications for patents that had been shunted aside and blocked for security reasons. That name also appeared in news stories on IsTac's "digital dream team," as well as on a list of visitors on a trade junket to Taiwan that included visits to several chip fabricators. "There it is, the Taiwan connection," she mumbled. "But I still do not understand what are we doing farming out manufacturing of critical military technology."

She did a quick search for other matches with Taiwan that turned up links to Tenido Industries. Among hits from searches linking IsTac and Tenido were a couple of requests for special access that were sufficiently unusual to have made their way to the upper reaches of Israel's defense decision makers. Both referenced the same familiar name.

"Not again, Karl Lustig. How is it that you can have such a talent for getting your nose into dark corners and your name on search results here at HaMossad?" She and her predecessor in Technical Services, her husband, Lev Novikov, had each worked with Karl on an ex-officio basis that was frowned on even though it had produced results. Anat had nearly had her post and security clearance taken away for the last episode, where she had run Karl as something between an outside asset and an inside operative in a manner that the then Director strongly disapproved. It had not helped that Karl was not Israeli but an American living in Israel.

On the other hand, Anat and Lev knew both Karl and his wife well and trusted them. The thought of that brought Anat up short. It was the people you trusted that got you into trouble. The first rule of intelligence work was to trust no one. It was a rule against which Anat had always chafed, not because it was not valid or useful but because it was not her. She could not go through life living lies and confiding in no one, which is why she had taken a desk-bound career path rather than becoming a *katsa* working in the field. There were many things about her work that she never discussed with Lev, but not because she couldn't or wouldn't trust him. If the need arose, she knew she would break protocol, even break the law, rather than let something come between them. On the other hand, the very fact that Lev was one of them, ex-Mossad, meant that he understood and would never ask her to violate confidentiality.

"So, where are you now, Karl Lustig? What are you doing that will make my work harder and my life messier? And how can we exploit you one more time?"

She knew she could always reach Karl by email or even call his cell phone, but some instinct told her to track him down without alerting him to her interest. Besides, she had access to information in databases around the world, including a good many for which she was not supposed to have access. The United States had publicly disclaimed the technology that, as part of its anti-terrorism enterprise, tracked and recorded all electronic traffic crossing its borders, whether as email, Web surfing, or voice communication. Anat and her colleagues knew that all this traffic was not only recorded but also permanently archived digitally. What the Americans did not know was that Anat's group had long ago hacked into American computer installations and could access pretty much anything that Homeland Security or the National Security Agency could.

Earlier, the Americans had collaborated with Israel on programming the Stuxnet software worm used to attack Iran's uranium enrichment plant at Natanz. In the process, Mossad's crack coding teams had used temporary privileged access to plant Trojan software that gave permanent backdoor entry to most of the US systems. This access had to be used judiciously and infrequently, lest it be detected, but it was there when needed.

Anat used Karl's passport number as a search key and immediately hit pay dirt. She had his entry into the US, his exit four days later, and his entry into the UK by way of London. So, he was in England. Anat remembered that Shira had grown up in England. Was she with him? Another query showed Shira Markham on the same itinerary. Anat sent a coded message to someone she knew in London.

Almost at the same moment, watchers at two facilities separated by ten time zones, scanned the summary of Anat's actions and concluded that they needed to take action as well.

▪ ▪ ▪

His name was Monchu to the Chinese he had just had dinner with, but it had also been Ahmed and Marcus and many others before, and it soon would be something else. To find out his new name and his next assignment, Monchu needed to check in with his handlers. He searched out a YouTube video on his laptop and watched it without particular interest as a browser add-in, a free download helper, saved off a copy to his hard drive. The video was popular, although it had yet to go viral. Some idiot young male with more daring than brains—plus an evident but unacknowledged death wish—was seen in quick cuts doing freestyle bicycle tricks at the edge of steep canyons, on narrow footbridges spanning deep ravines, and along the Jersey-barriers of under-construction highway overpasses. Longer and more revealing videos of the same self-styled adventure athlete could be found on YouTube and Flixxy, but the popularity of this relatively recent remix was in its clever quick-cut editing synched to a hip-hop music track.

Once the download was complete, Monchu closed his browser and began the protracted process of picking up his latest message. He launched a program from the Windows command line, sending the saved video file through software that extracted selected frames spaced according to a computer-generated sequence of pseudo-random numbers. Those extracted frames were left in memory to be retrieved by another program that picked out scattered pixels from the images and strung them together. These, in turn, had to be sent through another hidden program along with a key—a secret string of digits belonging to Monchu—to decipher the coded message hidden in the video and display it as plaintext that Monchu could read.

The system, a newly devised variant of visual steganography that his group had developed from technology "borrowed" from terrorists, enabled Monchu and his handlers to hide secret messages in plain sight by subtly altering stored images, each altered pixel forming part of the hidden message. Visually, it was impossible to tell where and how an image had been altered, which dot was not quite the right hue or was just a shade brighter or dimmer than it should be. The innovation that Monchu and his handlers used was not to hide a complete message in a single picture but to store only a few bits of information in each of a large number of frames from an extended video, making the alterations even harder to detect. A five-minute video at 30 frames-per-second provided 9,000 pictures in which to bury a coded message.

To pick up his messages, Monchu had to know which video to download, the seed number that told the system which frames to extract, and another seed number to identify which pixels in each frame were part of the message. All of these had been delivered to him in his previous message. Then he had to use the correct deciphering algorithm with his own private key. The whole process could be reversed to send a message back by posting altered "family" home videos via phony Flickr accounts and YouTube channels. With so many millions of videos online, outsiders looking for such communications would be doomed from the start, even if they knew what to look for.

Monchu had never met the particular people who were now on the other end of this technology-assisted conversation, although he knew who they were. He had been alone in the field for years, had worked in a dozen cities, and changed names almost as many times. He did not know why he was assigned particular tasks nor how they contributed to some greater good. Those matters he left to his bosses. He was only the instrument of a larger agenda, a well-paid mercenary but also a dedicated believer. For his belief in that larger agenda, he had left his homeland, trained in the Sahara and in the hills of Afghanistan, served under a rogue's gallery of temporary commanders, and learned to hide in plain sight like the messages in the videos.

Now he read and reread the message on his screen. He was no longer Monchu, but someone else, someone who spoke yet another language. He had always possessed a gift for language and dialect and had acquired a rich repertoire over his decades of exile. This time, though, it was a language of childhood memory, a residue of distant days of freedom and desperation, of hungry younger brothers who depended on his wits and bravado for their survival. For them, he had failed; everything since had been unconscious penance and conscious vengeance.

He memorized the location where he would pick up his new passport and the other documents of his latest backstory. The destination made no sense to him, no more than his current location. He was, by turns, a delivery boy and a fix-it man, a peeping tom and a thief, a roadside rescuer and an assassin. This time, in his new home with its old language, he was to be a street sweeper, cleaning up debris scattered from a previous operation whose precise purpose had been withheld from him against that remote possibility that he should ever end up in hostile custody. What he did not know he could not tell. He would now have to make certain that others could not tell the story either.

Chapter Ten

■ A cooling sea-breeze swept The Corner of the World. At the site where centuries of sailors and passengers had paused to refresh themselves in some inn or another, Karl, Shira, and Duarte sat around a small wicker table in front of The Golden Gate, a touristy restaurant in downtown Funchal, sipping *poncha*, the potent rum-and-lemon trademark of Madeira. Every table in the open air was now occupied, and a mix of locals and visitors strolled along the Avenido da Arriaga, its wide walkway paved with the island's signature mosaic of small white and black stones, everywhere laid in bold patterns: stark swirls, scallops and stripes, trefoils and braids.

Karl grinned across the table at Shira as the wind tickled his neck and ruffled her hair. Noticing his gaze shift to a spot beyond her left shoulder, she squeezed his hand. "What are you thinking?"

"I was thinking, here we are in downtown Funchal in Madeira, an autonomous region of Portugal, and we are surrounded by people speaking German, English, Russian, but not that many speaking Portuguese."

"What do you expect? We are in the tourist area, and it is during the Festival of the Atlantic, which is apparently a major summer draw for tourists."

"Yes," he said, dropping his voice, "but the people I was listening in on were not tourists and they were not talking about the music or the fireworks competition. They were speaking in Russian, negotiating the terms of a business deal, a very big business deal. Then they switched to Portuguese. I think the one on my left, your right, is from Brazil. The other, I don't know, his accent is heavy and my rusty Russian is as bad as my limited Portuguese, but I don't think this particular business deal is on the sunlit side of the law."

"Do you really think so? From the propaganda I've read, Funchal has no crime and no criminals."

Duarte, raised a finger as if calling for a time out. "You are right, Senhora Shira. We do not have much in the way of crime here. But it is also possible that your husband is right. Funchal is sometimes a kind of meeting point between South America and Europe. Customs and security are very—how do you say?—relaxed. The fact that it is quiet and safe here makes it an appealing place to meet for deals that are at the edge of the law."

"You're serious."

"Yes, it is true. My cousin Jorge is in the police. He says many millions actually flows through here, unofficially. It is not so much illegal traffic itself, not drugs, for example, or arms, but the profits and payments. Did anyone check you at the airport? No. It is very easy to meet to arrange deals or to pass sums of money. This is the side of Funchal that is not described in the tourist brochures, but it is real."

"Should we be concerned?"

"I think not. No one wants to make trouble here. It is the Portuguese way, not to make trouble. We were neutral during the Second World War, and Lisbon became the crossroads of dark dealing, a 'spy city' of watchers and watched and profit making all around. Here, in Funchal today, much goes on, but there is almost never any violence because if you shoot somebody, there is no place to hide." He gestured expansively. "It would be very easy to stop anyone from getting off the island if the police wanted to do that. Besides, if those really are bad guys that you overheard, at least they are spending money here and helping the local economy just like the many good tourists."

One of the men seated at the table behind Shira glanced toward Karl, who quickly pretended to be scanning the plaza appreciatively. For just a moment, Karl thought the man showed a sign of recognition before returning to his conversation. Karl shifted in his seat to face partially toward the street, allowing him to more easily steal glances their way while smiling at Shira. The man who had looked in their direction sat in casual awkwardness, the way the long-limbed occupy chairs designed for much shorter people. His short, wavy hair and close-cropped beard were jet black, like his eyes. His ethnicity was impossible for Karl to discern. He could have been from the Middle East or the Far East, from Central America or Brazil—or all of these—a swarthy mix of far-flung ancestors. And Karl could not help noticing the man seeming to be cleverly manipulating his utensils as he returned to his food, creating opportunities for fleeting looks again toward their table.

Duarte drew Karl's attention back to their own table and the present. "Funchal was once the crossroads of the sailing trade from Europe to Africa and to the New World. Where lines cross, people meet and make deals. I am sure there is a long history of this. Ah, and speaking of history, I have located a possible translator for your personal history. We have on the faculty a German economist, Professor Wilhelm Schottky. I showed him the letter you gave me, and he said it would be both easy and a pleasure to translate the letters for you if you don't mind that it will take him time to complete them all. I told him there was a thick packet of them. Anyway, here is your letter and the translation that he made. He apologizes that it is not perfect, although it should be good enough for you to understand the correspondence. He also said it was quite interesting, particularly because he is from Saxony himself."

Duarte handed Karl a large manila envelope, which Karl started to open, but Shira put her hand on his arm. "It can wait until we're back at the apartment, darling."

She nodded toward Duarte who spread his hands and said, "No, that's all right, please go ahead. I don't mind." Karl looked from Shira to Duarte but then deferred to his wife's judgment and tucked the envelope into the backpack at his feet.

Taking a last sip of his poncha, Duarte announced, "We should finish and be on our way if you want to visit the places I told you about. They are all the way across town, and one is beyond the Old City. If you would rather not, that is okay, too, but Shira said you might be interested in these spots—you are from Israel, no? There is, I am afraid, not too much to show, despite the long history of Jewish involvement on the island that stretches all the way back to João Gonçalvo Zarco. Zarco, you know, was the ship captain who claimed Madeira for Portugal and who himself descended from a Jewish family. Today, though, there is little left to show that there ever were Jews on the island."

Karl tried to act interested. "So tell me again why we are on this History Channel expedition in search of the last vestiges of Jewish history in Madeira?"

"Because my mother asked us to. You know she fancies herself something of an amateur historian. And because it's a piece of our collective past. How can you know where you are going if you don't know where you came from? None of the official guidebooks were any use, so I asked Duarte if he could help."

"I am afraid it is not much help, Senhora Shira. I know of only two remaining sites related to a Jewish presence on the island. Shall we go?"

At the open plaza of Praça do Municipio, Karl's slow circle around the central fountain with its cross-topped finger pointing heavenward earned him a puzzled look from Shira. "It looks pretty much the same from every angle, Karl."

"I know. Just practicing a little 'surveillance awareness.' I wasn't sure, but I thought we were being followed by one of those guys from The Golden Gate."

"Karl, they are probably just tourists like us, enjoying the very same sights of charming Funchal."

Karl shrugged but found another excuse to look back as Duarte led the way out of the square.

▪ ▪ ▪

"That's it?" Shira said. "That was once a synagogue?" They stood at the top of Rua da Ribeirinha de Baixo facing a modest three-story building on Rua do Carmo. In contrast with the simpler designs of its neighbors, the building's elegant façade and architecture, with tall windows in pairs and topped by circular openings, suggested a muted Moorish influence. The ground floor housed the *Lavandaria*

Brasileira, the Brazilian Laundry. In the circular portion of the window above the narrow wooden door to the left of the laundry, the panels formed a Star of David, the only remaining evidence that it had once been a synagogue, the last one in Funchal.

"I know, there is not much to see," said Duarte. "Some people have asked the City Council to put up a plaque or sign of some kind, but it never happens. It is the past. Someone else's past."

"The past belongs to all of us. What we do not know or remember is still important," Shira said. "Karl always kept meaning to ask his parents about their pasts. Then they were gone. It's all too easy to lose the past and our chance to know it. Before we know, history has become a laundry."

They turned their backs on the laundry as Duarte led them down toward the waterfront, then turned onto Rua de Santa Maria, a narrow, cobblestone street in the Old City lined with small shops, cafés, and restaurants. Eventually, they reached the Caminho do Lazareto, the road east out of town that hugged the cliffs overlooking the sea. A short ways up the road they stopped in front of the small *Cemiterio Judaico*, its padlocked doors marked by a brass plate in English, Portuguese, and Hebrew. Karl rattled the padlock on the solid metal doors. "I guess we are not going to see much here. Another anticlimactic pilgrimage."

Duarte shrugged. "It is very much in need of attention and dangerous because the edge of it is falling into the sea. The city wants to move it, to dig up the bodies and re-bury them in a Catholic cemetery elsewhere. Not a surprise, but Jews from the mainland have objected to these plans. And nothing happens, except more of the cliff falls away each year. I think the location here at the edge of town and perched above the sea would be very desirable for another hotel or something, and that may be part of the motivation for moving the cemetery."

"I want to look in," Karl said, walking around to the side and pulling himself up onto the wall that abutted the cemetery.

"Karl, please be careful," Shira told him.

"Hey, it is no problem. I just want to get some pictures before it gets too dark. I need to be able to prove to your mother that we were here. She'll ask, you know." He climbed atop an electrical junction box and looked over. The site sloped gently toward the cliff edge where part of the seaward wall had fallen away. A few dozen grave markers were visible amidst the tall weeds. In the far corner, nearest the road, a jacaranda tree stood guard over the grave sites.

"It is certainly sad to see it so neglected," Karl said, as he climbed down off the electrical box.

"It is too dangerous anymore for the caretakers," Duarte explained. "It will have to be moved eventually or the cliff face reinforced somehow. Or it will all fall into the sea."

"When was it last used for burial," Shira asked.

"I think it was in the thirties sometime," Duarte answered.

"No," Karl said, "at least as late as the 1970s. I understand there was a visitor named Albert Morse Goldberg who died while on holidays in Madeira and was buried here in 1971. And I think there was a Bettencourt buried here even later."

"You did some research, I can see. I thought you weren't interested in this ancient history stuff," Shira teased.

"Somebody has to take your mother seriously. Of course, she stood looking over my shoulder as she steered me to a site about the Sephardic diaspora. But it was interesting." He started lowering himself from the wall but slipped and landed on his backside.

"Hey, sport," Shira said, offering him her hand. "We don't want anyone else dying while on holidays in Madeira."

A short walk back down the road from the cemetery they passed a restaurant with an unlikely name. "Riso. Doesn't sound very Portuguese," Karl remarked.

"No," responded Duarte, "but Funchal is now very cosmopolitan. Besides, Madeiran food can be rather plain, at least to my taste. I was born on the mainland. This place, I hear, is very good, a mixture of influences: Japanese, Italian, Portuguese, whatever else the chef thinks will add to the experience. Everything centers on rice, different kinds: white, red, brown. I have never eaten there, but we could try it for dinner."

"Let's do that," Karl said.

"It is still too early for dinner in Portugal," Duarte said, checking his watch. "Maybe we can spend another hour or so walking around—if you two don't mind—and then we can have dinner."

■ ■ ■

Dinner had stretched into a three-hour marathon of talk about robotics and art, politics and language, punctuated by a succession of tastes and multiple glasses of wine. Although Duarte offered to drive them back to the apartment, both Karl and Shira said they preferred to walk.

The trek across town followed by the steep climb up the narrow streets back to the apartment left both of them tired but alert. At Shira's prodding, Karl began emptying his pockets and his backpack onto the small table in the kitchen and came across the translation from Professor Schottky.

"Aren't you curious?" Shira asked.

"Should I be? I mean, it's late."

"Go ahead, it's not that late."

He opened the envelope. Inside were his letter and two sheets of plain A4 paper with a small note in neat block printing paper-clipped on top. "Dear Professor Lustig," the note said, "I hope this will be useful to you. I will be glad to help with your family research. Although not dated, this letter would seem to be from sometime in 1944 or 1945. I think you will find it most interesting. Yours, Wilhelm Schottky."

"So, should I read his translation? I mean aloud?"

"Yes, my silly Karl. Read."

> Dear little one,
>   I love calling you that, even though you are the taller and only three years my junior. You will always be my little sister, my sweet love. I think of you often and am deeply sorry that I have not written before, but this is the first opportunity that I have had. Finally I have paper and a pen and fresh ink. And finally there is a proper roof over my head, although the roof is also too close to my head. The baby is sleeping

peacefully, his stomach full. I am awake and my stomach is empty. I am not complaining, though. I ate yesterday, and Dieter promised to bring me something tonight. I promised him to be grateful. Dieter is like the others and not like the others. He can be tender with me, even as he is demanding. He asks me questions but expects no answers. He is German, of course, but I have learned that not all Germans are bad, or at least that not all Germans are all bad. The same can be said of Poles, I suppose. We would not be alive and warm now were it not for the Poles and the Germans, but then, there would not be so many dead were it not for the Germans and the Poles. And the Russians. And the Austrians.

You would now speak of God, if you were in this tiny room under the roof of a small church in Saxony. And I would tell you that God is gone. He left Poland and Europe and now has abandoned the Earth. We are on our own, even as we have always been. But that is talk for another time, of another time, the talk of adolescent girls arguing the big questions as the grownups worried over whether they could steal more potatoes without being caught or whether it was worth risking a morsel of bread in hopes of snaring a songbird.

But you must be wondering what has happened and how I got here. First, I must thank you for lending me your coat. It has saved my life and kept us warm. I know how special it was to you, and I know what is secreted in the seams. Your father's magic crystals, you called them. I will see to it that they reach their destination, magic or no. That is the least that I can do for the loan of such a warm and wonderful coat.

I remember the first time we met. Do you? I thought you were a silly goose of a girl.

Our fathers were working on their "big project" and our families were sharing dinner to give them extra time to talk—to argue—over their work. Didn't they have enough time at the University, I asked. No, they insisted, there is never enough time at the University, because there are students at the University who want to be taught and donkeys at the University who stand braying at the front of lecture halls and think they are professors. And this, this big project, was the most important thing to come along in decades, perhaps in the century, and it would change modern life. Then Mama would laugh and your mother would laugh, and we would return to our games, and the men would return to their tiny, magic crystals and their arguing about politics and Poland and war.

Chapter Eleven

Krakow, August 1939

■ "It will come, I tell you, the Germans will attack. Soon."

"Everyone fears that, Chaim, but no one knows," Rivka said, standing in the doorway to the small kitchen. Her long, dark hair was held back by a patterned scarf, and she wore a simple white apron, but beneath it she had on an elegant, brocaded dress. It was an occasion. "It is not a certainty, not at all. And please clear the table of your things. Supper is nearly ready."

The bare dining table at the moment resembled one of Chaim's laboratory benches at the University, with spools of wire, an assortment of electrical parts, and tools spread over it. Rivka worried about the table's finish but knew it was hopeless to counter the men and their project. In the center of the table, a shallow wooden box, like an artist's case, lay open, exposing a web of wires and small electrical components. As Chaim Manczyk wound hair-thin wire around a wooden dowel, lining up each new turn neatly next to the last, Henrik Nowak used a folding, two-lens magnifier to study a small part.

"It is a certainty," Chaim insisted. "They will invade. I heard it, I have been listening."

His wife snorted. "You have been listening to what? Do angels speak to you and tell you of the future? Are you now a prophet, a prophet with a funny radio?"

"Herr Doctor Manczyk," Julianna Nowak said, gathering the courage to interrupt the adults. "Can you tell me of this radio that lets you listen to tomorrow?"

Her father placed his hand on her shoulder. "Do not pester Chaim with questions now. We have work to do, one more experiment to try. Play with the girls."

The girls were Chana and Symcha Manczyk, who played in the corner of the sitting room, half under a small table, making up stories about their dolls. Chana was only 11, three years younger than Julianna, and a skinny, silly girl who took nothing seriously. Symcha was a quiet, shy eight-year-old who did whatever her sister wanted. Julianna had no interest in their pointless play. She wanted to stay at the table with the men and her older brother, Jósef, and to learn what they were doing.

Jósef playfully tousled her hair and winked at her as he pulled her in beside him at the table. "Julianna has a head for numbers and science. She wants to be a professor, like her father, not a housewife like her mother. Don't you, Julianna?"

Julianna's face burned as she scowled at Jósef for betraying a confidence. They were close and affectionate sibs, more so now that both were teenagers, but Jósef had a mischievous streak and could not always be trusted. His hand slid down her back and around her waist. "Now, dear sister, don't be peeved. It matters not." He turned back to the business at the table. "And I, too, would like to learn about this marvelous, magical radio."

"It is not magic, and it cannot tune into tomorrow," Chaim said. "It is just very sensitive and very versatile. The magic is in the mind of the listener. If the listener understands both German and the Germans and knows which wavelengths to tune, if the listener is a genius like your father, a physicist who deciphers the secrets of matter itself and finds the secrets of neighboring Germany a far easier puzzle, then there is magic." He smiled over at Henrik, who accepted the compliment with a nod.

They were, in fact, speaking German, as they always did when all were together. Margit Huber Nowak had been born in Germany and had studied languages at university before meeting Henrik and moving to Poland. She was fluent in English, Spanish, and French as well as German and Polish, and she had insisted that her children become conversant as well. Julianna, who had inherited her mother's love of language and her father's quick mind, had not only mastered Hochdeutsch, the high German of learning and official-dom, but could flawlessly mimic the Schwabian dialect of her mother's homeland. Her English vocabulary was more limited, but her accent there, too, was flawless.

"It is not that hard to interpret their intentions," Henrik said, "but it was yesterday's staged raid on the German radio station at Gleiwitz that proved that war was certain and imminent. I heard the so-called propaganda broadcast after the station was supposedly captured by Polish soldiers. They were not Poles at all, but German agents speaking imperfect Polish. That was obvious. It was a sham, a pretense for the invasion that will come, and—."

"And that will be the end for the Jews in Poland," Chaim finished.

"Chaim," Rivka snapped, "not in front of the children."

"The children must know. They will live this future. The Germans hate us. We are the scapegoats for all their troubles."

Henrik spread his hands. "Chaim, my friend, we all will suffer. If you read the messages within the words of their broadcasts, you know what they think of all Poles and how they regard the intelligentsia. The Nazis want a nation of workers, of ignorant laborers to till the fields and man the factories, a nation to feed them and supply them with munitions and provide *lebensraum*, space to live. There will not be room for Polish physicists and engineers in their world, Chaim. It will not be just the Jews who suffer, not just the Jews." Henrik looked about, suddenly aware of the silent stares of the children, who were all turned toward him. "But now, we must eat, and celebrate while we can." He clapped his hands. "Come, Julianna, help your mother and Rivka with the food. Jósef, take these things and put them carefully in my valise and then move the chairs."

Chaim quickly but carefully completed winding the coil that he held. He slipped it into a vest pocket before folding the wooden box on the table. Closed, and standing upright, it looked much like any shortwave radio of the day, but thinner, with too many knobs, black knurled knobs that gave it a handmade, utilitarian look. Chaim set it atop the dark walnut secretary next to the china cabinet, attached a wire, and twisted a knob. Suddenly, the room was filled with the sound of the sea and the singing of woodwinds. Chaim twisted another knob, inching it first clockwise then back, until the hiss of surf faded and the harmonies of a Mozart symphony rang with clarity.

The two families crowded around the table and ate amidst a discussion of Mozart and opera and Schiller and poetry. After dinner, dessert, and coffee, the table was once more cleared and the men resumed their tinkering. Julianna could no longer contain her curiosity. She had always loved knowing how things work, why bridges do not sag, how coals can burn without flame, and how radios can claw music and words from empty air. Once, she had confessed to her father that she wanted to be an engineer when she grew up. He had laughed and said that girls could not become engineers. His friend and colleague, Chaim, had laughed, too, but then said, "Only in America. There girls can be engineers." In Julianna's mind, that moment had settled the matter and mapped her fate. Someday she would be going to America.

"Your radio," she began.

"Not my radio," Chaim corrected, "*our* radio. We are a team, your father and I, like the pair of mules that pull a plow. Your father is the scientist who figures out why things work the way they do, and I am the engineer who makes them work the way they should. Do you really want to know about this radio?"

"Yes, yes. Truly I want to know."

"Then I will tell you there is nothing special about this radio as a radio. Oh, I have improved some of the circuitry and devised a better way to tune it over many wavelengths—you know about radio waves and wavelengths?—good. The real difference is the valves. Here, let me show you." He walked over to the birds-eye maple cabinet of the old Elektrit console radio that now stood against the wall next to the door to the back stairwell. He turned it on and waited as it warmed up, the sound of a broadcast in English growing slowly from a whisper. "See, it is like Chana in the morning. It does not spring to life when called, but awakens slowly and grudgingly. And here is why." He pulled the cabinet away from the wall and turned it around to expose the open back. "Come close, here, closer."

Julianna knelt beside him and leaned toward the cabinet.

"What do you note, my future scientist, my engineer-to-be?"

Julianna leaned in closer. "It smells dusty. And there are glass tubes, like oddly shaped electric light bulbs, but glowing very dimly, red-orange, and in the corner, a cobweb."

"Wonderful. It does want for dusting," he said, as he wiped at the cobweb with his handkerchief. "Those glowing bulbs are valves. They change one kind of electricity into another and can make weak signals into strong ones. What else do you notice about the valves?"

Julianna reached out as though to touch, then pulled back her hand. "They are warm. No, hot."

"So true. And one of those valves needs replacing, which is why we can no longer tune the German broadcasts on this radio. Now go and turn on our magic radio and tell me what is different."

She started to rise, but Jósef, who was closer, snapped the switch before she could reach it. The room filled with the music of Wagner.

"Your radio is not like Chana in the morning," she said. "It awakens in an instant."

"And turn it around. What do you see."

Jósef twisted it and answered for her. "I see a staggered pattern of holes drilled in neat rows along the bottom and near the top."

"And if you look in the holes?"

They bumped heads as both tried to look at once. "Nothing, blackness," Jósef said.

"I can see nothing of the inside," Julianna added, showing off by trying to be as precise as possible in her observation.

"Exactly. The valves do not glow, they do not get hot, and they will never need replacing. They are what we are calling solid valves, small lumps of crystalline metal with tiny wires attached that do the work of the glass globes but do not break or wear out or get hot. That is our invention, your father and I."

"What a marvelous invention," Julianna declared. "You must secure a patent and tell the world and become famous and rich."

The two men exchanged a look and said nothing.

"Why, what is wrong?"

Chaim spoke. "When the Germans reach Krakow—"

"*If* the Germans reach Krakow," Rivka interrupted.

"*When* the Germans reach Krakow," Chaim repeated, "they would find our laboratory and our notes and our solid valves. They would use Henrik's brilliant theories of solidary physics and of traveling voids to help them make terrible machines and unstoppable weapons. No, we will neither patent nor publish our work. We have already destroyed our notes at the University, and we will soon destroy our lovely little radio. That is what we are celebrating tonight: the last stages of our project."

"But you can't do that," Julianna protested. "This is a wonder, an important discovery. You must share it."

"And we will, but not now and not with the Poles—or the Germans or the Russians, who have signed a pact and will devour Poland from the other direction. We have decided to bequeath it to the future, to give it to the Zionists in Palestine."

Margit sent a disapproving look toward her husband. "And you agree, Henrik? That the Jews are to be the benefactors of your work."

Henrik returned her look. "It is as it should be, since this is really Chaim's work. And before him, the experiments and ideas of that Russian, Oleg Losev. My work is numbers and equations, pieces of paper. All I did was add theory to practice. Chaim was the one who saw the potential, who took my formulas and turned them into a device by melding them with an idea almost as old as radio itself, what you would know, Jósef, as a crystal radio set. I am a scientist, not an inventor, so I gladly gave the rights to him. When, after Europe is at peace again, when it comes time to publish, then I will get the credit, too. And perhaps a Nobel, if I am alive to receive it."

"Of course, you will be alive, my Henrik," Margit said, annoyance contaminating her confidence. "This will not be a long war like the last one, or a bloody one. The Germans will swiftly bring a new peace to Europe, and a new era of culture."

"You still credit your Germans with more power and goodwill than they possess, dearest Margit. And it is not the Germans who are to be feared but the National Socialists. It is the Nazis who will rape Poland and raze Europe. Still, in any case, the decision has been taken. The notes are gone, the equipment dismantled, and, soon, our experimental prototype will be ash and molten metal. But, *die Gedanken sind frei,* as the Germans say: the thoughts are free. So, the ideas sail on, soon on their way to Palestine and a new generation."

"You have always been a Zionist sympathizer, Henrik."

"And you a believer in German culture, Margit."

"I left that culture to be with you, remember."

Julianna, uncomfortable with the rising tension between her parents, chose that moment to ask another question. "Can you tell me, Papa, about this theory. You said something about traveling voids. How can something that is nothing move?"

"Bring me the checkerboard and I will show you."

He opened the folded board and spilled the checkers on the table. He spread them out, then laid a dozen of them out in a straight line. "These are electrons in a wire, electrical charges that speed freely through the wire to heat the filament in a light bulb or power a radio."

"But some of them are red and some black," Jósef said.

"That doesn't matter; ignore the color. If we want to move electricity along the wire, we push an electron in at one end, like this, and an electron pops out the other end. So. But what if we have a substance, like our crystalline metals, in which electrons do not move so freely? Let's create a space in our line by removing one electron right next to the end. This is a void. Now, watch what happens as I shift the electron on one side of the void." He shifted one of the checkers over one position, leaving a new space another position farther down the line. He then quickly shuffled checkers, one checker, one position at a time, until the gap had been shifted all the way to the other end of the line. "See, a traveling void. That is how our solid valves work, not with a current of electrons but with traveling voids. The crystalline metals we use are neither conductors, like the wires in the walls that bring us electricity, nor insulators, like the walls themselves. Our crystals are something halfway in between, possessing what we are calling hemicon-ductance."

Jósef shook his head, but Julianna nodded and smiled. "Can I see one of these solid valves with its traveling voids?" she asked. Jósef, now bored of it, swept the checkers from the table into the open box, then walked away.

"There is not much to see," Chaim told her. He pulled something from his vest, a lump of rosin the size of a hazelnut, with three thin copper wires protruding. He used a table knife to break open the lump of rosin, exposing a sliver of polished metal inside.

"Where are the voids? Can I see them moving?"

Chaim laughed, a loving laugh. "They are too small to see, even with a microscope, but they are there." He brushed the pieces of rosin, bits of crystal, and metal into his cupped hand and poured them into Julianna's hand. "Here, a souvenir."

"So tiny, a carrier pigeon could deliver this to Palestine."

"A carrier pigeon will, when the time comes. Come here, my pigeon," he said, gesturing to Chana. She bounced across the room and slid into his lap. "What do you think of moving to Palestine, my *Tzipi*, my little bird."

"Do they have chocolate cakes in Palestine, Papa?"

"Yes, the size of your mother's hat."

"Then I will go. When do we leave?"

"When we can," he answered, "When we are ready."

■ ■ ■

In the tiny kitchen of the apartment in Funchal, Karl turned over the last page of the letter to find a postscript. He read it aloud to Shira.

> I remember the night in August when your father
> gave you your coat. You were perhaps ten or eleven,
> and though you were the tallest girl in your class, the
> coat was much too big for you. You were perplexed to
> be getting a new coat in August, but your father
> explained that things would soon be changing, that
> the Germans were about to arrive and that a harsh

winter was coming to Poland. You would need a warm coat on your journey to Palestine. You bounced with enthusiasm but protested that you would not need such a coat in Palestine, which was far to the south and therefore must be ever so much warmer. Then your father grew very grave and said that when you got to Palestine with this coat, you would no longer need it, so you would give it to his friend Mordecai Levitz, who was already there and would know what to do with it.

We all laughed to break the tension, but Germany invaded on the first day of September and our world shattered.

Shira sat in silence for many seconds. "This isn't the letter you started reading in the taxi, Karl."

"No, I must have given him a different one. Still, it's pretty interesting, I mean if it's true."

"Interesting? Is that all you can muster?"

"Well, okay, it's amazing, but I don't see how it can be about my mother. She was British, not Polish. I don't see that it has anything to do with me."

"We don't know that. We don't yet know the whole story. We must give the rest of the letters to Professor Schottky for him to translate. I want to know everything. How did Julianna get to Saxony and to London to meet your father?"

Karl sat, silent, holding the letter in his lap, staring out into a moving void that stretched across years and lifetimes. He was thinking about how little he knew and wondering who his parents really were.

Chapter Twelve

■ Israel's intelligence services were supposed to cooperate with each other, but like their counterparts in America, there was as much inter-service rivalry as collaboration, and each of the branches not only jealously guarded its own territories but also took what opportunities came its way to step over the line. There were exceptions, such as when Mossad had collaborated with military intelligence to help the Americans launch the cyber-attack on Iran. Still, it was with a certain amount of reluctance that Anat reached out to her contact at Aman, the country's military intelligence directorate. Colonel Barg was an old friend who had served in the Israeli Defense Force with Anat and been bitten by the same analytical bug that had sent her into intelligence work. Both had risen through their respective ranks to reach positions of modest influence and growing importance in a world in which technology loomed ever larger, and the old-fashioned techniques of intelligence and intrigue, although still necessary, were becoming bit players in the digital drama of satellite monitors and stealth software.

Yishai Barg headed a small group connected with the almost legendary Unit 8200, one of the largest units in Israel's defense forces and responsible for so-called sigint, or signal intelligence, and for the increasingly rich mine of open-source intelligence, information derived from public channels, such as newspapers, cable television, and the Web. Despite the growing importance of Anat's team, Mossad still relied on Unit 8200 for the greater portion of its intelligence information, particularly for analyses of the media, for which the much smaller Mossad lacked sufficient personnel.

Yishai and Anat had their official lines of communication, but for really important matters, they met at a small Moroccan couscous restaurant in Tel Aviv's City Center. It was always noisy and crowded, with generous helpings of authentic Tripoli-style cuisine at reasonable prices. A tiny table on the sidewalk was a setting both public and private.

Yishai leaned back in his chair and smiled broadly. He still had the dark, smooth skin and sculpted features that had attracted Anat when she first met him. Somehow they had ended up close friends but never lovers, which turned out to be best for everyone in the long run. "How's our boy Bulofsky doing now that he's camped on your side of The Hill?"

"Bulofsky?" Anat arched her eyebrows. "He's still obsessing over the obvious. But your assessment was right. Analytically he's very good, as long as he doesn't open his mouth. His written reports are perfect. But I have other things on my mind, like the recent crash of the F-16i—"

"What crash? There was no crash."

"The crash—"

"Look, Anat, there was no crash. It was shot down by friendly fire at the request of the flight crew. They ejected, but neither survived. They were so close to the border when they were shot down that some of the debris was recovered by the Jordanians. None of this is official, of course. The story 'leaked' to the media is that this is merely another case of human error. The families of the dead pilot and navigator are protesting and have gained a following of supporters demanding an inquiry, but nothing is going to come of it. Not any time soon."

"What really happened?"

"We don't know yet. The IAF has collected every piece of debris they could reach and is going over it with a microscope."

"What I want to know is if this was a test of the new *Zahav* avionics and flight control module."

"There is no *Zahav* module."

"Like there was no crash."

"Precisely."

"What is there then?"

"An old system with new components, but you know that because you have been querying databases about the 460 series chipset."

Anat froze. "Aman monitors Mossad, too?"

"Exactly as Mossad keeps an eye on our people. But in this case, we were already tracking queries on the topic. If traffic goes over the pipelines to and from Israel, we know about it. We can't do what the Americans do and track and record every damn byte on every damn channel, but we can track most of it and catch references on a pretty big subset."

"And the F-16i was flying with the new chipset in place?"

"From what we can tell, yes. And the Air Force is giving credence to the possibility that the chips failed somehow, because—and you did not hear this—the flight controls stopped functioning minutes before the hit. Frozen. The plane was out of control and headed for Jordanian airspace loaded with bombs we are not even supposed to have. And what is your interest, Anat?"

Anat, knowing the reliability of modern silicon technology and what went into the proving of microchips like those in the 460 chipset, doubted the failure scenario, but she said nothing about it. "Somebody is getting their hands on those chips and offering them on the illegal arms market. As of this moment, other than us, only the Yanks are supposed to have any."

"We never have been able to fully count on the Americans, and the current administration has not made the situation any better. Can we ... can they account for everything we've delivered to them?"

Anat shrugged. "Supposedly. I think the leaky pipe is upstream of the Americans, at least that's the angle I'm working today."

"And?"

"It's complicated."

"Meaning you have an idea but won't say."

"You know me, Yishai. I'm never short of ideas. Let's eat and leave things where they are. We've both gotten something from this."

"Yes, I get a free lunch. It's your turn to pay."

▪ ▪ ▪

At the University of Madeira, Karl dropped off the packet of letters for Professor Schottky, then headed off to prepare his next lecture in the temporary office he'd been assigned. He was staring at his laptop screen when Duarte popped in. "Ready for lunch?" he asked.

"Hmmm, maybe. I suppose I should eat." He started to close his laptop, then hesitated. "Tell me what you make of this, Duarte. You worked down at the silicon level before you got into robotics. If you didn't already know, what would you think you were looking at here?"

"Well, it's obvious a layout of some kind of microchip. This part of the chip is an array of some kind, the same little pattern repeated over and over. Could be memory, RAM, but looks a little too complicated for that. I don't know. Is it a gate array, an FPGA?"

"No, not a Field-Programmable Gate Array, or at least it's not supposed to be. It's supposed to be part of the new 460 series four-by-quad-core microprocessor that I delivered to you. I worked on security features of that architecture—I mean conceptually, not at the circuit design level—but I spent a lot of the time with the hardware engineers, and I don't remember anything about incorporating an FPGA capability. But this layout looks an awful lot like"—he paged to another image—"this one, which I took off the Web. This one is a gate array. At a glance, it looks like a very similar arrangement."

"Go back to the 460 image. Can we get a look over to the side there?"

"No, the image was cropped before it was sent to me. Why"

"Well, that looks like it might be flash memory on the chip, like to store the configuration for the gate array. Does this make any sense for this microprocessor?"

"No, for a whole bunch of reasons. First of all, FPGAs are slow and power hungry compared to hard-wired logic on the chip. Second, they multiply security risks because they can be reprogrammed at any time, effectively allowing on-the-fly rewiring of the computer, turning it into a completely different device or giving it new functionality. Finally, an on-chip static memory could defeat some of our built-in security logic. So, it absolutely doesn't make sense. This has to be the wrong image, a shot of some other microchip."

"They sent you the wrong picture."

"So it would seem. I emailed my pals at IsTac in Israel, but haven't heard from them yet. Wait. I've got another idea. Go on ahead to lunch; I'll meet you at Tecnopolo in a few minutes."

Duarte left and Karl started drafting an email to Heinrich Waldmeier in Dresden. If he simply came out and asked Heinrich directly for an x-ray ptychograph of the 466 microprocessor, Heinrich would have to get approval from IsTac who would have to clear it with government reps. He needed to create a plausible story.

> Dear Heinrich,
>
> I hope the Applied Radiation Physics Group is going well. I want to ask a favor, but it is a little embarrassing. I got one of your ptychographs from Yitzak Shuva back at IsTac but accidentally overwrote my original when I cropped the image. Any chance you could send me the whole image again? You can see the sequence number and time stamp in the lower right-hand corner of the attached file. Can you also confirm that I have the right image, a ptychograph of the IsTac 27U466? I can't get a reply from IsTac, and I need to teach a class this afternoon. If you can't send the file, I'll understand.
>
> Karl

When Karl returned after lunch, a reply email was waiting for him with a large image file attached and Waldmeier's confirmation that it was the IsTac 27U466. Karl dragged the image file to his desktop without noting the CC in the header of the email: y.shuva@pub.istac.il.

▪ ▪ ▪

In Tel Aviv, Anat Dorfman shook her head. "What are you doing now, Karl? Why are you making an end run around security to get an image of the internals of that chip?"

In Rehovot, Yitzak Shuva was wondering whether he should tell his boss about Karl Lustig's odd email exchange with the Technical University of Dresden.

In the Negev desert, at an isolated Unit 8200 installation not far from Kibbutz Urim, a flag popped up on a display indicating Internet activity related simultaneously to several persons of interest. The flag was linked to a standing alert order and triggered a coded message to Colonel Barg in Tel Aviv.

In the Parque das Nações, the permanent residue of Lisbon's 1998 international exhibition, Pedro Cabral, the man who was no longer Monchu, watched a fountain go through its programmed sequenced ending in a volcano-like eruption that sent a pulse of water shooting high above the palm trees. As the water settled and the spray drifted in the hot, noonday breeze, Pedro pretended to be interested in the newspaper he was holding, waiting for the moment when the fountain would restart its program and the climactic jet would draw, for a few seconds, the attention of those around him. As the water shot skyward again, he reached under the bench and withdrew the heavy package secured there. For a few more hours, he would pretend to be a tourist. Then, with some newly purchased aluminum luggage and a clever redistribution of the contents of the just-acquired package, he would fly back to the island to continue his cleanup work.

Chapter Thirteen

■ Karl sat in his temporary office again, talking with Rui and Duarte and two of their research assistants. Karl had called them in for what he referred to as a "special assignment."

Nuno, tall and very dark, was the younger of the two post-docs. The son of an Assistant Professor, a recent arrival from Angola who taught in the chemistry department, Nuno had himself only recently returned from Pittsburgh and defending his dissertation in computer science at Carnegie Mellon University. Tiago, whose great-great-grandparents had been born on the island, was short, round, and already, in his late twenties, beginning to go bald. Since completing his doctorate in mathematics at the University of Coimbra he had been bouncing from one research appointment to another.

"So, I have a challenge for you," Karl announced. "I wonder if you two could take one of these new microprocessor chips and reverse engineer it. I am asking you to hack into it to find out exactly what it does."

Nuno, who was the more confident of the two in English, spoke up. "But why, Professor Karl, why would we do that? We have the specs for the chip and the programming manual for the earlier version, the 455, which is already used in the computers for our submarine robots. And we have the C compiler to generate code for it, which is the same instruction set as this chip. What is there to reverse engineer?"

Karl leaned forward. "What if there were undocumented functions, features not on the spec sheets, instructions not in the programming manuals?"

A bright smile spread over Nuno's pitted tan face. "That could be interesting. Do we know what these undocumented features might do?"

"No, and if I knew, I couldn't tell you. But anything you discover on your own, that would be different. Your Institute has obtained the chips through legitimate channels. Since they now belong to the Institute, you all are free to make whatever use of them that you can. So, *não há problema*. Right?

"*Sim, é verdade, não tem problema*," Tiago said with a nod and a grin—yes, that is true, no problem. Karl could see that he had the young researchers hooked.

"And how do I justify letting you use my post-docs for advanced hardware hacking?" Rui asked. "They are supposed to be working on programming for semi-autonomous exploration in the open ocean. The grant that pays them as research assistants expires this year."

"You are right to object, Rui. But they also might find something useful for your programming. Besides, I am only here another week. If they come up with nothing by the end of the week, then fine. And, either way, I will introduce you to some people in Israel who might help you get that new high-sensitivity underwater camera you have been seeking. Okay?"

Rui nodded, shook hands with Karl, and left with the research assistants. Duarte hung back and closed the door after his colleagues departed. "This is about the image you showed me, right? This detective work, not so?"

"Yes, come look at this." Karl turned on a large-screen monitor attached to his laptop. It displayed a high resolution x-ray ptychograph of the 466 microprocessor, a complete image rather than a cropped one. "Can I trust you, Duarte? I mean, can you keep what we are talking about just between the two of us?"

"Yes, of course. Is this defense-related stuff?"

"No. Yes. My work on this chipset is top secret, but I am not going to say anything about that. I want to share my suspicions with you about something that could be very serious, but because it is only my speculation does not exactly constitute a violation of confidentiality. Not exactly. We have known each other since long before you returned to Portugal and ended up here. I just want our conversation not to go beyond this room."

"I did not 'end up' here in Madeira. I came here after working at the Institute for Systems and Robotics in Lisbon because I wanted to start an Institute of my own. I have succeeded, and with men like Rui Delgado, I am preparing for the future and for my exit. I want to retire here in a little *quinta* and grow grapes and bananas and grandchildren. My daughter is working on that even now.

"Congratulations on that. *Parabens*, I should say. I must keep practicing my Portuguese. When is the baby due?"

"In August, a summer baby. Mercifully, it is never too hot here as it could be on the continent. But back to your question. If it is important to you, I will swear on my mother's grave to tell no one about what we speak of here."

"Good, then look at this." He zoomed in on part of the image. "As you suggested, it does look like it might be a field-programmable gate array supported by a small on-chip flash memory to store its configuration." Karl dragged the image sideways. "Here. And up here, we have shadows from another layer that I do not remember but makes me think of a digital signal processor. And there's more. Components and connections that just seem out of context, stuff that might even be analog circuitry rather than digital. It makes me think of software radio. Of course, it's impossible to be certain just by looking at an x-ray of the chip, particularly a slightly fuzzy x-ray with all the layers on top of each other."

"So, what do you really think this is about, my friend?"

"I am very hesitant to say this, but I don't think what is in that package is the 466, at least not the system that I helped IsTac design. It's something else, or it's been modified after the design was frozen, sometime after I left the project."

"Maybe there were late design changes, new requirements. That's possible, isn't it? This is really a military part, and defense people are notorious for piling on new requirements. I know, because ISR did some defense work. And our roving submarines can be used for military as well as scientific purposes."

Karl stood and started pacing in the small space behind his desk. "That might be true, and I am not ruling out some late design changes or even specs that were outside of what I was permitted to know, but one thing just makes no sense in this architecture: the FPGA. If it really is field programmable, it pretty much defeats all the work I did designing new security features. And it would be slow, when everything in this new design—from the 4-by-4 core architecture to the size of the components—was designed for speed."

"What aren't you saying, Karl?"

"Only what I don't feel I can say."

"Do you want me to say it for you?"

"Yes."

"You think the design was somehow hacked into, compromised by hostile parties."

"That is what you think, Duarte. I can't say what I think without skating around the edges of my security clearance. Which is why I have the post-docs playing code cracker with our chip. I hope they come up with an answer, something useful. The big question is about what the design really does. And why does it do it?"

■ ■ ■

Two days later, when Karl plugged in, booted up his laptop, and logged in at the university, his in-box held an email from nuno.rodrigues119@gmail.com that had arrived in the small hours of the morning. It outlined the procedure Nuno and Tiago had used to probe for undocumented features and appended a two-column list of supposedly illegal instruction codes and incorrectly format-ted data that led to what the researchers had labeled in the second column as "interesting results." At first Karl was elated. He had not expected results so quickly nor results with such clear implications. Then he felt suddenly crestfallen. He should have told the researchers to hand deliver the results to him, not to use open, unencrypted email, certainly not sent from a web-based service.

Chapter Fourteen

■ Tiago held out his spare motorcycle helmet to his friend. "Nuno, we promised, and that is what we are paid for."

"Or what we are not paid for. I do not consider a research stipend a salary. It is a sop to poor students who are actually slaves." He did not reach for the helmet.

"Slaves who get to work on interesting problems, like reverse engineering that microprocessor. Admit it, you had fun."

"Exhausting fun. I am so tired. Two days and hardly any sleep. I am getting too old for this."

"You are 26. What do you mean, too old? I'm old, almost 30 and losing my hair."

"Why are you still a lowly post-doc then, working for nearly nothing?"

"Because it's fun, and it is better than a real job, and because I can't seem to get a real job. This is my fourth post-doc. I'm becoming a career research assistant. At least this time I am back home. A year in Norway at the University of Trondheim was enough cold and dark to last me a lifetime. And the prices! I could afford a glass of beer only a few times a week and never any wine."

"Some career," Nuno scoffed. "But, yes, this assignment was fun, especially what we learned after we sent the email to the American. Wait until Monday when we tell him and Professor Duarte about the digital signal processor and what we found in the microcode."

"Good, until then we have maintenance work we promised to do in Porto Moníz." He thrust the helmet once more at Nuno. "I told my cousin about you and that we were coming. She wants to meet you and is inviting a friend she thinks I will like. My cousin is tall, like you, and pretty, not like you. We will first go to *O Centro Ciência Viva* to get that stupid ecology computer game running properly, and then we will have fun with the ladies. So, let's get on my motorcycle and get going so we can finish debugging whatever crap code those stupid masters students left on that PC. Then we can enjoy the afternoon in the tidal pools and the evening in . . ."

▪ ▪ ▪

At São Vincente on the north coast of the island, Tiago turned west toward Porto Moníz, then faced the split between the fast, regular road, and the "old road," a narrow, disjointed alternate, no longer properly maintained since the completion of the series of new tunnels that made the trip faster, safer, and considerably less scenic. The old road hugged the steep mountainside and ran along the edges of cliffs with unguarded drop-offs to the rocks and sea below.

As they approached the exit with its warning sign, Tiago slowed and twisted his head to shout to Nuno. "Old or new?"

"Not more tunnels, please. My ears are still ringing from the last one under Boca da Encumeada."

Twisting the accelerator and leaning right, then left, Tiago took them onto the first segment of the one-way old road toward Seixal and Porto Moníz. The sun was almost directly above, and the headwind fluttered his jacket. The road soon rejoined the main route, then split again. On the second segment, they almost immediately faced a fresh breakdown pile of dirt and rocks from the slope on the left leaving less than a meter on the right between the pile and the precipice. Tiago slowed, negotiating the narrowed passage easily but coming out into the clear again too late to see what was waiting in the road. His right hand and foot applied the front and rear brakes as he tried to hug the rock wall to his left.

▪ ▪ ▪

There was a knock on the door to Karl's office. Rui entered. "I have news," he said.

"Yes, I know. I got the email from Nuno. Pretty exciting."

A puzzled expression painted Rui's face. "I don't understand. I just talked to Nuno's father. It was terrible."

"What do you mean?"

"I mean Nuno and Tiago. They were together on Tiago's motorcycle. They were on the old road to Porto Moniz not far out of São Vincente. You wouldn't know it. That is the narrow road that winds along the cliff edge rather than through the tunnels that were drilled later.

"Anyway, Tiago struck something—the police don't know for sure, maybe a rock slide spilled across the road—but they went tumbling over the edge onto the rocks below. It took hours to recover their bodies."

"That's terrible news. I am so sorry. I was referring to the email I got from them with the first results from their reverse-engineering project. And now . . . I had no idea they were dead."

"Yes, it was a tragedy. They were so young and with such futures. They were also, I am sorry to say, so reckless, like so many young men. The police said they were going much too fast for the old road."

There was a long moment of silence between them; Rui broke it. "I have to go and pay respects to their families. It is such a terrible blow. And I don't know what we will do at the Institute, but those matters will have to wait." He started to leave. "Oh, with all this happening I almost forgot. Professor Schottky asked me to give this envelope to you. He said it was another translation."

Karl folded the envelope and slipped it in his pocket without thinking. His thoughts were on the two researchers. Rereading the email message from Nuno, he realized that it must have been sent only hours before the two had taken off for a joy ride. Some ride, no joy. He felt sick.

▪ ▪ ▪

The former Monchu, now comfortably Pedro and back on the island, sat in his hotel room with a view of the ocean and worked his way through the succession of steps to send a message confirming his arrival and describing the situation he faced. His message, hidden in the frames of an iPhone video, was short: The streets were littered with debris and would take some time to sweep clean. He had already started to work, scrubbing the gutters, clearing away the trash.

▪ ▪ ▪

With his spirits dragging and his anxiety rising, Karl had no desire to go out for dinner and even less desire to cook in the apartment's tiny kitchen. Before hiking back to the apartment, he stopped for take-away pizza at Tecnopizza, the small café opposite Tecnopolo that was popular with University students and younger faculty. With no real appetite, when it was his turn he took the easy route and said, "*Queria o mesmo, por favor,*" thus asking for the same pizza that the student in front of him had ordered. He had no idea what was in the large, square box handed to him ten minutes later, but he paid for it and started the up-and-down hike back to the apartment.

▪ ▪ ▪

On the veranda at the apartment, Karl and Shira sipped vinho verde and watched the late sun dropping behind the next block of buildings. Between bites of pizza topped with tuna and herbs, he told Shira about the research assistants.

"How terrible," she said, "but you seem to think there is more to the story."

"I do, and I feel terrible. The two just finish a marathon bit of extracurricular research for me, and hours later they are plunging off a cliff. I checked with some of the others at the Institute, and everyone said that Tiago was a skilled and sober rider. He grew up on the island, learned to ride here, and had motorcycled all over Europe without so much as a close call."

"Knowing you as I do, there is probably no point in saying you have an eye for seeing causal connection where coincidence is all the explanation needed."

"I suppose. Still . . ."

They sat watching the growing shadows as they ate. Shira broke the silence. "You said you got another letter. Why don't you read it while the light is still good. I want to know what happens."

Karl set down the crust from the slice he was finishing, wiped his fingers on a paper napkin, and slipped the translated letter from his pocket.

> Dearest Hannah,
>
> I should tell you how I got here, how I ended up in Saxony. Dieter, the man who hides me, is not the soldier who brought me to Germany. Dieter is a bookkeeper for the government who was studying theology at university in hopes of one day becoming a Lutheran minister. In Bavaria! But he was friends since a boy with Father Warnking, whom he thinks has always hoped to convert him to the one true church. Everyone is so certain they have the single key to the kingdom to come. And I think there is no key because there is no gate, and you, my young deist, believe that all keys fit the lock. Your Rabbi back in Krakow would be so disappointed in you.
>
> So, I am here, hiding beneath the rafters in an empty, half-burned Catholic church, because Dieter's priest once convinced the Nazis that, owing to his pronounced limp from a boyhood fall, he was unfit for duty as a soldier carrying a rifle across the fields but fit enough to serve the Reich by carrying numbers from one column to another. Dieter took pity on me when he found me searching for scraps in the alleyway. His Christian charity almost fled when he discovered that Karl was with me, not only because it would complicate his fantasies, but because Karl had not been changed or washed. He tolerates the baby's presence now, so long as Karl does not choose the occasion of Dieter's visit to fuss or demand my attention. I try to time things so that Karl is fresh

asleep after nursing before Dieter arrives, and I try to distract Dieter right after he gives us whatever he has brought.

I hope you understand, my sister. Dieter, too, thinks that I am a German girl escaped from Poland, and he has promised to get me papers so that I do not have to hide, but I know these promises are made of fog, like the cloud that escapes his lips in the cold attic air when he repeats them. He has no interest in ending my hiding, because he would have to say goodbye to his private prostitute who services him for bread and sausages. He calls me that, *meine kleine Hure*, my little whore, but says it with a wink in hopes I will take no offense. At least I am not a Jew, he says, with a hint of worry in his voice. I reassure him that I am no Jew but a good Catholic, a good German girl. I quietly sing a hymn in German or quote the Latin Mass, a bit which I remember from the time Beatka took me with her. He affirms that I am very good and also adds that at least I am, thank God, not a good Lutheran girl turned to sin—or a filthy Jew.

The first night of my long journey here was difficult and frightening. After leaving our cottage in the wood and taking a long way around, I huddled under the stone bridge less than a kilometer away, as the snow turned to freezing rain and the wind whipped pins of ice against us. Karl awoke at what must have been around midnight and was inconsolable. I put him to the breast, but the strange surroundings or the howling wind distracted him from his usual concentration on the one thing in the world that mattered to him. If there were any way I could have returned to the relative warmth of the cottage, I would have, but you know that was impossible. The village was several kilometers distant, still, and walking in the dense wood on a stormy, moonless night would be far too difficult. In any event, there was no one in the village to whom I could turn, and there might even be more soldiers there.

I had, as yet, no plan, save to get away and survive. How I would do that, a young girl with an infant, in a world at war, I did not know. Plans would come later, when there was an opportunity to plan. At that moment all I could think of was surviving the night, and then the next day, and then the next.

Karl would nurse for a few minutes, then arch his back in protest and start to cry again. I tried to shush him, bouncing him, and pressing him to my breast, but he would have nothing of it. Then the soldiers arrived.

Chapter Fifteen

Western Poland, January, 1945

■ Julianna hugged Karl tightly against her and pulled as far back into the shadows under the bridge as she could. Karl nursed intermittently: a few draws, a pause to lift his head toward her as if to be convinced she was still there—a voice, a face attached to the breast that suckled him—then back for some more. She could hear the soldiers getting nearer on the road above, foot soldiers ahead and, farther back, motorcycles or small vehicles. She dared not speak but bent her head to keep a soft and steady shushing in Karl's ear, praying that it would calm him and be unnoticeable amidst the sound of the sleet and the water bubbling under the ice of the frozen brook at her feet.

And then there was the sound of many booted feet on stone paving just above her head and more in the wet snow and brush to either side of the narrow pathway. Karl shook his head back and forth before letting out a cry.

Suddenly, a soldier standing not three meters away, shouted at them. "*Halten Sie! Wer ist da?*"

"*Nicht schießen! Ich bin deutscher.*" Julianna held her hands aloft and kept repeating that she was German, begging them not to shoot. Karl, slung suddenly back against the makeshift sling of her jacket and lost in the folds of her heavy outer coat, started screaming.

"What is this? A baby in the woods?" The young soldier waved his rifle and shook his head in agitation. "Come quickly," he called to those behind him, "and see what I have found hiding under the bridge in the snow." The soldier waved to his comrades with one hand while keeping his rifle trained on them with the other. "I think it is a Jew-girl and her Jew-baby we have found. Come quickly."

Several soldiers now faced her, all with rifles aimed at her chest where Karl squirmed and screamed.

"No, I am not a Jew. I am German. I was born in Heidelberg, but my father moved us to Poland to help teach the ignorant Poles. My father was a lover of lost causes. My parents were killed by Partisans. I think the Partisans are all Jews or Jew-lovers,"—she spat for emphasis—"and Zionist sympathizers. And, of course, they hate all Germans, so they hated us. We were going to return to the Homeland, but my father was too slow about it and kept putting it off. He wanted to keep teaching the ignorant in the secret schools, but he was the one to be taught how the ignorant repay his service." She hoped she was not overacting.

"And you? How is it that you are here if they were killed?"

"I," she lowered her head in shame, "I was with my lover, my beloved soldier. Gerhard promised we would be married and would return together to Germany after the war."

There was hearty laughter all around, which startled Karl into crying again. "A soldier's promise, eh? To a Polish girl."

"I am not Polish. I told you, I am German. Can you not tell."

"Perhaps you are from Germany. Your accent says that may be true, but you are a Jew, I think, and that is why you are here hiding in the wood with no husband and a bastard Jew-baby. Give him here."

"No, not my Karl! Not my baby!" She lowered her hands and hugged Karl tightly through her coat. Around her, the clicking of rifles being readied fought against the sound of an approaching motorcycle. The motorcycle stopped suddenly, just short of the bridge, and a tall German climbed out of the sidecar. As he picked his way down the bank, the soldiers in front of her opened up to let him through.

"What is this? Why has the column stopped?"

"*Oberleutnant*, we found a Jewess, hiding under the bridge. She has a baby with her."

Julianna seized the moment to remove her woolen cap and step boldly toward the new arrival. She did not know the German ranks well, but he was clearly in charge. "Do I look Jewish to you, Lieutenant?" she said, shaking her head to draw attention to her blonde hair. She hoped that there was enough light spilling from the headlights of the motorcycles for him to see also the deep blue of her eyes. "We are Aryans, both. Like you."

The grim look left his face for only a moment, but he continued to study her as she edged subtly toward him and let her lips part a fraction of an inch.

"Let me see the baby," he said, his voice gentle but commanding. He held out his hands, waiting, his eyes locked to hers.

Julianna opened her coat and lifted Karl, by now too tired to fuss any more, and untangled him from the makeshift sling fashioned from her jacket.

The Lieutenant took him gently, and while holding him expertly in one arm, tugged at the swaddling in which he was wrapped. "Whew!" he said, wrinkling his nose. "Certainly not Jewish but most definitely in need of cleaning." The soldiers laughed as he turned Karl around and held him up to show his exposed genitals to the group.

"*Obersoldat*, here, take the baby and help this German girl."

"What?"

"Help clean him up. You heard me. And quickly."

"Jawohl, Oberleutnant!"

"Thank you, Lieutenant," Julianna said, so quietly that no one else could hear.

He looked down at her and something flashed in his eyes. "You remind me," he started to say. "But, you cannot stay here. We are being sent back to the Homeland. The war . . ."

"I want to get back also, to Germany, to take my Karl to meet his grandparents, who still live in Heidelberg." She let her eyes drop to his lips, then return to once again fix on the man's eyes.

The Lieutenant blinked, then closed his eyes. "We were to bivouac tonight outside the miserable little village at the foot of this mountain. We were delayed. You can ride in the other sidecar with the baby. *Leutnant* Braun, this young woman will take your place in the motorcycle sidecar until we reach the village."

"Yes, sir," he saluted sharply, but with his voice expressing just a hint of annoyance.

▪ ▪ ▪

The column shortly reached the outskirts of the village and set up camp in an abandoned farmstead. In the farmhouse, *Oberleutnant* Kolbe at last introduced himself to Julianna. "I am Maxim, Maxim Kolbe. You will sleep there, in that room, for the rest of the night. In the morning we will decide what happens."

"I am Julianna," she said, extending her hand. She almost said Julianna Nowak, but quickly recovered. "Julianna Neustadt. You already met my son, Karl."

Maxim's smile broadened slowly into a grin. In the light of the oil lantern now glowing on the table, he began to notice how young she was and, for the first time, to appreciate how sweet was her face. She turned reluctantly from him and opened the door to the room. A tattered mattress on the floor almost filled it. She lay the sleeping Karl in a sagging hollow, then wrapped herself around him, curling into a ball with them both under her heavy coat, their trapped breath quickly warming them.

The sky had not yet lightened when she felt Maxim against her back, one large hand reaching around under her, cradling her belly, the other turning like a wedge between her legs. He took her quietly from behind as he whispered, "Elise, Elise," and then he was gone.

▪ ▪ ▪

In the morning, the freezing rain redoubled, keeping the soldiers in the burned-out barn and the officers in the farmhouse through the day. Maxim waited until Karl was asleep after his afternoon feeding, then decided to send his two subordinates to lead a patrol to commandeer supplies from the village. As soon as the sound of the motorcycles faded, he grabbed Julianna and shoved her backwards toward the kitchen table, sweeping aside the maps spread there, then lifting her legs and skirt so that she was balanced, the rough edge of the table cutting into her buttocks. This time he was neither quiet nor gentle. He took her face in both hands, then squeezed her throat as he climaxed, shooting panic through her along with his semen. But it was over quickly, and his hands lifted. Afterwards, he stood and looked down at her turned face. "The war will soon be over, and I will be out of a job and maybe much worse. You want to be back in Heidelberg. I cannot take you that far, but if you have the fare, I can get you into Germany. For now, until the border, you will take care of me, and I will take care of you."

"And Karl."

"Yes, I suppose, and the baby. You are an educated girl, I can see, and you can work. You will make yourself useful, which will give me an excuse, a thin one, to take you on to help. The men will laugh and disapprove, but I don't care anymore because we will soon enough be scattered. Or dead. At this point I no longer care what is in store. A firing squad, a Russian bullet from a partisan sniper, a mine where it shouldn't be. It hardly matters. I died long ago."

■ ■ ■

On the veranda in Madeira, Karl read the last paragraphs of the letter with a growing ache in his throat:

> Lieutenant Kolbe got us into Germany proper, but once back in "civilization"—German civilization, that is—it was no longer possible to continue as his camp-follower. I waited until he was distracted and his men were mostly occupied. Then I simply walked away. I think he knew that I was going, but he didn't turn and no one made a move to stop me. I walked and took rides from soldiers and farmers, dairymen or lorry drivers, sometimes paying in the universal currency that men seem to seek, sometimes merely thanking my drivers for simple kindness. I didn't know Germany all that well, so I simply kept moving west, toward some fantasized future that lay beyond an ocean whose very existence I could only accept on faith. There was no ocean around me, only Germany at

war and by this time losing that war, which made them more desperate and even more dangerous. But I was one of them, an orphan, a young woman whose husband was killed by Russians, or by Poles, or by murdering, marauding Jews. The story changed depending on what I thought would best get me what I wanted or to where I wanted. Always I had to find ways to avoid checkpoints or roadblocks where I might be asked for papers.

Once, a young man with a stump for a hand let me ride with him in his farm wagon, then told me to quickly hide under the straw in back as we approached a bend in the dirt road. The wagon stopped, and I listened as he chatted amiably with a couple of bored soldiers. He stopped after turning off the road toward his parents' farm, wishing me good luck but asking no questions. I never knew who believed my stories and who saw through them but chose to help me anyway. What I did find was that, with time, I could tell who might be either trusted or easily fooled. Like with my Lieutenant, I didn't care which way it went, only that it went. And always I was grateful, grateful for such a warm coat and for such an easy baby. I knew he would soon grow less easy, and I would have to reach someplace and be somewhere.

When I arrived in Dresden because my last ride took me there while I slept in exhaustion, I realized that the cities offered opportunity as well as danger, but disappearing into the ebb and flow of wartime life was far easier there than in the open countryside. Then Dieter found me, and life took on a semblance of settled—for a time.

I am out of paper, and I don't know when Dieter will next bring me more, but I will write again then.

With all my love,
Julianna

Chapter Sixteen

■ With neither meetings nor lectures at the University for the day, Karl proposed to Shira that they strike off on their own. After a very Madeiran breakfast of coffee and a cheese sandwich on the veranda, they headed down the narrow street leading into town, dodging the *Horários do Funchal* buses that were almost as wide as the street, and keeping eyes to the ground to avoid deposits from the many feral dogs of the area. A longer than expected hike out Estrada Monumental, a wide street leading west, put them at the EuroDrive agency on the western edge of Funchal. There they picked up their rental car, a baby-blue SmartCar.

"Why get such a tiny car?" Shira asked. "Shouldn't we have a bit more horsepower for the steep roads of Madeira."

"Oh, you will see. This baby is a spirited little thing and really, really easy on the gasoline, which is very, very expensive here. Besides, I wanted to give it a test drive on Duarte's recommendation. It has a completely computer-controlled engine and drive train. It's actually a manual transmission but drives like an automatic when you want. The computer operates the gear shifting and the clutch as conditions demand, turns off the engine at stops, and instantly restarts when you press the accelerator—just amazing."

"You know, Karl, you are so predictable," she said, giving his arm a squeeze. "Always the geek."

Karl managed to navigate the pretzel turns and backtracking necessary to get from the rental garage to the on-ramp for the VR-1 highway that would take them on the short drive west to the fishing village of Câmara de Lobos. There they parked for a stroll around the town and *uma bica* at an outdoor café, where they stretched the espressos out with tiny sips. Getting into the slower pace of a day without destination, from Câmara de Lobos Karl took to the smaller secondary routes that he preferred, putting the sporty little car through its paces on the switchback turns of the narrow roads that climbed and twisted all the way to the lighthouse at Ponto do Pargo. There, at the western-most tip of the island, they left the car and walked down a dirt path below the red-and-white lighthouse to look out over the ocean. "There, that direction, the next stop is Florida." Karl waved. "Hi, Bini. Hi, Shoshi." From Ponto do Pargo they headed north in no hurry, stopping on the way at every point of interest and widening of the road that afforded a view of the ocean or the valleys peppered with *quintas*.

At Porto Moniz, a jagged volcanic arm jutted out into deep blue, roiling water that might as well have been a different ocean than the smooth gray seas they had left behind off Funchal. Like a layered pastry in an outstretched hand, a multi-colored mound of rock sat at the end of the point, and in the geologic forearm a network of interconnected tidal pools within the ancient lava flow hosted swimmers and sunbathers. From the parking area, Shira ran ahead toward the tidal pools, where she quickly changed into her swimsuit and dove in. The water trapped in the pools had been warmed by the sun shining on volcanic rock the color of ebony, but there was a shriek as Shira's head popped out of the water. "C-c-cold!" she shouted. "It's . . . it's wonderful. Come on in."

Karl had his doubts but followed her in and immediately turned back. Despite the chill water, there was no persuading Shira, who was determined to try as many of the interconnected pools as she could. While she continued to swim, Karl dried off, dressed, and retrieved his camera from his backpack. Offshore, swells gradually raised their heads and rolled in toward the rocky coastline to strike half-submerged barriers sending explosions of spray high into the air. Fine mist settled slowly back toward the sea, creating transient flashes of rainbow color before the next inbound wave crashed against the shore. By the time Shira, blue and covered by goosebumps, finally emerged from the pools, Karl's SD card was filled with shots of the rocky coast being pounded by waves, and they were both very hungry. A sign on a hotel up the road beckoned them to its restaurant, where they settled in for a leisurely seafood lunch overlooking the crashing sea.

On the drive back, Karl suggested that they stop again at Câmara de Lobos for a light, late dinner at a restaurant recommended by Rui. "Just before we get there, we have one more sight to see. It will not take long, but I hear it is quite special."

With the sun so far north in midsummer, the overlook at Cabo Girão was already in shadow when they arrived. Karl parked the SmartCar at the side of the road above the overlook, and they walked the rest of the way down toward the cliff, which was marked by a stone ledge stretching across the cobblestone path and, at the edge itself, a safety barrier resembling a wrought-iron garden fence, its thin metal fingers silhouetted against the graying sea.

Karl, instantly entranced by the near-vertical drop, leaned out to get a better view nearly straight down to the beach and sea below. "Look down," he said, "isn't that amazing? You feel like you are suspended in space."

Shira stiffened. "No, thank you. I don't want to look down," she said, burying her head in his shoulder.

Karl put his arm around her. "You don't have to. But isn't this incredible? So beautiful. You know, this is one of the highest sea-cliffs in Europe, over 1800 feet straight down."

"Karl, I love you, but you have such a wonderful way of being reassuring to a wife who is mildly afraid of heights and who puts little faith in guard rails and pylons and other marvels of civil engineering that hold her husband in thrall."

"Okay, I'll shut up." Karl leaned out again over the waist-high railing atop the fence and stared down at the narrow stretch of gravel beach in the shadows far below. The wind had picked up and the sea offshore was frosted with scattered whitecaps. Karl leaned out farther still, trying to follow the contours of the drop below them, then straightened up again as Shira tugged at him. They stood, arm-in-arm, gazing out over the darkening sea, with the warm wind caressing their cheeks.

The quiet was broken by the sound of squealing tires and alarmed voices behind them calling out in Portuguese. Karl turned just in time to see a car speeding away and a driverless blue SmartCar rolling toward them, gathering speed as it approached. Karl shoved Shira to the right ahead of him, putting a tree between them and the car hurtling toward them. The light car struck the low stone ledge. Tall and stubby, the oddly proportioned vehicle upended on impact, tumbled over, and slammed into the railing whose thin metal bars gave way under the force. The car, with its undercarriage entangled in the bars of the fence, swung out over the edge, wrenching the railing on the far side from its anchors and twisting their side out over the void. The falling car ripped free from the railing and tumbled noisily down into the shadows toward the sea.

Shira screamed. She was flattened against the fence to the side, her leg caught in the bars stretched out over the edge of the cliff. Karl scrambled to reach her, but the cobblestone paving at the damaged edge of the walkway gave way under him, and he found himself slipping over the side. Someone grabbed his arm and shouted something in Portuguese. Karl, his feet now dangling in empty space, tried to get purchase with his knees. Above him, a second young man reached for Karl's belt, and the two pulled him up onto intact pavement. Karl looked to his left to where Shira had been seconds before. The entire section of the fencing had been pulled from the stone post and was gone.

"Oh, my God. Shira!" he shouted into the emptiness.

"I'm over here, by the tree. I scrambled up, like on a ladder, before the fence broke off. Are you all right?"

"Yes, I'm okay, thanks to these young men." He faced them and bowed slightly. *Obrigado, muito obrigado.* I thank you so much. You saved my life."

"*Não tem de que,*" said one of them. The other said, "He means it was nothing. We just helped you up."

"Shira, are you hurt?"

"I have some scrapes, but I am okay," she said, limping slightly as she approached. "What happened?"

"I don't know. I am certain that I left the car in park, and I took the keys. It was unlocked—it's Madeira—but . . . I don't know what happened. And that's what I am going to tell the police when they get here."

After one of the bystanders telephoned the police for them, it was not ten minutes before officers were on the scene, looking over the side of the cliff and shaking their heads. "You are very lucky, *Senhor e Senhora*," said one of the officers. "*Sim*," said the other, "but that will be very expensive to retrieve what is left of your automobile."

"It's not my car; it's a rental."

"Oh, I am sorry to hear that."

"But we had full coverage, so the insurance should cover everything."

"Oh, I would not say that. It depends on the contract. This is a single-car accident. It might have been better if you had crashed into someone. But, maybe you rent from a company that doesn't care if you drive their car off the cliff."

"I didn't drive the car off the cliff. If I had, we would be down there and not up here."

"Most fortunate that you jumped out in time."

Karl tried to explain that they were not in the car when it rolled, on its own accord, down the path and over the cliff.

When the police were finished taking his statement and noting down all his details, Karl returned to where Shira was sitting at the side of the road, well back from the gap at the edge of the precipice. He put his arm around her, and a shiver went through them both.

"So close," he said. "We were very lucky."

"No thanks to computer-controlled cars," Shira added.

"What did you say?"

"I was expressing my reservations about smart cars run by dumb computers."

Karl suddenly turned from Shira and walked back to the patrol car where one of the police was talking on the radio while the other filled out a report.

"What will happen to the car?"

"It will be recovered and looked at to see if maybe the brakes failed, although it is very strange how it could roll of its own accord on nearly level ground. Perhaps you will not have to pay for it after all."

"I am at the University, a visiting Professor. I want some of my colleagues to have a chance to look at the car. Is that possible?"

There was an almost instantaneous change in demeanor as the officer pulled himself erect. "Oh, of course, Senhor Professor," he said. "If you have a business card, I will have you called when we have recovered the car. Where are you staying? I will need it for my report. I can call a taxi for you, also."

Karl walked back to where Shira sat at the side of the road. "What was that all about?" she asked.

"I think it is a good thing to be a professor here in Madeira. Anyway, he is getting a taxi for us. Not a very good ending to our first day exploring on our own."

"These things happen, Karl; they just happen. We were very lucky. Besides, there will be other opportunities to explore."

■ ■ ■

The sun was already beating directly down on the plaza between the University and Tecnopolo when Karl arrived the following day. He had spent the morning filling out forms and answering questions and generally being made to feel that he had done something wrong. Most bizarre was that it seemed the police had still wanted to charge him with failing to wear the required safety vest after an accident, which was a violation here. Regardless of how many times he explained that his car was on the rocky beach below Cabo Girão and that it would have been impractical, to say the least, to have retrieved the safety gear from the car, the police had seemed insistent that he had failed to abide by the law. When Karl said that he would call the U.S. Embassy in Madeira, the police officer interviewing him had laughed. "The Embassy? It is in Lisboa, on the continent, 900 kilometers distant. I do not think it will help much to call them." However, after that the man had suddenly softened and allowed Karl to go "pending further investigation."

As Karl headed for the entrance to the University, Duarte was coming from Tecnopolo.

"*Bom dia*, Karl. Are you trying to get into a Red Bull video?"

"Good morning, Duarte. What are you talking about?"

"Your car. I understand you drove a rental car off Cabo Girão. Like that famous base jumper in the YouTube video who drove his motorcycle over the edge and parachuted to the beach below."

"How do you know about the car?"

"It was on the television. 'Wreckage on the beach. Visiting Professor drives rented car into the sea.' Very dramatic. But no video of the plunge. You must be some driver."

"It drove itself, Duarte, which is what I want to talk with you about. You said you knew people in the local police. Still?"

"Yes, a cousin."

"I want to get access to the event log on the SmartCar I rented. Can you arrange that?"

"Perhaps. What model was it, what year?"

"Brand new. The sport two-seater, with the convertible roof. Less than 500 kilometers on it."

Duarte slapped him on the back as they entered the building. "You are a terrible person, my friend. You destroyed a defenseless baby car."

"I am telling you, Duarte, it committed suicide. Can you get me the computer log?"

"On those new models, there is more than one log. Besides the event log, there is a separate command log in the computer itself. Not everyone knows this, but I have studied the on-board systems on my own SmartCar."

"Great! Just get me access to those logs. And see if your cousin can get the police to get off my back. Tell him that I had nothing to do with that car going off the cliff."

■ ■ ■

Karl spent what remained of his day preparing for his next lecture. Shira was off exploring on her own but had promised to meet him downtown for dinner. He was about to pack up for the walk back to the apartment when Duarte arrived waving a sheaf of A4 paper.

"I got them. Here they are?"

"Here are what? Oh, right, the onboard computer logs. Great, let's take a look."

Duarte came around to the other side of the desk and spread the sheets of paper in a fan.

"But these are just numbers, codes. What do they mean?"

"This is all I could get from my cousin, a raw printout. We jury-rigged a cable set to download to an office computer, but we didn't have access to the Daimler diagnostic equipment."

"How are we going to make sense of these?"

Duarte's eyebrows arched into semicircles, and he shrugged.

Karl grunted, stretching it out into a gravelly groan. "Can we get the files from the police computer? No? Then do you have a secretary or someone who could transcribe these into a computer file?"

"No, but I can scan them and crank them through optical character recognition. OCR should be pretty reliable with nothing but a bunch of numbers. Why, what do you have in mind?"

"More contacts in Germany. The last time I did work with this one guy I know, it was still DaimlerChrysler, but it's worth a try. It would be great if you scan and convert these for me, then email— no, wait—put the files in a drop-box where I and Klaus can pick them up. I am beginning to distrust open email."

"What do you mean?"

Reflexively, Karl lowered his voice. "Hours after they send me email about their reverse engineering of the microprocessor, Nuno and Tiago have a, quote-unquote, accident. The next day a rental SmartCar goes rogue and almost takes out Shira and me. I don't like this, not one bit."

Duarte scowled as he tapped his chin with his left hand. "The drop-box folder," he announced, "will be on the departmental server, not the MIRI system. It will be called PASTA and the password will be LASANHA, Portuguese spelling."

Karl smiled at the thought of how little difference this would make to people like his Mossad pals, but he nodded and patted Duarte on the shoulder. "Good, that's the way to think. And be careful."

Chapter Seventeen

◼ Anat took the steps two at a time, but this time turned left, down the short hall, and into the Director's office. From the size and the appointments, no one would conclude that this was the office of the senior-most person in HaMossad. Anat stood in the doorway, waiting to be acknowledged. Without looking up, the director waved her in and gestured toward one of two chairs haphazardly placed facing his desk.

"Well?"

Anat smiled. "Never one for long introductory clauses, are we? Did you know that the manufacture of Israel's new avionics chipset is being outsourced to a company in Taiwan." The director said nothing. "I'll take that as a yes." As he continued to look at her, she found his expression as unreadable as if it had been encrypted. Still, even an undecipherable message in code made a statement about the sender. As McLuhan had so quotably said it, the medium itself is the message. "Then the question is why?" she continued. "Which I assume you are either in no position to answer, in which case you will pretend not to know, or you have no intention to answer, in which case you will feign ignorance."

The director blinked but remained impassive, waiting.

"I think Taiwan may be the source of the contraband chips, although that would seem to be rather too obvious, and the growing availability would suggest there is probably at least one other leaky pipe. I also have someone I want to start keeping a close eye on."

"Lustig."

Anat was surprised by this, but determined not to let on. As her boss had done moments before, she assented with ambiguous silence. "I know we are short staffed, but I think we need someone in Taiwan. I assume that's Dror's department, and—let me guess—we already have someone there."

The Director continued just to look at her, poker-faced.

"How long would it take to get one of our people into Portugal, then, someone fluent in Portuguese?"

The Director snapped his fingers.

"Meaning?"

"He's there, in Madeira. That is where your asset is, isn't it?"

Anat realized she should have anticipated all this when the Director had given her free rein on tracking the chips. She was also thinking that, in the sense she and her colleagues used the term, Karl was no asset. Assets were tokens to be played in a shifting game, to be used, traded, discarded if necessary. She could never burn Karl, sacrifice him, so, therefore, he was not an asset. Or she was no longer a member of the team. Well, she thought, two can play the game. She said nothing.

"Taiwan," the Director said, appearing to change the subject, "is Dror's territory, Madeira is not."

Anat was wondering just who was calling the shots in Madeira, but she asked a different question. "I thought you were relying on me. Don't you trust me?"

The Director didn't answer, except with more loud silence, then he started on one of his infamous tangents. "You know, don't you, that I was a mathematician? I finished my military service, signal corps, and left. Not like so many of the people on your floor who made a beeline for our headquarters as soon as they got out of the military. No, I went to the Technion, got a PhD in maths, studied with the best and brightest in the field, including no less than the duly infamous Dr. Felicity Gold, a name I imagine you remember from the caper on the Temple Mount. She is, of course, still in prison.

"I specialized in ciphers and encryption, but not for the content or application, just for the simple joy of abstractions to be constructed and puzzles to be solved. Then I was recruited. I didn't pound on any doors, the doorway came to me. 'Lift high your lintels, o you ancient gates.' The Institute opened its gates for me, they trained me, and they sent me into the field. I never looked at another equation in my life, except when it comes to fudging the budget and trying to persuade the Knesset that what we do is a bargain for the State of Israel.

"My wife says that nothing has changed, that I am calculating and always have been."

Anat realized that her question had been answered, which immediately took her to her own next calculation, that she should trust the Director—exactly as much as he trusted her. After decades in the bright light of overhead fluorescents and desk lamps, she was finding herself suddenly thrown back into the game of shadows, looking over her shoulder without turning her head. She rose to leave, then stopped at the door. "We have field operatives who speak Portuguese? Amazing."

"Sephardim," he said. "Dutch Jews, South Americans. What you want, we got."

"Madeira seems such an unlikely place to position one of our all-too-scarce *katsas*. I suppose there is a reason, that it makes sense."

"We only put people where they are needed, where something is happening."

"Am I interrupting something?" It was Bulofsky standing in the doorway, his perpetual look of disapproval deepening when Anat turned to see who it was.

"We're almost done here," the Director said. "Come back in a few minutes."

"I can wait. Go ahead."

"Come back in a few minutes, Bulofsky."

"Oh," was all Bulofsky said as he backed away.

The Director coughed, looked heavenward, and shrugged in one stream that spoke reams, a nonverbal version of "What can you do? Bulofsky is Bulofsky."

She echoed his eye-roll. "Look, I'm out of here; I have plenty to do sorting this one into piles."

"As you sort things, don't always take the labels too literally. Sometimes the discard pile has useful scraps."

Anat, at a loss for words over his cryptic advice, stood and clicked her heels in an unconscious salute. In the hall outside the Director's office, she found David Bulofsky pacing back and forth.

"I need to talk with him," he said.

"I'm sure," she said. Her footsteps echoed down the hall as the Director waved Bulofsky into his office and reached for his secure telephone.

At the stairwell, Anat was met by Dror Magen coming up. As he pushed past her turning toward the Director's office, he twitched a half smile in her direction. "Meeting," he mumbled, as if an explanation were needed, but he neither slowed nor elaborated.

As she paused before starting down the stairs, Anat heard snatches of a heated conversation that was unsettling.

▪ ▪ ▪

She was already deep in thought before reaching her office. What was the Director trying to tell her? If she couldn't trust him, who could she trust? Maybe that's his message to her, that she was on her own with a case that was bigger and more complicated than she had previously thought. She needed to talk this through with someone, and she knew who that someone was.

Appearing busy for the rest of the day was the hard part for Anat, whose work ethic might as well have been tattooed across her breasts. She knew that her next move would be tricky, that there was no way out of Israel that would not draw attention to herself. And she, of all people, knew that any communication via any medium would be monitored and flagged. If she could track Karl Lustig, for her colleagues to follow Anat Dorfman would be like tracking an electric menorah carried in a Hanukkah parade.

Over dinner, she did something she almost never did: she talked shop with her husband. It was all cast in vague and indirect terms, but Lev, who had become a successful author of espionage fiction since retiring from Mossad, had never lost his nose for intrigue. He immediately caught on to where she was leading the conversation and told her that he had no interest. "Let's go for a walk," he said, "It will do us both good."

Half a kilometer from the apartment, he reopened the conversation. "Okay, what's troubling you? Talk."

She outlined what had been happening, leaving Lev to fill in most of the blanks. "I heard part of the conversation after I left the Director's office. He was speaking of the need to plug the holes at whatever cost. He used that phrase—plug the holes at whatever cost—more than once. This was right after his conversation with me about my tracking of Karl Lustig in Madeira. And before that, he had let me know, indirectly, that he was not putting any trust in me."

"Okay, assume they are keeping an eye on you," he said, "and will watch everything you do, so just do it openly. My dear friend Migdal, may his memory be a blessing, ran his controversial Trade Now initiative with the Palestinians while his ex-buddies in HaMossad dogged his footsteps. He made openness and transparency an art form. As long as they could always see his hands on the table, so long as his every move was open and above board, he figured he was safe. If he acted suspiciously, he would be a goner. Same game applies here and now. Don't hide anything. Work in the open and let them watch."

"You, Lev, are the best partner. And you certainly have given me something to think about."

Chapter Eighteen

■ Duarte sauntered into Karl's office and immediately walked around the desk, leaned over Karl's shoulder, and shook his head. "No, that is the wrong command. You are rusty. You haven't been doing enough programming lately."

"I haven't been doing any programming lately, not for many years. It's far easier to think big thoughts and then write big words to explain it all. And finally to submit big invoices."

"You mock yourself too easily, Professor Karl. But, please, let me do this. We will get the codes translated faster."

Karl stood up and offered his chair to Duarte, who started typing even as he was seating himself. Duarte submitted the short program to be compiled and run, but it returned an error. He scrolled rapidly through the instructions, retyped one of Karl's lines, and submitted the program again. This time it compiled and started executing. When it reached end-of-job, Duarte opened the output file with Excel. In neat columns were the original code from the dump of the car's log files, the simple symbolic translation, and an extended explanation.

"This is from the event recorder," he said, pointing. "It shows what we would expect. It confirms what you told the police. There, this code is when the car was stopped, then when it was put in park, here the doors closed. Then it starts again, accelerates quickly, shifts up, decelerates even more quickly—that's the impact—the airbags deploy, and ... yes, these error codes are because the accelerometers exceeded their limit settings as the car flipped over. It's all straightforward, except for the car starting. See, back there is the 'key removed' event, but there is no 'key inserted' event before the car starts again. Obviously something interesting is going on there. Now, let's look at the internal computer log. That," Duarte said, pointing to a line a third of the way down the screen, "is the most interesting of all. Do you see what it is?"

"Yes, a program update, according to the notation column. They must have serviced the car sometime and updated the firmware."

"Look at the time stamp. That would be after you arrived at Cabo Girão, not before you rented the car. The embedded program was modified after you arrived."

"How is that possible?"

"Look at the lines just above, 'Mobile telecommunication access to head unit.' Then into the multimedia system, from there, a link into the car's CAN bus—that's the Car Area Network—and on to the on-board computer. That's how."

"This stuff is supposed to be secure."

"In principle, but just like factory controllers and cellphones and desktop PCs, there are unplugged holes and tunnels under the firewalls. If you know what you are doing and the vehicle is online, there are ways in. Not just this car, but any vehicle that's online, reachable by phone, or connected by Bluetooth. No one in the industry wants to own up to the vulnerabilities, but they are there."

"So, this suggests somebody hacked into the on-board computer and reprogrammed it while we were enjoying the view. The only people there, that I remember, were those two students. But why would they have hacked our car, sending it hurtling at us, and then save my life."

"Perhaps it was just a hack and not intended to hurt anyone."

"Doesn't make sense, but neither does an intentional intrusion, unless it's part of something bigger and more sinister."

"I am thinking like you, because look down here, the next-to-last record in the log file. That command would reset the computer, which would clear the log and restore the factory-default configuration. It would have erased their tracks."

"Would have? What went wrong?"

"The very last line is an error code. Their hacked program threw an exception. There was a bug of some sort, so the program never successfully executed the last command. They are not quite the super-programmers they must think they are."

"Lucky for us."

"But Karl, this does not seem very lucky. Somebody hacked into your car and bricked it. And almost bricked you."

"Are you sure you want to hang around me?"

"I want to hang around, yes. And tomorrow I will drive you to Rabaçal as I promised, but I will take my son's car, which is an old Ford Focus with a manual transmission and no on-board computer to be hacked into without wires.

"Oh, here," he said, reaching into his jacket pocket, "I have another letter for you. Enjoy the rest of your day. Tomorrow I will be at the apartment at eight hours to take you to Encumeada and Rabaçal."

■ ■ ■

In Tel Aviv, Anat and Lev were taking another stroll on an evening that threatened hardly to cool at all.

"Why would we have an agent in Madeira? That's what I want to figure out," Anat said. "And what does this have to do with China stealing our latest avionics technology? And is it just coincidence that Karl is in Madeira with Shira?"

"Too many questions to answer from here, especially if you think the Director is not being straight with you. You have been sitting on your wonderfully skinny little tuchas for too long, my love. You need to go where the questions are if you want to find the answers."

"How can I do that if they are watching every move."

"As I told you before, if they know every move, just move, hide nothing. You did say the Director gave you free rein. Use it. While you have it, use it. You're a chief now, not an Indian. Buy the tickets and go. If they don't want you to go, they will stop you. If they don't stop you, then you are in the clear."

"Go with me."

"I'm retired. I only write about cloak-and-dagger stuff these days. I'm too old."

"Karl Lustig is retired, too. Or at least he should be. And maybe you shouldn't be. Come with me. Keep me company. Watch my back."

"I'd rather watch your front."

She deliberately bumped into him. "Too old, eh? I'd say you are as young as ever, with the same young man's interests as always."

Lev stopped and waited for Anat to turn around and face him. "Okay, I'll go with you, if you insist, but if you get me killed, I will never forgive you. And one more thing."

"Yes?"

"There is a man with a phased-array microphone sitting in a blue Fiat just down the block. You should have noticed him."

"I did, dearest one. As you said. Nothing hidden." She turned to shout over her shoulder. "Hello, Director. Goodbye, Director."

▪ ▪ ▪

In Funchal, with a freshening breeze promising a cooler evening, Karl sat with Shira on their veranda and unfolded the newly translated letter.

> Dear Hanna,
>
> [translator's note: the writer uses a different spelling here and is inconsistent in this letter]
>
> I have been thinking of the late spring day you arrived at the cottage in the wood. I had no idea how you had found us or what had brought you there. It was, I suppose, a modest miracle. You, always the believer, would not suppose but would be certain.
>
> You were such a forlorn sight when I opened the door: your hair a stringy mess from the rain, your shoes and the bottom of your coat caked with mud, and the look on your face one of utter despair. I pulled you in quickly—the rain had stopped, the sun had not yet set, and we knew there were patrols in the region. Then I fussed over you as I got you out of your wet clothes. I remember feeling silly about my reaction when I saw how much you had grown, how your

breasts were now bigger than mine, and how, when you stood, you looked me in the eye. I never did tell you of the wave of shame and embarrassment that swept me when I realized how much I enjoyed looking at your body. I had to concentrate while toweling you off, ordering myself to keep moving and not linger too long over your slim hips and long legs. When I kissed you on the forehead, I really wanted to kiss you elsewhere, everywhere.

You stood there, frozen for a moment. Then the knock came on the door—three slow, a pause, two fast, pause, and again—Józef's little Morse code joke: oi, oi!

Chapter Nineteen

Western Poland, spring 1944

■ Józef knocked in code, waited a moment, and pulled on the latch. He almost dropped the young fox from his hand when he saw his sister with a naked young girl. The girl was slim to the point of being skinny, but then, nearly everyone was that way these days. He dropped his eyes in respect, but not without pausing to appreciate her breasts, which were firm and somewhat larger than his sister's, and then to her feet and a furtive glance back up to note the small, dark patch of hair between her legs. Her skin was covered with goose bumps and her chestnut nipples were contracted from the cold—firm little buttons, inviting. As if suddenly but belatedly aware of his presence, she grabbed at the towel Julianna was holding and clutched it to her chest.

"I'm sorry, I . . ." he said, holding out the fox. "I caught a fox. Fox meat is not very good, but then you probably know that. We haven't had meat for weeks, though, so this is, well, good. I'll, I'll go and, ah, dress it."

Chana stared, unmoving, as he backed away. "You've grown a mustache," she said, trying to keep the tremolo from her voice. He shrugged and backed out of the cottage.

At dinner, a woody potato from last year divided in five and a handful of early greens were made festive by the fresh, if gamey, meat, Chana told her story in a narrative rush.

"We were among the few families not deported from Kraków when the Germans first declared it was to become a 'clean city,' free of Jews. Father had left the university to work for the electric company, reasoning that it would be seen as essential, but we were forced to move into the Kraków Ghetto with the others. Then Mama and Papa and Symcha were brought to Zgody Square to be relocated in the second wave. I knew what that meant, despite the lies that people told themselves—and me. I was not with them because I was ... with a friend when they were taken away. I don't know where they were sent, but Mordko told me that he saw them being boarded onto a train in Prokocim.

"I had already left the ghetto—it was not too hard—because Papa said I had to get to Palestine and join the Zionists, that I had to keep the coat, whatever happened, and get to Palestine with it. He had sent me to Tadeusz, who was Catholic but said he was a Zionist sympathizer and would help get me to Palestine. I stayed with Tadeusz for a few months. He kept telling me of his connections with the Partisans, but I never met any Partisans and Tadeusz was not a nice boy. I finally left Kraków and wandered through the countryside, hiding, stealing food, moving from farm to farm, hoping to find the Partisans. But I never did. I hid and moved until I was caught. But the Karsickis were good people, who bleached and straightened my hair. They pretended I was a niece and called me Anika. They fed and clothed me until they were caught out because the childless neighbors had become jealous and suspicious of the niece who helped them. I was in the meadow when the soldiers arrived. I saw Stefan and Katrine pulled from the farmhouse and shot by the road. Little Cyryl, ran, his short legs pumping, but they shot him in the back. Then the soldiers saw me, but I ran and was too fast for them. I just kept moving, always moving, hiding to avoid the patrols, stealing, always moving.

"Finally, one day, I recognized where I was, a turn in the road that I remembered. I knew the path, and where to find it by the berry bushes and the boulder shaped like a cow's rump. I remembered this place, the woodsman's cottage, your retreat in the wood you called it. So I hiked here."

"You came by foot, all the way from Kraków?"

"Not all at once," she laughed. "It's taken many months. I didn't think I would find you here. I had thought that you were ... like the others."

Henrik reached out to her. "Well, you are welcome here. You can sleep in the loft with Julianna. You already know how to steal and forage and not get caught. Józef will teach you how to trap and dress what you catch."

Margit lowered her head, as if to trap her words, "She's a Jew. If we are caught hiding her . . ."

"If we are caught, whether hiding her or not, we are dead. But I think the war is nearly over, and we will not have to hide here in the wood much longer. When I last slipped into the market, I heard rumors that the Americans were in Europe or soon would be. I predict the end is near."

"You are always predicting, Henrik, always."

"And I am nearly always right."

"Less and less often are you right."

Julianna, ready as always to defuse the tension between her parents, rose from the table and tugged at Chana's hand. "Come, I'll show you the loft where we sleep. You have to climb these pegs on the wall, but it is cozy under the rafters, and the heat from the fire rises, at least at first. We only make a fire after dark and only when we absolutely must, but still, it is not too bad up there. Mama sleeps on the bench over there and Papa and Józef have to sleep on the floor.

"You can be my little sister, the little sister that I have always wanted." She shot a glance not at her parents but at her brother. "We will sleep together, like sisters," she said, looking straight at Józef. She led the way up the pegs and reached back with her hand to help Chana up the last bit.

▪ ▪ ▪

In the dark of the night, with quiet settled over the cottage, Julianna turned toward Chana. "There is so much to tell you, my new sister," she whispered, as she put her arms around Chana and snuggled close.

"And I have many things to tell you," Chana replied. "But please don't ask me to tell you everything. There are things I do not want even to recall. Do you understand?"

"Oh yes, there are such things for me, too. You cannot believe how glad I am to have you here with me, to have you to talk to, and to keep me warm at night, safe at night."

The change in the tone of the tiny household was not immediate, but it soon was evident to everyone. Józef and Julianna ceased to squabble quite as much, and both became very attentive and protective of Chana, who, because she was Jewish and looked the part, was not permitted to roam far from the cottage. Julianna was both envious and relieved by the shift of Józef's attention to Chana. He even sometimes brought wildflowers—"to brighten our drab cottage," he would say—but always he handed them to Chana with a fleeting smile.

"After the war," Henrik mumbled one evening, "who knows." He nodded toward Chana, then Józef.

"After the war, she will still be a Jewess," Margit answered quietly.

■ ■ ■

Chana was the first to notice, even without Julianna telling her. She asked, but Julianna only cried quietly in the night and said nothing in response. But the day arrived when it was no longer possible for Julianna to hide her condition. Amidst tears, she told her mother of being caught stealing eggs from the farm at the bottom of the hill. Jan, the farmer's youngest son, had threatened to turn her in unless she lifted her dress for him. She had no choice. He was clumsy and inexperienced, and ended up slipping out and spilling himself on her dress. But his father, who had heard the grunting, was more skilled and more demanding. He sent his son away to pull weeds, then kept her at the farm for the rest of the morning. When finally he let her go, he took back the eggs. She had lied to him about how she had arrived, saying she had come from a village that she thought he would not know, and when she left, she left in that direction.

This was what she told her mother, and this was what her mother told her father. This is what they believed and chose to believe. They started making plans for the baby, as if the times were normal and they were not living in hiding in the woods and their only daughter was not carrying the bastard child of an ignorant farmer.

Julianna was nearly to term when Józef suddenly announced that he was leaving. "I have heard that there is a group of Armia Krojowa bivouacked nearby. The resistance may have been slow to start, but the AK is growing in numbers and around here they have become bolder in their escapades. I have decided to join up with them."

His father, who hated killing anything and admitted to having been a pacifist while at university, said, "Good," then walked out the door. His mother cried and tried to convince her son that the resistance was doomed, then that it was unnecessary, then finally that they needed him at home.

"I am in the way here, Mama, another mouth to feed. With the baby coming, there will be no room. I want to fight for my country. It is an embarrassment to be this old and not be part of the fight for our freedom." He said these passionate words without passion, then lifted his knapsack and started out in the direction of the deeper woods.

Julianna looked to her mother for some clue as to what was going on, but her mother turned away. Then Julianna turned to Chana, who was sitting in the corner, head bowed, saying nothing.

In a flash of recognition, it all made sense. Julianna ran out the door, after her brother. In her condition, it was all that she could do to catch up, but she stumbled through the brush and finally was able to grab at his knapsack. He whirled around and said, "What? Want to say goodbye to your beloved brother, a final kiss?"

"I want to kill my beloved brother, my stinking bastard brother. How could you? She's just a girl." She grabbed him, but he shrugged her off, turned, and started out again along the all but invisible trail.

"Józef, I am speaking to you. Why? Why, you bastard, why did you rape her?"

He turned back. "It wasn't rape." He spat out the words. "She wanted it. It was not like with you. You never wanted it. But who cares? And who knows? No one. You were so clever with your tall tale of the farmer and his son."

She struck at his face with all the force she could muster. He did not flinch, but when her other hand came out from her jacket, he grabbed her wrist, twisting it, shaking the pocketknife loose from her grip. "My beloved sister," he said, as he bent to retrieve the knife. He folded it and tossed it to her. "Here, you never know when this might come in handy. Maybe you can cut the cord with it." He turned once more and started back down the path.

"You keep it, Józef. You're the one who wants to fight for Poland." She opened the knife again and lunged.

He jerked and clutched at his shoulder where the knife handle protruded from his jacket just above his shoulder blade. He cursed and pulled it out. The wound was not serious, but it was an inconvenient start to the journey. And it was starting to hurt like hell.

▪ ▪ ▪

In the twilight in Funchal, Karl looked up at Shira. "There is another postscript," he said, struggling to keep his voice level.

> I got word from one of my German soldiers—that is another story I will tell in another letter—that an AK patrol tried to ambush a German cavalcade on a road a few kilometers north of our cottage. One of those killed in the brief firefight was a young recruit with a moustache and a bandaged left shoulder who was carrying an empty knapsack. It was obviously our Józef, and the German soldier remembered him because he had been so poorly trained and poorly equipped. He had rushed an escort motorcycle with an unloaded pistol.
>
> Do you remember the day Karl was born, barely a month after Józef left? You were so eager to help. By then Józef was probably already dead, so my Karl was fatherless, which was for the best. I did so love Józef, you know, even though he betrayed that love. I know you also loved him. I did not cry when he left, but I did when I heard of his death. It is funny how much both

his sons looked like him. Neither Mama nor Papa would ever say anything, although in your case they certainly knew, because there was no fictitious farmer on whom to lay the blame, and you were never far from the house. Still it was never spoken about.

Although you hardly showed until quite late, I knew, of course, because you would press against me at night and would rise early because you felt unwell. And then, only months after Karl was born, your little Mosje, your Moishele, arrived. You despaired that there would be no bris for your son, and my father refused to serve as mohel. He admitted to me that he considered the practice of ritual circumcision a superstitious barbarism, but he said to you that the risk of infection was too great under the circumstances. He was probably right. I did my best to persuade you that an uncircumcised Jew was still a Jew. I still do not know if you were convinced or merely dropped the subject, but you never raised it again.

Yours,

Julianna

Karl gasped as he put down the letter. "So, now we know who my real father was. I know that's not politically correct to say it that way, and it's unfair to the father who raised me, but I am just not used to dealing with all this. Do you realize what it means? Do you understand? My father was my mother's brother. My God. Incest. I'm not just a bastard, I'm a, a, what the hell is that word? I'm a . . . what is it in Hebrew? A *mamzer*. I'm unclean, unfit."

"That isn't what it means, Karl. It is a very old biblical concept. And, in your case, it does not apply because you are not Jewish. Besides, this is just a letter, telling a story from far away and long ago. We don't know how much of this is real or how much of it is true or how much of it is about you."

"And you were the one who kept telling me to believe in this story. Now that I do, you want to cast doubt?"

"What does it matter in the end. Whatever the story, you are still you, and I still love you. Let's get some sleep. Duarte picks us up early tomorrow."

Chapter Twenty

■ From Encumeada, where they had stopped at the *miradouro* to gaze down from the overlook on the clouds below—wispy ghosts floating over tree-covered mountains and pouring like aerial rivers down blue-green valleys—they headed west. The route incongruously led them over open high plains, past platoons of giant, arm-waving white sentinels lining the island's wind farms, and through flat surrounds that reminded Karl of the open chaparral of the American Southwest. Horned cattle grazed on the gently rolling terrain strewn with boulders and low brush, completing, for the untrained eye, the impression of them all being suddenly transplanted from a mountainous, subtropical island to the middle of Arizona or Utah.

"We are almost there. And that," Duarte said, pointing toward a roadside restaurant called Jungle Rain, "is the weirdest name in the world. There is no jungle on the island and here it is mostly dry. That is where I will wait for you."

"Are you sure this is okay?" Shira asked. "We seem to be putting you to a lot of trouble."

"It is no trouble. This is a really good levada walk that you should definitely do before you leave Madeira, but you have no car and I hate hiking. Besides, the Jungle Rain has free Wi-Fi, so I will catch up on my email while you walk to the fountains and back. This is fine."

Karl and Shira had intended to drive a rental car to Rabaçal but had learned that no agency would rent them a car after the well-publicized incident at Cabo Girão. They were now completely dependent on buses, friends, and shank's mare for their remaining days on the island.

Duarte dropped them off amidst a handful of cars and a few butterscotch cows grazing in the parking area at the top of the road leading down to Rabaçal, the start of the levada walk to Vinte e Cinco Fontes. "You can walk down from here," he said, "or pay for a shuttle bus. It is about two kilometers. Perhaps you will take the bus on your return."

"Perhaps we will."

"Yes, and I will be back here waiting in about three hours, or you can call my cell phone if you give up earlier or are speed-walkers on the levada."

"We are definitely not speed-walkers, and we are not quitters, so we will meet you here in three hours or so." Karl slapped the top of the car roof as he smiled at Duarte.

The serpentine paved road leading down to the trailhead at Rabaçal was easy enough walking downhill but steep enough to make Karl wonder about what the climb back out might be like after a strenuous hike. Rabaçal itself seemed to be no more than a single building. They followed the signs for Vinte e Cinco Fontes, which took them to the start of a downward trail steep enough to require stone steps. After several hundred of these that had Karl's knees complaining loudly, the path leveled out and joined the levada itself. There the subtle slope that kept the water flowing made for easy walking alongside the channel.

The levada was part of Madeira's vast and exquisitely engineered network of narrow waterways carved out over nearly four centuries to carry water from the rainy north side of the island and the many springs in the mountains to the thirsty southeast. Through woodland and brush, along the edge of steep canyons, and over narrow bridges, the levadas offered the hiker ever changing scenery and spectacular vistas. Shira had picked Vinte e Cinco Fontes because the walk rewarded persistence with arrival at a canyon ringed by spectacular waterfalls—the twenty-five fountains of the name—that sprang from its steep rock walls and tumbled into a deep, boulder-ringed pool.

It was early enough in the day so there were not too many others already walking the trail. Duarte had warned them to start early if they wanted to avoid a logjam of late-sleeping tourists that would make hiking less fun.

The levada itself, a manmade concrete creek, varied little. It was a boxy trough as wide as a forearm and about as deep, nearly level, but sloped just enough to keep the water flowing steadily. Here and there were signs of recent repairs, which was the real reason for the trails: to give workers who maintained the levadas needed access. The trail beside the narrow channel was never the same for long. For some ten meters it would be a wide, sandy footpath in the open, then become arched over by low trees forming a shaded natural tunnel. Some places it consisted of stone paving abutting the levada, other sections took them on a muddy detour that climbed over and around exposed tree roots. Always to their left was the vertiginous drop: here a steep slope through brush and over boulders, there a sheer cliff falling away for hundreds of meters.

They reached a point where the trail narrowed, barely wide enough for single-file passage, and where the sharp drop-off to their left was protected by a pair of steel cables strung between angle-iron posts set in the concrete shelf forming the walkway. A party of Japanese tourists approached them, chattering away on their return from the fountains. Shira climbed up onto the edge of the levada to let the group pass, and Karl followed suit. As they waited for the last of the Japanese to pass below them, Karl took the opportunity to turn on his camera and snap a few pictures just as a pair of hikers approached from their rear. Shira hopped back down and started up the trail again, but Karl hesitated for a moment as the sound of voices speaking accented Russian neared. He turned toward Shira, intending to ask her to wait up, but she was nearly around the bend ahead. As he started to step down from the lip of the levada, Karl's foot slipped, twisting his ankle. He tried to regain his balance, but tumbled headfirst toward the safety cable. Before he struck the cable, the first of the walkers lurched forward as if to grab him but only succeeded in pushing past, propelling Karl toward the precipice.

Karl caught the upper cable squarely in the stomach as the adjacent angle-iron posts gave way and the whole assembly twisted in its anchors to bend out over the near-vertical drop. Karl somer-saulted over the cable, holding on with all his strength, but the momentum tore his hands free.

Shira, hearing shouts, turned just in time to see Karl crashing down through the brush that grew almost horizontally from the steep side of the mountain.

"Karl!" she screamed, pushing past one of the men.

"I tried to catch him," he said as he backed away, continuing down the trail as if nothing had happened.

Shira reached the spot with the cable fence now tilted almost horizontally out over the void. She squatted and forced herself to look down. At first she couldn't see Karl, but then she spotted him, lying face up against a boulder at the edge of a stream some fifty meters below. He was not moving. "Karl!" she shouted. "Karl! Oh, my God, my God."

"Are you all right?" A young man in a black, Universidade da Madeira hoodie stood over her. "What happened?"

"My husband," she pointed. "He fell."

The young man stretched and leaned out over the edge. "Oh, this is not good. Not good."

"We have to get help." she pleaded. "We need a helicopter or something to get him out of there."

"Oh, I am afraid there is no helicopter, Senhora."

"There must be a mountain rescue team or something."

"No, there is only the *Bombeiros Voluntários*."

"The what?"

"The volunteer fire department. I will call them." He pulled an iPhone from his pocket. "There is not a good signal here, but I will try."

Shira fished her own cell phone out of her backpack and handed it to him. "Here, I have three bars. Try this."

The young man took her phone, looked at it for a moment, and then dialed a number. "I have not seen one of these in years," he said, as he put the phone to his ear and waited for an answer.

The conversation in Portuguese went back and forth for several minutes. Then he handed the phone back to her. "I had to explain exactly where we are. They will be here soon."

"How soon is that?"

"They said maybe an hour. Maybe."

Shira threw up her hands. "An hour? An hour? That's crazy. My husband is down there, injured. We need help right away. You have to get somebody here now."

"There is nothing I can do. The *Bombeiros* must get their special team together and their equipment, and then they must drive to Rabaçal and hike to here with their ropes and everything. They will come as fast as they can. They know what they are doing."

"We have to go down and get to him."

"No, there is no way down, Senhora. We must wait for the *Bombeiros*."

Shira lay down on her stomach on the trail and looked again over the edge. "Karl, Karl, please be all right." There was no movement. "Hang on Karl, don't leave me. Please don't leave me. You can do it. Hang on." She continued to talk to him for what was the longest 45 minutes of her life.

A team from Calheta, four men and a young woman in yellow hardhats and bright red-orange jackets, was the first to arrive, pushing past the crowd of gawking walkers that had begun to clog the trail. They talked rapidly with the University student, then walked up and down the trail looking for the best spot from which to climb down. They set up a belay at a wider point about ten meters back on the levada, and one of the men immediately started rappelling down over the side.

The young woman came over to Shira. She had green eyes and wavy brown hair that stood up when she took off her helmet. "My name is Ligia. We will get to your husband. Do not worry. We will do our best." She reached to take Shira's hand. "I will stay with you."

Shira watched, afraid to turn away, as the rappelling volunteer worked his way down through the brush and over rocks. When he reached Karl, she held her breath. A long minute passed before there was a shout from far below, then another shout and a thumbs up sign. "He is alive," Ligia said. She reached for the walkie-talkie clipped to her waist and started a rapid exchange in Portuguese. "I will go down to help take care of him," she said to Shira. "I am a nurse."

"We have to get him out of there."

"Yes, but we cannot bring him up. Another team from São Vincente is approaching from below along another levada. They will carry him out from there."

"Is he, is he going to be all right?"

"I will know more when I get to him. I must go down now. I will call on the radio and tell Carlos here, and he can tell you."

Shira watched as the young woman rappelled down to join her teammate. She could see Ligia and the man talking and doing something with Karl, but it was hard to tell what exactly was going on. A large canvas bag was lowered toward them, but it snagged on a bush part of the way down, and Ligia had to climb part way back up to free it and drag it down with her. When Shira saw them fitting a cervical collar around Karl's neck, she inhaled sharply and whispered, "Please, God, no." The team worked rapidly but without haste as they fitted a splint to Karl's left leg before wrapping him in a bright silver blanket.

A short man with pale skin and a dark beard approached Shira and took off his hardhat. "I am Carlos. They call me from below and tell me that I should say his skeleton is broken."

"You mean he has broken bones?"

"Yes, bones. That's right, many bones, I think. The team from São Vincente is almost there, and they will carry him out."

"Where are they taking him, to São Vincente?"

"Oh, no, to Funchal, Senhora, to Cruz de Carvalho. That is the central hospital. There is an ambulance ready to meet the *Bombeiros*, and the hospital already knows they are coming. You should be going to there to meet him."

"Oh, God, I forgot about Duarte. I need to call him." She looked back over the precipice to where Karl was being loaded onto a stretcher to be carried out. She paused to say a short prayer. "Please, God, be with him," she finished.

▪ ▪ ▪

Escorted by a police patrol car, Duarte made record time getting them back to Funchal. He pulled up outside the white curve of the large hospital and had barely come to a full stop when Shira opened the door and trotted toward the entrance. As soon as she identified herself, a doctor came out to meet her.

"Senhora, I am Dr. Oliveira. Your husband is all right," he began, "but he is now still in serious condition. We have already finished the x-rays, a CAT scan, to identify his injuries. He has many. We have dressed wounds and set broken bones in his leg and arm. He hit his head and has a concussion. Also seriously, his hip is shattered, and it will take major surgery. Our orthopedic surgeon thinks that he will need a new hip, a complete artificial hip, but it is complicated because of the broken bones. He will be in the hospital for some time."

"Can I see him?"

"Yes, but he is not awake."

"You said he has a concussion. I always thought you shouldn't let someone with a concussion sleep."

"Trust me, it is okay. We now know that is not necessary, only to check regularly that the patient is okay. We are watching him carefully, Senhora. Please, come with me. We will take you to him."

Except that the signs were in Portuguese, she could have been in a modern hospital in Jerusalem or Miami. The men and women in white walking the long, wide corridors, the carts and gurneys along the walls, the lighting, and the disinfected smell: these were all universals.

Karl was in an intensive care unit, surrounded by monitors and with a bag dripping fluid down a line into his arm. His face was tracked by scratches and partially obscured by a clear plastic oxygen mask. His right eye was swollen shut, and he seemed to be breathing with some difficulty.

A momentary wave of panic passed over Shira. It was now all on her. What happened next was up to her. She couldn't consult with Karl. There was no one else in Madeira whom she could really turn to. She straightened her back and started thinking about what she would need to do. Putting Karl through major surgery and an extended stay in a strange hospital on a small island in the middle of the Atlantic did not seem like a real option to her. He should be back in Haifa, with the best surgeons. Or in Miami. How? Who could she call?

She thought of her mother in Miami, but knew that was a no go. Her mother would only turn her own panic back on Shira and spread it to the kids. The family would have to be filled in about what had happened, but not yet.

She thought of Anat Dorfman in Tel Aviv. She was fishing around in her pocket book for her cellphone, when she spotted the red-brown card with its odd, Internet-style name, the words all run together. Karl had given it to her just before they left Israel, and she had tossed it into her purse. She had told him before that she thought it a needless expense—after all, they already had medical coverage—but Karl had gone ahead anyway. "Look," he had said, "I'm the road warrior, flying around the globe for decades now. I've been a subscriber to this service for years, because what if something happened when I was overseas? What if I had a heart attack? How would you get me back from Taiwan or Bangladesh if I were seriously ill?"

"You don't fly to Bangladesh, and from Taiwan you'd book the next flight to Tel Aviv."

"I could do that only if I were well enough for ordinary travel, but I don't think you realize what a medical evacuation entails. The logistics could be a total nightmare, and it can cost hundreds of thousands of dollars. Anyway, as I said, I've carried this service for years. All I did was bump it up to a family plan, which wasn't too expensive."

Shira now stood in the hospital at Karl's bedside, holding the card: MediFlightGlobal. She flipped it over and scanned the brief instructions.

"Karl," she said, bending over to kiss him on his bruised forehead. "I'm going down the hall to the nurses' station to get some information. I'll be right back."

Chapter
Twenty-One

■ "Hello, this the MediFlightGlobal medical emergency line. I'm Jason Tanner; I'm here to help. First please tell me your name, the name of the MediFlightGlobal member, and the telephone number you are calling from in case we get disconnected and need to call you back."

"I'm Shira Markham, the membership is in my husband's name, Karl Lustig." She had trouble remembering her cell phone number, so she told him she would have to look it up on the phone. "I'm sorry about that."

"No reason to be sorry. When you are ready, just read off the numbers to me, including country and city codes."

Shira told him the number. "That is a number in Israel," he said, "is that correct? Are you in Israel now?"

"No, we are in Madeira. The city is Funchal, in Madeira, Portugal, the island, Madeira, I mean."

"You are calling from a cellphone. Is that correct? I can call you back, if you would prefer. That way you can save on international roaming charges."

"No, that's all right; we have a plan."

"Okay. And the patient in this case? Is that your husband, Karl? Okay. Please tell me, briefly what happened to him and what is his condition, to the best of your knowledge."

"He fell, from a levada, a footpath, down a mountain. He has multiple injuries, broken bones, a concussion. I don't know. He's unconscious. The doctor said he is in serious but stable condition. I think."

After she gave the man the name and telephone number of the hospital and the name of Karl's doctor, he said he would call her back. As she waited for her phone to ring, she paced up and down outside Karl's room, trying to calm herself and think of her options.

▪ ▪ ▪

"Okay, Mrs. Markham, our on-call doctor has spoken with the physician in charge at the hospital there and confirmed your husband's condition. We have located the hospital in Cruz De Carvalho and have established contact with the hospital administration."

"You work fast," she said.

"Well, this is what we do, and we are here to help. The next question is where you would like your husband to be transported to."

"I am trying to decide. We live in Haifa and have full medical coverage in Israel; everybody does. The hospitals there are really good. But right now, our children are with my mother in Florida. Miami. It's complicated. I only know that I don't think we can stay here. What do you suggest?"

"We don't make those recommendations, but your membership covers medical evacuation to the hospital of your choice, whether it's in Israel or the United States. Some countries are easier to deal with in terms of logistics, but you should make the choice on the basis of the best medical treatment for your husband and your own comfort and convenience."

Shira knew he was reciting policy, which was no help to her under the circumstances. What she also now realized was that leaving Funchal was motivated by more than just the matter of an unknown hospital in a foreign country. Madeira, peaceful and beautiful Madeira, no longer felt safe, and suddenly she had a mother's impulse to be with her children. "Miami, I want to get my husband to a hospital in Miami."

"Which hospital would you prefer? I'm showing on my screen that there are 74 in the Miami-Fort Lauderdale area. And, of course, it depends on whether there is a bed available, whether they can accept an admission."

Shira's impulse was to ask Karl what he suggested, but he was unconscious, with a concussion and a shattered hip. Where was it that her mother had gone for her hip replacement three years ago?

"There's a top-rated hospital in the Miami area," she said, "with a Jewish-sounding name, but I can't remember it."

"Are you thinking of Mount Sinai Medical Center, in Miami Beach?"

"Yes, that's it. So how do I find out if they can take Karl?"

"We'll take care of that for you. In fact, we take care of everything for you; that's our job. So, I am going to start the paperwork and make the necessary inquiries. I will call you back as soon as I have more information. In the meantime, if there is anything you need or you have any questions, just call me at this number again. If I am not here, whoever is on dispatch will immediately know all the up-to-date details. All you have to do is say who you are."

Shira held the cellphone in her hand, staring at it. When she looked up, Duarte was standing in front of her, waiting politely. She looked up into his dark face and reached out to hug him, determined not to cry.

Behind them, there was a slight commotion, and a nurse hurried across from the nurses' station to enter Karl's room. Fearing the worst, Shira closed her eyes briefly as she walked in. When she opened them, she saw Karl's head turned toward her. He was blinking and trying to raise his head. She kneeled beside the bed, bent over, and tilted her head to match his, beaming a smile at him. "Welcome back, skydiver," she said.

He lifted his head off the pillow and tried to say something, but the mask over his mouth and the hiss of the oxygen supply covered up his faint words. The nurse put a reassuring hand on his arm and said something in Portuguese, but Karl squirmed and tried to raise his head again.

"Camera," he said. "Camera. Shot."

Shira placed her cheek against his and spoke softly into his ear. "Don't worry about your camera. I'll see if I can find out what happened to it. Okay?" He nodded the tiniest of nods. "Just rest and let the doctors take care of you. Everything is going to be all right."

Shira stared into the pillow under his head and bit her lip before straightening up. She forced herself to smile reassuringly. "My sweet Karl, just rest. I'll take care of everything. Okay? Just rest now." She wanted to stay at his side, but she had work to do. She rejoined Duarte outside the room.

"Two things: Can you use your police contacts to find out from the *Bombeiros* whether they recovered Karl's camera and what happened to it? And, second, can your cousin arrange for police protection for Karl. I think somebody may be trying to kill him." Once it was spoken out loud, to another person, the threat seemed to become real, and Shira was both shaken and galvanized by the reality.

"Duarte, you go see what you can do. I'm going to stay here with Karl. I can catch a taxi back to the apartment when I need to. I'll see you here tomorrow?"

Duarte nodded with a grim expression. "*Sim*, I will be here tomorrow."

In her mind, Shira started ticking off theories and possibilities. It seemed obvious to her that the threat must have something to do with Karl's recent consulting work for IsTec or his presentation here at MIRI. What linked them was the microprocessor chips that Karl had delivered to MIRI. Was somebody trying to steal them? No, that would have been easy. Karl, not the chips, must be the target. She had work to do, and she didn't want to be doing it alone. She immediately thought of Anat, but something told her not to contact Anat at her work email. She needed to start thinking like Karl, who was compulsively methodical and constitutionally distrustful, which was a big part of what made him a good consultant and sometime spy. She would use her Gmail account to contact Lev Novikov, with a message between the lines for his wife, Anat.

■ ■ ■

Shira and Duarte were walking back toward Karl's room when her cellphone rang.

"This is Amanda Delacroix calling from MediFlightGlobal. I've taken over your case from Jason. I have some good news, Mount Sinai has a bed open and will accept your husband as a patient, but they can only guarantee admission for a short time. We are now working out logistics, whether to arrange for a flight out of Lisbon to pick the patient up or to fly a crew out from the U.S. and back to Miami. But that is our problem. We do need to apply for medical visas for your entry into the United States."

"We don't need visas."

"I thought you were from Israel."

"We are, but Karl and I are both Americans by birth, and we are traveling on U.S. passports."

"Great, that simplifies things and could save some time. After I verify your passport numbers, I will turn you over to Karen Pedroncelli who will brief you on how the transfer will take place and what to expect. We are still working things out with your husband's current attending physician who seems reluctant to release him, but there does not appear to be compelling medical reasons why not to, so I am sure we will get that taken care of soon. Is there anything else I can do before I turn you over to Karen?"

"Yes, how do we get to the airport? Do we hire an ambulance or what?"

"That's our worry, too. You've heard of door-to-door service, right? Well, we have something better; it's called bedside-to-bedside service. You have enough to worry about. The whole process will be under our control."

▪ ▪ ▪

In Atlanta, what had started to look like an ambitious but fairly routine point-to-point evacuation had begun to unravel. Before the handoff to the next shift, Amanda decided to bring in the head of operations, Hal Turnbull. Turnbull, a smallish man with a big Texas accent who had learned the business as a paramedic and then as a pilot, often took a hands-on role in the small company. He wheeled a posture chair over from across the operations room and sat down beside Amanda.

"We have a two-part logistic problem that we are trying to work out," she told him. "Whether we work with one of our air ambulance partners here or contract service with a European company, the problem is Madeira to Miami with the patient. We can stopover in the Azores to refuel, but Ponta Delgada in the Azores direct to

Miami is beyond the range of the Learjet 35As commonly used by so many of the air ambulance services. We could dog-leg via Boston, which is the nearest continental landfall from Ponta Delgada, but that, too, is uncomfortably close to the range of the Learjet. And it would add about another 400 nautical miles to the total trip."

Turnbull ran his hand through imaginary hair that no longer topped his bald head. "So, we move to service with longer range aircraft, maybe a Bombardier 604. Or an extended range 36A. So what's the other problem?"

"The problem is Portuguese air regs, which require special pilot certification to land at Funchal in Madeira. It's considered one of the toughest airports in the world."

Hal glanced down at his clipboard for inspiration, then back up. "What if you use a Portuguese crew out of Lisbon or Porto?"

"We're trying. So far we haven't located a Portuguese company with both pilots certified for Funchal airport and equipment with the needed range."

A few minutes later, Jenna, the operations analyst at the next desk leaned over. "Hal, I think I may have something. I have been combing through databases for business-jet pilots with Portuguese-sounding names, and I spotted one Antonio Gomes who recently retired from TAP, the Portuguese commercial airline, and now flies for EuroBizi, a fractional-ownership service based in Madrid. They have Learjets and Gulfstreams. Gomes also has flown for MacAero Services in the UK. With the historic British links with Madeira, could be we have a winning combo. I'm checking now, trying to get someone from the Spanish company on the line, but we are hampered by the six-hour time difference." The analyst flipped the mike on her headset back down and started talking on the phone again.

"Okay, I have reached a 24/7 line for EuroBizi," she said, flipping up the mike again "Their records show Gomes is still certified for Funchal airport even though he is no longer with TAP."

Amanda was typing away as Jenna worked the phone. "All right, I have the information on MacAero, but they don't do medical evac, that's handled by a sister company, Macallister Air Ambulance.

Okay, bingo, they fly Learjet 36As. I'll drill down and see what else I can find out."

Jenna returned to her call, then muted the mike. "The operator at EuroBizi says their pilots are on exclusive contracts and can't fly for Macallister. I'm trying to fight my way through layers of the European corporate onion to get a home number and appeal on humanitarian grounds to their top dog."

It was nearly midnight before they were able to track down the needed number. Amanda and Jenna went together to Hal's office.

"Okay," Amanda said, "here's the deal. Macallister has a 36A fitted with two after-market mods: the Raisbeck Engineering ZR LITE performance package and the Avcon extended wing tanks and empennage strakes. Together, it ups the takeoff weight and range enough to put them well within the safety margin for a direct flight between Ponta Delgada and Miami with adequate reserves."

"That's great. Now what about the pilot?"

"Jenna's call was the alarm clock for Jose Manuel Diego Garcia, the head honcho at EuroBizi. He's holding on line three; he wants to talk with you. He tells me that EuroBizi will let Macallister in England take them on as a subcontractor for 'special navigation services.' And I don't think you are going to like what he wants to charge."

"We don't really have much choice, it seems. We have to get a plane into and out of that airport. In any case, that contract would have to get approval from the COO or CEO. I'll talk with the EuroBizi guy, but you better get Roy or John on the line with this Spanish dude."

It took another hour and a half of back and forth shuffling of tradeoffs and working and reworking of the numbers before a deal was struck. Gomes would fly to England to join the air ambulance crew, land the air ambulance in Funchal, pilot again on takeoff, then hop off in the Azores to catch a commercial flight back home to Madrid. Since the Learjet had to land in the Azores anyway, it did not increase the load on the air ambulance or its crew, and the Portuguese pilot would not need to leave Portugal. Everything looked good until Macallister checked with their insurer, who balked.

This time both the CEO and the COO got on the phone, in a conference call with the heads of Macallister, and EuroBizi. In the end, a multilateral deal was struck in which Macallister paid EuroBizi for the loan of the services of Gomes and billed them back to MediFlightGlobal. This made Gomes a temporary contract employee of Macallister, which covered them with their insurer.

Hal, Amanda, and Jenna breathed a collective sigh of relief and started to schedule arrivals and departures and arrangements for the on-board medical staff.

Three hours later, as the bright morning sun rose in Miami, Antonio Gomes was catching a commercial flight from Madrid to London. In England, he joined the air ambulance crew—two UK pilots plus a paramedic and a critical-care nurse. After a procedural briefing, they took off in a Learjet 36A extended-range air ambulance bound for Funchal, where it would arrive in the late afternoon.

▪ ▪ ▪

In Funchal, when Shira went to check on Karl at the hospital, she was stopped by a uniformed policeman who insisted on seeing identification. "What is the problem? I'm his wife," she said.

The policeman didn't answer, but held out his hand waiting for her identification. He examined her passport, held it up to compare to her face, and then checked her name against a list in a small notebook. "You may visit him."

Karl was still sleeping, so she sat by the bed, watching him breath. He was no longer wearing the oxygen mask, but he was still festooned with cables and tubes. When Duarte showed up a few minutes later, she greeted him with a hug.

"Thanks for arranging for the guard," she said.

"Guard? Oh, yes. It was nothing. It just took finding the right way to ask."

"And the camera? Did you find out anything?"

"Yes, one of the *Bombeiros* remembered it hanging from a cord around Karl's neck when they found him, but he doesn't know what happened to it. He suggested we check with the hospital. They would have whatever was with Karl when he was brought in."

At the front desk, they learned that, in addition to Karl's clothes, which were badly torn, dirt stained, and spotted with blood, the hospital had an envelope with his personal effects: his wallet, broken glasses, and a battered pocket camera, its lens cracked and its display screen in shards.

"I think he will have to get a new camera," Duarte said gravely.

Shira pried at the bottom of the camera and managed to extract the SD card. It had a hairline crack running through the case, but she slipped it into a pocket of her jeans anyway next to the letter she was carrying.

When they reached Karl's room, he was awake and managed a smile at them.

"How are you, my love," Shira said, as she pulled up a chair beside the bed.

"Beaten up, hurting, itchy, but really glad to see you."

"I have some news. The good part is that we are getting you out of here later today; the bad part is our vacation in Madeira is being cut short. We're headed for Miami."

"Fill me in."

"That medical evacuation service you subscribed to is sending a private jet to ferry us back to Miami where you are being admitted to Mount Sinai, the same hospital that did Mother's hip surgery last year. They are going to turn you into the bionic consultant with your own new hip."

"Oh, goody. I have always wanted to be bionic. Will I be able to run the marathon in sub-five time?"

"Only if you ride the camera car. I have been talking with the people here and this morning had a brief chat with Doctor Rosenblatt, the orthopedic surgeon in Miami. They will know better when they get you there, of course, but things look good for getting you up and walking again fairly quickly. But, I am afraid your dreams of setting a new senior-division record in the Boston Marathon are probably not going to become reality."

"I am so relieved, particularly since I never liked running, and I was afraid I would have to start training." He winked at Shira as she beamed at him.

"We have a few hours before your private jet arrives, sir. Would you like me to read another letter to you? Our dear German professor gave me another one by way of Duarte and promised to mail the rest to us in Miami. I gave him my mother's address."

Karl nodded and Shira unfolded the letter from her pocket.

"It starts with a note from Prof. Schottky. 'Dear Prof. Karl,' it says. 'It seems that you have a connection with Portugal. Perhaps it is the deep pull of *saudade*, the longing for home, that has brought you here to the University. But I will let the letter tell you the story. Schottky.'" Shira turned the paper over and started to read.

> Dearest Hanna,
>
> Life is so terrible and wonderful. It takes from us and gives to us at the same time. I am writing now from a hotel in another country, and my life is utterly changed. You would not recognize me with the way I am dressed and the life I am leading. I am warm, truly warm, for the first time in many months, and I have enough to eat. I also have work of sorts, a job that is easy and exhausting at the same time.

Chapter
Twenty-Two

Dresden, early 1945

■ Stealing the pram was easy. Frau Kohl, in Aachener Straße, the next street but one, always returned from the market in the morning and left it on the stoop while she stored her produce and readied herself and her baby for their morning promenade at the small park at the end of the street. Julianna waited until the front door closed, checked up and down the street for watchers, and then simply wheeled the pram away. Back at the church, she made small modifications: removing the polka-dot skirt, scuffing the corduroy in places with a bread knife, bending the collapsible hood so that it no longer fit perfectly when up nor folded all the way down. It was not such a fine pram any more, but it was hers, and so long as she stayed away from Aachener Straße, it would remain hers.

She had learned to time her walks with the baby by the rhythms of the nearby neighborhood. No one else lived on her end of the street, with its crumbling buildings and the partially burned out church, so she had learned to simply appear by exiting into the alleyway and rounding the corner. When all the mothers were out shopping or taking the air with their young children, Julianna busied herself in the attic room. When the street cleared of pedestrians, Julianna would bundle Karl into the pram, maneuver through the rubble in the alley, and take to the streets. She had papers now, not proper ones, but a residency relocation notice that might satisfy a nosey civilian. The police and the military were simply to be avoided. Dieter was not happy with her going out, but Dieter worked and could not keep her locked in a building without locks. He had begun to return during lunch on some days. He pretended that it was to bring her bread or a newspaper, and she pretended to believe him.

For Julianna, the weather this day was perfect: overcast, with dark clouds that threatened snow and a chill wind that kept casual walkers off the streets. Those who were out were either hurrying back or going somewhere with swift purpose. Karl was awake and babbling away happily as she smiled down at him and chatted quietly.

"You are such a handsome boy, my Karl, you are. Yes, and I am your ma-ma-ma-ma and that is your ba-ba-ba-ba." The ball, sewn from scraps of cloth with thread salvaged from those same scraps and stuffed with bits pulled from their tattered mattress, was Karl's only toy. At its heart was a nut, its shriveled seed still inside making a satisfying rattle when Karl waved it. "That's it, shake the ball. Shake, shake."

"Your English is very good," said a voice behind her.

Julianna whirled in panic. Already she was furious with herself for her lapse. At least she had not been speaking Polish with Karl. The man who had approached from behind her was tall, with dark brown hair showing beneath his cap. His goatee was coarse, the color of shoe leather but flecked with gray. He touched the brim of his cap and nodded without smiling, clearly waiting to hear her response.

She answered him in German. "My mother was a linguist. She believed in starting children young with many languages. I am continuing a family tradition with her grandson."

"You mother *was* a linguist?" he said in English. "And what is she now?"

"Dead. My family, including my husband, were killed by Russians in eastern Poland. They were in the way, I suppose. I am German, so I made my way to the German-controlled area and was repatriated."

"I see. And do you speak other languages?"

"Besides German and English, I can manage in Polish. I also speak French and Spanish, although I am out of practice."

"And by any chance do you know Portuguese?"

"Yes, of course, it is a dialect of Spanish," she said, confidently making up her answer. "I speak Portuguese quite well enough, as you can easily see." She spoke in rapid Spanish, hoping that it would suffice and not knowing why she felt the urge to impress this gentleman.

"Well, I do not speak more than a few words, so you have convinced me." He reached into his pocket and withdrew a leather case, which he opened to show his identification. Diplomatic corps. Julianna's heart raced. "Papers?" he said.

"I . . ." Julianna stuttered as she fumbled in her coat. "I think I have only this with me. But I can get them at my home."

"You should always have your proper identification with you at all times, Frau Fuchs," he said, reading off the relocation form. "Surely you know that. Come with me, please."

"My baby."

"Bring him. Of course, bring him." He looked down at the forged paper and slapped it against his free hand. "You do not live in a very good area, Julianna Fuchs. We shall have to detain you. In a more central location."

Julianna considered her options. She could hardly run while pushing the pram, and even on her own she could not outrun this man. She would have to talk her way out. "The papers, let me explain."

"There is nothing to explain, Frau Fuchs. You have not the proper papers, and the document you do have is a forgery, a rather crude one. This is a crime, a most serious matter."

Julianna's eyes closed, and she let out a quiet sigh. To have come so far, to have survived so many close calls, only to be caught now, on the streets of Dresden, because she had spoken to her son in English.

"You will have to come with me, Frau Fuchs. Please, no scene."

"The papers, I want to tell you—"

"Papers? Papers are nothing. you will have to get new documents anyway."

"I don't understand. I am being arrested."

"You are being recruited."

"I really do not understand what you are talking about."

"Frau Fuchs, I am not with the police. My papers are, like yours, faked. Except for the one I showed you. I am with the diplomatic corps, and I am to be sent to Portugal, to Lissabon. This is such a stroke of luck. You speak English and Portuguese. And, clearly, you have practice in pretending to be something you are not. I am improvising, it is true, but I am also short on time and do not, in the future, expect to be in a position for my superiors to question my actions. Even the baby—it is perfect, this, utterly beyond suspicion. Who could have doubts about a man traveling with his young wife and child."

"Your wife? Now I see."

"No, you don't, but there will be time to learn of all that later. First, let us get you and the baby off the street before we are stopped by other authorities. I have an apartment near the market where you can stay for now, but not for long, only long enough to get you some new clothes and fix your hair. We must leave for Berlin almost immediately. You will need a passport and a visa. There are many things to be taken care of and little time, so please, come with me now, and when we are at the apartment, I will explain. But no more talking here on the street, just come with me, my deferent and admiring young wife." At last he smiled, with a twitch, a half-wink in his left eye. "I will push the baby." He offered her his arm as he swung the pram around with one hand. "I am Otto, Otto Krause. And you are from this moment Frau Krause, should you be asked. But defer to me and let me do the talking should any talking be necessary before we reach the apartment."

Julianna obediently took his arm and smiled up at her husband, the man she had only just met, who was taking her to Berlin and to Lissabon. Lisboa. Lisbon. It was a magical name in any language. It was a port, a port on the Atlantic Ocean and another step closer to America.

▪ ▪ ▪

The Julianna who carried her son into the first-class compartment on the train to Berlin a week later was a different

Julianna. No longer a Nowack or even a Fuchs, she was Frau Krause, Julianna Krause, wife of an Austrian business man, a dealer in metals. She had a German passport and a visa for entry into Portugal. She was dressed in a wool suit, a tasteful, muted plaid. Her hair was done up and topped by a jaunty feathered hat, and on her wrist, a silver bracelet, a gift from her admiring spouse. Her son, dressed in blue and brown, shook a resin and metal rattle in one hand and chewed on a carved wooden cow in the other.

From Berlin, they would fly to Lisbon. Fly. On a plane. The very thought of it made Julianna tingle. There was some rush to get this particular plane to Lisbon, accompanied by Otto. He would not say exactly what its cargo was, but she had gained the clear impression that it was of extreme importance. It was a puzzle to her, considering that Germany was losing the war and might be on the very verge of surrender. Something needed to be gotten out of the country before Germany became occupied territory.

Simply put, Otto was a spy. It was not a term he used, but it did not take a university professor to discern the true nature of his work. She and Karl were part of his disguise and she was his ears, a listener and translator in a city where the conversations of greatest interest to Otto would be in English and in Portuguese. He had not been trained in espionage but was being pressed into service for this one specific mission. How long it would take for her own subterfuge to be exposed she could not know. Perhaps her Spanish would be enough to get by in Portugal. She would know in another day after the night flight from Berlin to Lisbon.

▪ ▪ ▪

The chubby, four-engine Condor stood on the runway, glistening in the light spilling from the partially hooded lights at the edge of the field. Otto stood under the wingtip, engaged in some argument with a member of the crew, finally throwing up his hands in desperation.

"What was that about, dearest?" she asked when he returned.

"There is no room for the baggage. We can each take one suitcase and the small bag for the baby, but the rest will have to be sent later, by train. With the way things are going, it could be weeks, perhaps a month, before our things arrive. And I am supposed to be stationed there for . . ."

She nodded, thinking to herself what she needed. She was not used to traveling with more than she could carry. For the journey to Lisbon, they had among the three of them, seven large cases and three smaller ones. For the first time in years, she actually had possessions—spare clothes, books, a curling iron, makeup, toys for Karl, a portable bassinet, too many things to list—and she was feeling the weight of them all. "It will be all right, Otto. What we need immediately, we can buy or borrow in Lisbon."

"Yes, I suppose, but it is a bother, nonetheless. At any rate, we must board. We cannot miss this flight. It will be the last, I am told." He gestured toward the plane. At the stairs just forward of the plane's tail, Otto took Karl from her and followed her up the steep steps. Inside, the cabin was laid out with wide, comfortable seats, two on the left and one on the right. The rear-most rows on the right side had been replaced with a cage of metal mesh, through which Julianna could see stacks of small wooden boxes.

Otto and Julianna made their way up the incline of the aisle to their seats at the front. There were no other passengers.

"Why is there no room for our luggage, Otto? The plane is empty."

"It is not room that is the problem, but weight. The cargo is rather heavy. More I cannot say. You understand. It is business. One might say a golden business opportunity."

Karl, who had fallen asleep during the ride to the airport, awoke when the plane roared down the runway for takeoff, then screamed with the pain of changing air pressure as the plane climbed into the night sky. Julianna nursed him in an attempt to calm him, which seemed also to help with the pain in his ears.

The flight, which Julianna had anticipated so eagerly, was boring, with nothing but blackness below and the endless drone of the four engines throbbing in her ears. Karl, lulled by the steady vibration and the pedal-point music of the thrumming engines, slept through the night, the only one to get more than fitful sleep. In early morning fog, they finally landed at Lisbon's Portela Airport, where they were met by someone Otto introduced as a "business colleague." Julianna realized that, from the moment they were on the ground, they were also on stage.

▪ ▪ ▪

In the hospital, Shira checked to see that Karl was still awake as she finished reading the letter.

> Our departure from Germany was literally at the last moment. The very day we arrived in Lisbon, the Allies started to fire-bomb Dresden. As word of the devastating attack raced through the German community here, everyone lamented not only the great loss of life but also the destruction of such a beautiful city. I did not know what they were talking about. My memories of Dresden were of a cold attic in a partially burned church at the end of a run-down street. They tell me that now nothing is left of that area, and I wonder if Dieter is all right. He exploited me, but, then, I exploited him as well. I had no affection for him, but neither do I wish him ill.
>
> For now, I will close this letter. I am to meet Otto for lunch with some "very important people." I will tell you more of my new life in the next letter.
> With Love,
> Julianna

Chapter
Twenty-Three

■ It was nearly the dinner hour when an ambulance pulled up at the hospital in Cruz de Carvalho and two men extracted a gurney from the back. They were nonplussed to find a police officer standing outside Karl's room. "We are here to transport the patient to the airport," the man at the front of the gurney said in Portuguese. "It has all been arranged."

"This patient? The American? He cannot leave," the officer said emphatically.

"We have orders to pick him up and take him to the airport. The hospital has discharged him to us."

"Not this patient. He is in custody."

Shira, just returning with Duarte, approached the group queued up outside Karl's room. "What is the matter here."

"Senhora, the police, he is saying we cannot take your husband to the airport."

"The patient is charged as a suspect in a crime," the officer announced, sounding as if he were reading a memorized passage from a police manual for dealing with difficult English-speaking foreigners. "He is in police custody pending a full investigation."

Shira turned to Duarte. "Do you know what this is about? I thought you had friends in the police."

"I do. That is exactly what this is about. I could not get what you would call police protection for Karl, so I arranged for him to be charged as a criminal. That way they have to watch him." He grinned proudly. "I am Portuguese. We are practical and clever and always find a way."

"This is not that silly business about wearing a safety vest after an accident."

165

"Oh, no, this is much more serious. Reckless endangerment, destruction of public property, interfering with a police investigation: those are the important ones."

"That's great. Now my husband is a criminal."

"Not to worry." Duarte nodded and smiled enthusiastically. "My cousin assures me this will work. The charges will all be dropped eventually. In the meantime, he cannot leave, of course, but he is also police protected, which is what you wanted."

"But Duarte, we cannot wait for a trial or even for some judge to rule. He has to be evacuated now, today, or the hospital in Miami won't take him."

"You say he has to?"

"Yes, that's what I said."

"Okay. Okay. No problem. I will just call my cousin." Duarte opened his cellphone and started walking away from the room. As he paced up and down the hall, speaking into his phone, the radio carried by the policeman at the door started chirping loudly. The officer held it in front of his face and started a rapid conversation in Portuguese. He was still talking as he started down the hall and broke into a trot.

"Okay," Duarte declared. "Let's get Karl to the airport."

"You fixed it? Just like that? Karl is released?"

"Oh, no. I just had my cousin call the officer away for an emergency. Karl is still a prisoner in police custody, but in a few moments he will be an escaped prisoner."

"What have you done, Duarte? Now Karl will be an international fugitive from justice."

"Oh, they will never, how do you say, extradite him over this. But probably you should not come back to Madeira too soon. Right now we should get you both to the airport. The emergency the officer is handling could be a short one."

▪ ▪ ▪

As they rode to the airport with the lights flashing all the way, Shira kept listening for sirens and looking out the back, checking to see if they were being followed by police. Karl, who had been lightly sedated for the flight, took in the whole proceedings with chemical detachment.

At the airport, they were stopped by security, then escorted directly out onto the tarmac where they pulled up to a sleek Learjet with the red-and-white Macallister Air Ambulance logo on the tail and a blocky red cross on its flank. A trim, middle-aged woman with dark brown hair in a military-style crew cut stepped out of the open aircraft door, smiled, and held out her hand to Shira. "Hi, I'm Sylvia Bates. I'm the emergency and critical-care nurse on board. And this is Josh Spielman, our paramedic. I'll introduce you to the rest of our crew after we get your husband and you boarded."

While Shira waited, still watching for police, the ambulance crew helped shift Karl onto the gurney from the plane, which was then boarded and locked in place on its mounting pedestal running along the far side of the small cabin. After the nurse and paramedic hooked Karl up to the onboard monitors, they helped Shira up the steps.

"It's a little tight in here, but the seats are comfortable. You have to keep your head down and make yourself skinny to get past the gurney and our seats along this side. For now we'd like you to take one of the two seats at the back, by your husband's head. Seated next to you is Andrew Cowell, our co-pilot. He's English. Up front we have our Scot, Captain Mallory. Her name is Abigail, but everyone except her husband calls her Mal, and she won't say what he calls her. She's the blonde with the long hair, our regular pilot. Say hi, Mal. The brunette with the short hair and beard is Captain Gomes. He's Portuguese and the one in charge for the moment. He's the pilot who will get us off this rock." The man in the left seat turned and gave Shira a half-hearted salute and a big smile. "They wouldn't let Mal land here—special rules—but Captain Gomes brought us in beautifully, angling down the runway like a Calgary Flames forward skating to a hockey stop just short of the boards."

The co-pilot, seated at the back next to Shira, leaned toward her. "In case you don't speak Canadian, she meant there was such a crosswind that we had to land sort of sideways, rather heavy on the rudder, but as slick as a pro skater. You're in good hands with that pilot. Now we're waiting for a SATA flight from the mainland to land; then we'll be cleared for takeoff. Once airborne, we're a little over an hour and a half out of Ponta Delgada in the Azores. Then after a short stop to service the plane, just over six into Miami. Weather looks good all the way. Should be a smooth flight. So just buckle your seat belt, sit back, and enjoy the trip."

Shira laughed. "You sound like those pilots on the airlines."

Cowell bowed. "I'll take that as a high compliment. Did you hear that up there, Mal? Maybe one of these days I'll get the patter down and delivery well enough to graduate to the big jets."

Josh, the paramedic, held his hand beside his mouth as if making a confidential aside to Shira. "Don't let him jerk your chain, ma'am. Andrew flew for Virgin Atlantic for sixteen years before taking an early-retirement buy-out to join us and do some real flying."

▪ ▪ ▪

The man who was now Pedro watched from behind the chain-link fence on the road overlooking the airport. As the Learjet sat on the runway, broadside to him, waiting for final clearance for takeoff, he knew this was a last chance. Whatever course he took would be ever so much harder were he in America. In America, no one could ever get this close to an active runway with clear line-of-sight to the aircraft. Stooping low between his rental car and the Ibiza parked next to it, in a position that would be difficult to observe except from head on, he opened his aluminum computer case and quickly reassembled the custom, 7.62-chambered Arms-Tech TTR-700 whose pieces had been smuggled in from Lisbon. With the lightweight Take-down Tactical Rifle at this close range, he would not even need his ballistic computer for a targeting solution. He adjusted for range and estimated wind velocity and sighted in on the precise point on the plane's tail assembly that he had figured out from the Learjet maintenance and engineering diagrams re-trieved off the Web. It was all there, he thought, waiting on the Internet, accessible to the persistent professional or ingenious amateur.

Pedro noticed that the tail configuration, with its extra set of fins below, did not exactly match the pictures he had seen, but he kept his focus and waited. If he waited too long, he would miss the shot, as the Learjet engines could spin up from idle to 100% in under four seconds. If he fired too early, the impact would most likely be noticed.

He listened with his scanner locked onto the tower frequency, waiting for the confirmation that the plane was cleared for takeoff. The image in his scope wobbled as the twin engines were throttled up. He squeezed off a shot. The image jerked slightly just as the plane's brakes were released. He squeezed off another shot. With the long suppressor in place, the sound of his shots was swallowed up in the roar of the revving jets less than fifty meters away. Hardly more than a second after firing, he watched the plane start down the runway, accelerating. The agile jet rotated in half the length of the runway and, once airborne, climbed quickly and banked out over the ocean. The damage was done. If it accomplished what was intended, it would finally lead to catastrophic failure someplace over open ocean, where evidence for the cause of the crash would be all but impossible to recover.

Breaking down the TTR was like brushing his teeth—something he could do half-conscious. He shoved the case into the back of his rental car, then watched as the small plane faded into the distance. He did not jump at the sound of the voice behind him, but his hand was reaching toward his back, preparing to retrieve the tactical knife stashed at the ready. He was already surveying the terrain and comparing options for disposing of a body quickly and with little chance of it being discovered until after he was long gone.

■ ■ ■

Anat Dorfman was half-way down the gangway from her delayed SATA flight out of Lisbon when two police cars, sirens whining and lights flashing, pulled out onto the tarmac at the Funchal airport. While armed guards trotted out from the terminal building to meet up with the police exiting the patrol cars, the uniformed escort at the bottom of the stairs spread her arms and told the disembarking passengers to wait. For the next several minutes, as Anat and the other passengers waited on the stairway, they watched a scene of confusion and chaotic conversations as airport officials and police milled about, argued, and gestured in every direction. Then, suddenly the crisis was over and the idling police cars circled and drove away as the guards strolled back to the terminal.

"Do you know what that was all about?" Anat asked the escort as she reached the bottom step.

"I couldn't say. Maybe the Americans who just took off after we landed."

Figuring that she could find out soon enough on her own precisely what had transpired, Anat let the matter drop. With no bags to reclaim, Anat went straight through baggage claim and out of the terminal.

As she was getting into a taxi at the front of the terminal building, a man on the uphill side of the airport was facing a boy with a skateboard, chatting with him in easy Portuguese, smiling, feeding him a tall tale about an experimental x-ray camera that looked like a gun but fired a narrow beam to take pictures of the inside of equipment or machinery. Would the boy believe him? Would he tell anyone? It didn't matter. Now all that mattered was that the boy leave smiling, quietly, before Pedro Cabral had to steel himself to use the tactical knife that still waited at the ready. The kid was ten or so, about the same age as Pedro's youngest brother had been when the four of them had been caught in an ambush. Pedro had walked away; his brothers had not. Pedro was still walking away and would today, regardless of how this encounter went down.

As suddenly as his inconvenient companion had interrupted Pedro's exit, the boy shrugged, smiled, picked up his skateboard, and started carving carefree arcs down the steep road. Had he swallowed the story? Pedro, deciding to assume so, got back in his car and headed for Funchal, waving to the boy as he passed him.

■ ■ ■

Anat opened her carry-on case on the bed, extracted her laptop, and logged into the hotel Wi-Fi to send a Web-mail message to Lev telling him she had arrived safely. She had decided at the last minute that there was no need for Lev to hold her hand or watch her back, but that it might be handy to have someone back in Israel. With the message off to Lev, she used the prepaid cellphone she had picked up in Lisbon to call the hospital. Pretending to be Shira's mother, she was told that Karl had already been discharged that very afternoon. By using her rusty Spanish to chat up the woman on the phone, Anat was able to piece together the gist of Karl's accident, which had happened while she was skipping from airport to airport on her way to Madeira.

Using an anonymizer and a private-mode browser, Anat queried some non-public but accessible databases and learned that the flight departing just as she arrived in Madeira was a Miami-bound charter operated by Macallister Services Limited doing business as Macallister Air Ambulance. The filed flight plan had them bound for Miami via the Azores. By this point, she had guessed that Karl and Shira were on their way to the States for medical treatment. Switching to a one-time use email account, Anat posted a message to Shira telling her to hold tight and that Bini's "aunt" from Tel Aviv would see her soon.

Using a credit card that matched the identity on her spare passport, Anat booked the earliest flight out the next day, back through Lisbon, to Newark, and then down to Miami. She knew her small subterfuges would not stand up against close tracking, but they might impede the casual inquirer.

With nothing else to do until her early morning departure, she left the hotel to explore downtown Funchal and look for something to eat. At the Golden Gate, she was sipping a glass of the house red and waiting for her order of *espada preta* to arrive when she recognized a man walking on the other side of the street. He turned away up a side street next to the *Jardim Municipal* before she could recall how she knew him. For a moment, she was torn in indecision, then she quickly stuffed some euros under her wine glass and walked away. She pretended to be a curious tourist as she tried surreptitiously to spot the man through the thick plantings in the gardens. Crossing the street diagonally, she slipped between yellow-and-blue cabs in the long line at the taxi rank and entered the gardens at the far end. She could not see her target, but in her mind kept estimating his position by his last heading and how fast he had been walking. As she circled the sunken amphitheater at the top of the gardens and realized that she had lost the man, she remembered the context in which she had seen him before. She had glimpsed the face only once, at the first Mossad briefing on the contraband computer chips. It had been in one of the photos on the page in Dror's folder.

▪ ▪ ▪

Working late, the Director sat in his office staring at his monitor screen. He let out a cough of acute annoyance as he tapped the monitor's off button, then closed the folder on his desk. "Another damned near miss in Madeira," he said to his visitor. "In training they try to convince you that our work is a matter of persistence and intelligence, but they lie to us. They want to heighten our sense of agency, convince us that we are in fact in charge of our fate, when in truth, Fate is in charge of us. Without persistence and intelligence, we fail, true, but neither is enough. It is always a matter of timing, of mindless chance. Arrive at an intersection five minutes late, or too early, and you don't see what you need to see, the contact gets away, or the asset is burned before he can be debriefed."

Yishai Barg nodded, his head tilted at a noncommittal angle. "Next time, then."

"If there is a next time. If we are not there when the goat is taken, we will not know whether it was the lions or the jackals—or some Bedouin thieves—who made off with it."

"A lot is riding on our one goat and our one lookout."

"You know full well that it is imperative we keep it this way. The circle of trust. You, me, them."

"What about this American?"

"Not my choice, but he volunteered, in a manner of speaking, by alerting us to the problem. And both Novikov and Dorfmann have vouched for him. Besides, his role is limited. He's merely the opening act to get them in the tent. After that . . ."

"And the wife?"

"Not someone we have to factor in." The Director turned back to his screen.

Chapter
Twenty-Four

■ The Learjet turned to chase the setting sun and leveled out at 38,000 feet. Twenty minutes out of Funchal, Tony Gomes switched on the autopilot and climbed out of the left-hand seat. "She's all yours, Captain Mallory." Mal slipped in to take over the controls. "Hey, good job, Tony," she said over her shoulder. "You definitely have the touch. Take a break in back and send Andy up here. You're a passenger now."

"Thanks. The pleasure was mine. A chance to do an in-and-out at Madeira is something I couldn't pass on, especially with such a fast turnaround. And the pay is not bad, either."

For the modest hop into Ponta Delgada, the teams in the front and back quickly settled into their separate routines. In the cockpit, with the plane on autopilot until they neared the Azores, Mal and her first officer were mostly just extra pairs of eyes. In back, with Karl stable and dozing off, the nurse and paramedic were similarly reduced to watching LCD panels and monitoring vital signs. Shira had taken on the hardest job, worrying over every grunt or snort from Karl and each thump or click from the plane.

Karl, who had drifted in and out of sleep since shortly after take-off, awoke again. He reached out and took Shira's hand. She gave it a squeeze, then laid her other hand atop it. Karl opened his mouth behind the oxygen mask, but Shira said, "Don't try to talk. Just rest, we're getting corporate jet service to Miami. How's that for class?" Karl smiled and closed his eyes once more.

Shira turned to the nurse and paramedic. "I wanted to thank you all for letting me come along with him."

"Oh, we prefer it this way," Sylvia said. "It helps keep our patients calm to have family along. But your husband is doing great, so why don't you lean back and close your eyes, too. We've still got a long haul ahead of us."

▪ ▪ ▪

After landing at João Paulo Airport in the Azores, they all said goodbye to Captain Gomes. Mal had decided to keep things simple by having everyone else stay on board while the plane was refueled. She completed her walk-around inspection but noticed nothing. In just under an hour, they were ready for take-off again, queued behind a delayed charter 767 bound for Africa. Despite generous spacing, Captain Mallory had to struggle some against the turbulence trailing the jumbo.

"The rudder seemed a little sloppy," she remarked to her co-pilot as the plane climbed, "but none of the annunciators are on, and it seems okay now. After we reach altitude, I'm going to hand-fly it for a while just to feel how it behaves."

Twenty minutes was enough to convince her that if there was any problem with the controls, it was too subtle for in-flight diagnosis and not worthy of worry. She switched on the autopilot again and went into watchful waiting mode.

They were approaching the halfway point in their plan of flight, when the plane was briefly buffeted by rougher air. The autopilot did its job for a few minutes, but then started lagging behind in responding. The plane bounced and slid into a slow slalom of intertwined roll and yaw, subtle at first, but gradually building in intensity. Both Mal and Andy noticed it.

"Dutch-mode roll?" Andy said, waiting to hear Mal's assessment and to see whether she would take the controls.

"Feels like it," she said, "but that shouldn't be happening with our configuration. Unless the autopilot is somehow generating it."

"Yaw dampers?"

"Not engaged, because it's not needed with the Avcon strakes on the tail. I thought you knew this model."

"I do. Just trying to puzzle this out. Shouldn't hurt to try it. The system is still in place and operable."

Mal flipped a switch on the control panel and immediately got a warning light. "The yaw dampers think we have a malfunctioning rudder, but the autopilot is still trying its best." She turned off the autopilot and twisted the yoke to take the plane through the beginnings of a gentle S-curve, working the pedals controlling the rudder in synch with banking the plane. It was instantly clear that something was seriously wrong. "I've got no rudder. No, wait. Now I do, but it's too much." She shifted the rudder pedals back to compensate, but there was a delay in response and then an overshoot. She worked her way through standard procedure, switching hydraulic systems, but the rudder continued to behave erratically. "Now it's jammed. I'm going to follow procedure and take us down to find smoother air and counter the Dutch-mode yaw." As the plane descended and then leveled, a shudder ran through it.

"That's it. We've now completely lost rudder control." A throb of tension was beginning to creep into Mal's voice as she quickly assessed the situation. "If the autopilot was fighting a bad rudder and somehow did not detect it, we've probably been flying dirty for hours. With our nose not always headed true, plus the Dutch-mode oscillation, we've been burning extra fuel, although the fuel totalizer does not look too far off. The headwinds have been lighter than expected, which could explain that. Now, at lower altitude, we are going to be burning even more fuel. Better check our consumption. Which gives us two questions. Can we still make it to Miami, and can we land without a rudder?"

"Or should we turn back for the Azores?"

"We are damn close to the half-way point, but we had crosswinds coming out of Ponta Delgada. Landing with no rudder is no picnic; with a crosswind ... Have you ever landed one of these without rudder control?"

Andy nodded. "More or less. I've done a practice run without rudder control using differential thrust down to 200 feet, but we didn't do an actual landing. It was hard enough to pull off heading dead straight into the wind. You?"

"Not part of standard training. But I know what the flight manual says, which is not much: Ailerons to control track, differential thrust with the engine throttles to control yaw and minimize sideslip. Maintain power to touchdown and do not flare. After landing, use differential braking for directional control and don't retard power if using differential thrust until direction is under control." It was an almost word-for-word recitation.

"That's the story. I also know some horror stories about loss of rudder, but I'm not going there now. I've never ditched in the ocean either, but I know the drill."

"We're not that desperate yet. What say on the fuel?"

Andy looked up from his calculator. "We can still make it to Miami if our present rate of consumption holds. The margin is better heading back to Ponta Delgada because we would have tail winds, but there is also now a storm system closing in on the Azores. We might beat it, we might not. Your call, Mal."

"Okay, Miami it is. We stay on course for another half hour and then recompute. If we are using fuel too fast to make Miami, we can divert. At that point we'll inform air traffic and fill in Sylvia and Josh on what is happening, but we'll spare the passengers any worry until just before we land—wherever that is."

■ ■ ■

Andy was flying the plane when Captain Mallory called to Sylvia and Josh, gesturing for them to come forward and lean in close. "Listen carefully because I don't want to awaken our patient or his wife. We have lost rudder control. We don't know what the problem is, but the rudder was behaving erratically and now has ceased to function altogether."

Josh sucked air through his teeth. "That doesn't sound good."

"It's not. To reduce the risk to the plane, we've been flying manually and avoiding any use of the rudder."

"That *really* doesn't sound good. You can do that, fly with no rudder?" he asked.

"Yes. We use the engines for yaw control—left-right twist, to you—to compensate for sideslip when we have to. As long as we don't touch the rudder pedals, we seem to be fine, and performance does not seem to be deteriorating. Because we have had to fly at a much lower altitude, we are burning fuel faster than planned. Miami is now at the very outer edge of our range at this rate. From our present position, we are about equidistant from Boston and Baltimore-Washington, I have decided to change course for Baltimore, which will be a shorter hop down to Miami. I've already contacted both MediFlightGlobal and our boss back in England. Another air ambulance is flying up to meet us in Baltimore and take our passengers down to Miami."

Sylvia turned to Josh. "You've done an emergency landing before?"

"Yes, but not since joining Macallister. What are we in for?"

Mal turned in her seat. "It is an emergency landing, yes, but it should be relatively routine as these things go; all the rest of our control surfaces are operational. Plus, we have the advantage of this aircraft being configured in a way that adds stability." She was putting on a brave face for the sake of the passengers and crew, but it would be far from easy.

"The airport will be prepared with emergency crews ready, of course, but we shouldn't need them. By working the engines independently—what's called differential thrust or asymmetric power—we can keep the nose pointed more or less how we want it and avoid slipping sideways. We will have to come in hot, a little faster than normal, and we do not flare—the little nose-up, bird-style landing we usually do. Control over our heading is a little clumsier and slower, but Andy here has done it before and we will both be handling the landing. We've already been practicing coordinating our actions."

"I don't want to raise anxieties back there, so we'll wait to tell the passengers until we are on approach. Okay?"

Josh and Sylvia nodded and returned to their seats opposite their patient. After buckling in again, Josh turned to Sylvia. "You've done this a lot longer than I have. What do you think? I've read about loss of rudder control. It's pretty hairy. Mal's act was not completely convincing."

"I wouldn't call it an act. She's a professional, just like we are. Staying calm and focused is what we are paid for. We'll do our job back here taking care of our patient; they'll take care of the plane." She bit her lip and made a show of checking on Karl.

■ ■ ■

With the go ahead from the cockpit, Josh reached back and placed his hand lightly on Shira's shoulder. "Shira, I hate to wake you, but we are about to start our approach, and there are some things we need to tell you."

Shira blinked and looked around to get her orientation. "Is there a problem?"

"Not really a big one, but we have had to divert to Baltimore-Washington International Airport because we have been burning extra fuel. This will not be a real problem for you and Karl because we have another plane already on its way to ferry you down to Miami."

"Is there some reason we have been burning extra fuel?"

"There is a problem with one of the controls, which has required the pilots to fly at a lower altitude, which uses more fuel. But they tell me we have plenty to complete the landing safely in Baltimore with fuel to spare."

"And what aren't you telling me?"

"Well, it's an emergency landing, but—"

"Emergency?" Karl, suddenly awake, tried to sit up but was constrained by his safety harness. "What sort of an emergency?"

"It will be all right. We lost rudder control, but Mal and Andy are old hands and they can land this thing with or without a rudder."

Karl tilted his head back to get a glance at Shira, who was pulling at her ear, a nervous habit that signaled she was trying to act nonchalant. He looked back at Sylvia. "Is there a reason we are coming into BWI rather than some less crowded airspace?"

"Mal says she wants the longest available runway for the landing, plus the best emergency resources. Just in case. Air traffic control has vectored us straight in on a runway that is wide and almost two miles long."

■ ■ ■

Mal and Andy ran through their checklist for final approach, using the orderly routine to help calm their nerves. Despite her cool exterior, Mal's grip on the yoke kept tightening up. As they ticked the last of the items, Mal added, "Just remember, you are handling yaw with the throttles; I get everything else. Let's see. It's a calm morning. We have wind at 10 knots from the west, which shouldn't be too hard to compensate for, plus runway 28 is 200 feet wide. As soon as we touch down, we'll brake and use the brakes for steering, but stay on the throttles until we are clearly under control. Once we're below 45 knots, I can steer with the nose wheel."

"Can we really do this?"

"We have no choice, so the answer is yes. Absolutely. So let's bring us down safely."

They kept up a crisp back and forth without realizing they were calling out in steadily rising voices. In the final minutes, fickle Nature decided to throw them a curve. The wind dropped some, but then shifted almost broadside to them, with gusts out of the southwest. Andy advanced the right throttle as Mal banked left. With the runway coming up at them, Mal had to level the wings again. Andy juggled the throttles forward and back as he and Mal tried to control their speed and keep the plane on the glide path. "Right," she called. "No, right more. Left throttle." The plane shuddered through the last of the descent. Owing to the extra corrections, when the rear wheels touched down, then bounced, they were farther down the runway than intended and hot by over 30 knots. Mal fought to settle the nose wheel.

Mal worked the brakes, but had trouble trying to both steer and slow the plane.

"We're too hot," Andy snapped. "We're going to run out of runway."

"Okay, we use our ace in the hole." With a close eye on their speed, Andy reached awkwardly with his free hand and felt for a handle to the right of the engine throttles. The moment he saw the speed drop below 150 knots, he pulled up on the release to deploy the drag chute. Mal had to keep letting up on one brake or the other, fighting to compensate for the tug of the chute that was slowing them but also pulling them to the side. Andy disconnected the chute early as Mal tried to straighten the plane on the runway. They were now angled right and still too hot for nose-wheel steering. At 50 knots, Mal decided to chance it and try to steer the nose around. The nose landing gear collapsed as the plane veered off the right edge of the runway.

The plane pitched forward and the right wingtip tank dragged, but they skidded to a stop without flipping over. Andy killed the engines and hit the extinguishers.

Sylvia called out from the back. "Somebody ought to teach you how to land this crate, Mal."

"Everyone all right back there?" Mal asked.

"Looks like we're all fine. Shook up, maybe. But you guys better help get that jammed door open before the fire brigade kicks it down or gets out the heavy artillery."

Mal turned to her co-pilot and saw blood on his hand. "You alright?"

"Yeah, just ripped some flesh on that bloody chute release handle."

Once the door was opened, the ground emergency crew helped get Karl out and into a waiting ambulance. Josh and Sylvia followed to go with Karl and Shira as they were whisked away.

Having kept her composure and focus throughout the crisis, Mal now fought to keep from shaking. After busying herself with procedure and checking to make sure everything was shut down properly, she was the last out of the plane. She stood for a moment staring at the ground as she took an extra deep breath.

She was letting it out slowly when a firefighter in full turn-out gear called out from behind the plane. "You know, it looks like you left part of your plane on the runway." Mal walked away from the plane to skirt the wing and saw that the entire rudder was gone, ripped from its mounting on the tail.

Chapter
Twenty-Five

■ Karl had lucked out, thanks to Shira's quick thinking. Mount Sinai Medical Center turned out to be a mecca for hip and knee surgery where some of the best surgeons had been perfecting minimally invasive techniques that allowed them to work medical miracles through small incisions. After a thorough workup, fresh MRIs, and a series of consultations, the surgical team had decided that there was nothing to be gained by delay.

When Karl awoke from surgery and was wheeled from recovery back to his room, Shira was waiting. For the longest time, they held hands and looked at each other without speaking.

"It's going to be all right," Shira said at last. "They said you'll be up and around in no time and will be able to lead a normal, active life."

"Oh, goody. I've always wanted to lead a normal, active life. Believe me, after recent events, a shot at normality is very seductive."

"You," she said, tapping him on the head, "are as corny and funny as ever."

"Hey, careful there with the tapping. Remember, I had a recent concussion. Another head injury too soon and the brain melts into blancmange."

Shira waived her small fist in front of his nose. "I'll concuss you, Mister." Then her brave front collapsed, and Shira awkwardly tried to hug him despite the tubes and monitors. "I have been so worried about you. Worried. And so alone."

Karl managed to work one arm free enough to place his hand on her shoulder where it stayed until he drifted back asleep.

▪ ▪ ▪

The afternoon sun was shining a mustard yellow through the Miami haze when Shira returned. "I hear you've had a busy day, already up and about."

"It's this modern medicine. They used to keep patients bedridden for weeks; now they kick you out right after major surgery. The docs tell me it makes for a faster recovery, but I know it's about revenue maximization. If they keep me here another week, all they get is the room charges, meds, and physio. If they bring in a new patient, they get those astronomical upfront lab and surgery billings."

"What's that sticking out of your purse?" he said, craning to see.

"Oh, our German friend in Madeira sent this to my mother's place by courier, bless him. She sends love, by the way, and a promise to visit tomorrow."

"Your mother sends love? Surely a figure of speech. Or did falling a hundred meters finally prove myself worthy of her only daughter?"

"It was not a hundred meters, and don't pick on my mother. Oh, yes, the kids are fine. Bini is actually a little disappointed that we are back early. Seems he's made a friend. An American. A girl. Our very grownup and oh-so-responsible teenager has been leaving Shoshi mostly in my mother's care. Which might explain why she is glad to have us back early. See, that's why she loves you now. You brought the cavalry to her rescue."

"Where's your horse, my dear?"

"No horse. It's an armored division, silly. So, what about the letter? It's another translation with a note from Professor Schottky. I thought you might be distracted from itching stitches if I read it to you. Should I?"

"Yes, do."

> Dear Karl,
>
> This is the last of the letters, or really the first from the set, as your wife explained. I want to thank you for giving me this opportunity to practice my skills as a

translator and to be a part of such a remarkable discovery. It has been a privilege to be privy to the story of your mother and her journey. I was born too late to know the Germany she describes, so I cannot attest to any of the facts. I grew up in a post-war world of guilt and resentment: guilt over what my country had done and resentment for being made to feel guilty for a page of history in which we personally had no part. Some of my generation went bravely into the bright light, staring history in the face without blinking or flinching. Others turned to denial and to the same dark impulses and self-serving storylines that fueled the rise of the Nazi Party and the Holocaust that it unleashed. This time they turn their hatred to the Turks and Islam, but it is the same sad part of us, a part that is hardly limited to Germans.

Forgive me for the personal comments, but I have been so moved by your mother's letters. She must have been a remarkable person.

Yours,

Wilhelm Schottky

Dear Hannah,

It has been such a long time since I wrote to you and so much has happened. Where I have been working I have met the most wonderful man, an American. He is with the Corps of Engineers, and they are here for now helping with reconstruction. He speaks German but with a very distinctive accent. He is passionate about engineering and passionate about me. The most wonderful thing is that he shares what he knows and learns from his job with me, as if I were also an engineer. Of course, he explains that he is only called an engineer now, a term used by the American Army. But he wants to return soon to the United States and study at a university to become a structural engineer, a real engineer. When I told him that I wanted to do that, too, he did not laugh at me or dismiss it. He takes me seriously, as did your father. And he is taking me to America! Yes, I am going to America, and I am going to become an engineer.

But I am jumping so far ahead, for I have not told you how I got to London and how I changed my name. Again. This time I am Julianna Ryesdale, and this time I do have papers and can prove it.

Chapter
Twenty-Six

Lisbon, early 1945

     ■ Julianna and Otto Krause began their work immediately, with a series of welcome dinners and casual gatherings at various cafés in the heart of Lisbon. The city had prospered during the war, a conflict in which neutral Portugal had traded heavily with both sides and benefited from its pivotal position at the edge of the Atlantic. At the heart of this trade was the strategic metal, tungsten, with Portugal's ore reserves fueling a bidding war and giving it leverage with the Allies and the Germans. Portugal was on track to become the only European nation to finish the war far wealthier than it had begun, its vaults bulging with gold bullion paid by Germany from plundered gold laundered through Swiss banks and layers of concocted commercial transactions.

Lisbon, the wartime City of Light, had also become the dark nexus of Allied and Axis espionage, with German and British spies rubbing shoulders with Salazar's feared and hated secret police in a high-stakes game of information and disinformation. The stalked were following others, and the informants were compromised in a round robin of clandestine charades and games of deception.

Julianna knew only sketches of Otto's mission, an outline gleaned from overheard conversations or from the times she had helped as casual translator. She knew he was looking for a ship to Brazil, that he was negotiating for both cargo and passage. The cargo she assumed to be the heavy containers that had accompanied them from Berlin; the contents she assumed were Nazi gold. She was not keen to be headed for South America, but it was America, nevertheless, and the right side of the ocean for her larger agenda.

In this elaborate stage improvisation, she was Otto's wife, but only in public. Unlike nearly all the men encountered in her long journey from Krakow, Otto made no move toward her. He was sweet and casually affectionate, but slept in the sitting room of their hotel suite. Whatever his interests were—and she had begun to suspect his eye was for men, or boys—he was discreet, in keeping with his profession.

■ ■ ■

Rafaela, who was to stay with Karl while she and Otto dined at a popular restaurant, had shown up late and full of apologies.

Julianna bent over Karl's crib. "My Karl, my boy, Mama has to meet your daddy for dinner, so Rafaela is going to stay and play with you. You be a good boy and do not cause her trouble, okay?" She rubbed noses with Karl as she talked with him.

"He understands you, Senhora? He is just a baby. Does he know what you are saying?"

"Perhaps not, but if I don't talk with him, how will he learn?"

Rafaela was fifteen, not much younger than Julianna by the calendar, but very young in experience. She was the daughter of one of the porters at the hotel, and earned extra money for her family by watching over the children of guests.

"I will take care of your *bebê*, Senhora. I will talk with him so that he will learn Portuguese." She grinned in triumph.

■ ■ ■

The restaurant Chave d'Ouro, overlooking brightly lit Rossio Square at the heart of the city's social life, was crowded with well-dressed patrons savoring an evening of good food and spirits, a life far removed from the realities of war that kept other European cities darkened at night. Otto ordered drinks for the two of them, then excused himself to make the rounds of other tables. He had been trying to set up a meeting with Ricardo Espírito Santo, head of one of Portugal's leading banks and a driving wheel in the country's wartime financial machinery.

While Otto worked the crowd, Julianna swirled the ice in her drink and pretended to be bored as she listened in on conversations in German and Portuguese at nearby tables. Otto would quiz her about what she had overheard when later they were alone again. Suddenly, one fragment of a sentence leapt out at her, spoken in quiet English barely audible in the multilingual din.

"... being pulled back to London. The Americans ..."

She glanced quickly around to try to get a fix on the source, but saw no one that seemed to be speaking English, none that fit the voice, with its gravelly resonance that carried through the noise even when pitched low. Then she heard it again.

"... a BOAC flight at week's end ..."

They were behind her. She raised her eyes toward the ornate chandelier in the center of the room, then let her gaze follow around the balcony filled with more diners, scanning as if taking in the scene, turning to catch it all, sweeping the upper level with its somewhat lower echelon of wartime society. She continued all the way around, full circle, arm over the back of her chair, as if she might be looking for a particular face in the crowd above. Without lowering her eyes, she took in the two gentleman seated at the table behind her, both dressed in British tweeds and sipping whiskeys. The younger of the two had a handsome face shaped like an acorn, with bright red, wavy hair forming the cap. As she swiveled past, he spoke again to his companion with the quiet, resonant voice she had heard before.

Julianna pushed her chair back from the table to make room to cross her legs and to lean back with her drink, putting herself almost on top of their table.

"I'm British," she said, turning slightly and leaning back farther still. She held her drink at the ready near her mouth to hide the fact that she was speaking. "I'm a British subject. I've had my passport confiscated and am being held against my will by the Germans."

Behind her, the voice answered, soft, resolute, "Get up, pretend to be leaving for the loo, continue down the hall and exit through the last door on your left. In the street, head toward the train station, then turn right. Wait just around the corner. I will meet you there in five minutes."

Julianna panicked. What did he mean? "The loo?"

"Yes, the WC. Pretend like you are looking for it. Ask a local if you don't know where it is. Go. Now. Your companion is coming toward you."

Julianna looked up to see Otto, across the room, making his way between tables. He smiled at her. She picked up her pocketbook from the table, held it up, and gestured with it as she stood. Otto nodded back in recognition.

She followed the directions, turning away from the tree-lined Avenida da Liberdade and ending up in a narrow side street, just beyond the glare of the Square. Bare shouldered, without her coat, she shivered in the chill night air. It was more than ten minutes before the red-haired man arrived, opening the passenger door as he stopped his car beside her. "Get in. I'm taking you to the embassy before anyone knows what is happening."

"No, we have to stop at my hotel first. My son is there. And I need to grab my coat."

"Which hotel?"

"Hotel Tivoli."

"Of course, the German favorite. Unfortunately, that is the wrong way, north. The embassy is west. We will have to get your son later. Just get in. We can't chance it now."

"Then I will walk there and get my son. You meet me at the lobby bar in half an hour."

"Don't be an idiot. Get in. We'll go to the hotel. Oh, by the way, I'm Julian, Trade Attaché at the embassy."

"I'm Julianna. What a coincidence."

■ ■ ■

At the Hotel Tivoli, she left Julian in the car and went alone to the front desk. "My key, please, room 211."

"Both keys are gone, Senhora. Your husband . . ."

"My husband?"

"Yes, he just returned, to relieve the nanny, who has not yet returned the key she had. He must be there now. He can let you in. Do you want me to ring the room for you?"

"No, that will not be necessary. I'll just go up." She started toward the stairs but then changed her mind and decided to check in with Julian.

"That's impossible," he said when she told him about the key. "How could your husband get here ahead of us? I'll go up with you."

Outside room 211, Julian signaled to her to be quiet and to stay to one side of the door while he went to the other side. He tested the door, then knocked and stepped aside. There was the sound of scrambling inside, and the crash of furniture. Julian stepped directly in front of the door and kicked with all his force. The door bounced open.

A man whom neither of them recognized was trying to finish pulling on his trousers while Rafaela frantically redid buttons on her blouse. "Please, Senhora, say nothing of this to my father. Please. He will kill us both."

"I will not tell him if you will say nothing." She nodded toward Julian. "Now, go quietly with your boyfriend and find some other place."

"Thank you, Senhora, thank you. I will say nothing. We will say nothing."

"Here, Rafaela, take this." She held out some folded escudos. "And get another boyfriend. This one is much too old for you. And far too clumsy."

■ ■ ■

"The letter continues," Shira said.

> Karl and I hid in the British Embassy for two days waiting for the next BOAC flight from Lisbon to Whitchurch, outside Bristol. Julian had the Embassy prepare a Letter of Transit for me, a genuine document even if obtained under false pretenses. I had to think quickly when he asked for my full name, so now I am Julianna Warwick. He reassured me that my lost passport could easily be reissued once I filed the proper paperwork. He had been willing to take a chance on me because, poor boy, I think he was

instantly smitten. After the numerous loveless liaisons and the sexless gallantry of Otto, I found Julian's boyish crush quite charming. He was always the gentleman, and I am quite certain he had no idea what to make of my sudden disappearance once we were in England.

And there I was, once more a homeless waif with a young babe, this time in a London that was still under air attack, the target of a new German long-range rocket. In what I learned was a very British fashion, London had already begun the post-war rebuilding while the last days of hell still reigned on the continent.

How I met the Ryesdales is another funny little story. It was because of the Germans that I was spared having to search out someplace for Karl and me to sleep on our first night in London. We were fortunate to spend that night huddled in the London Underground, sheltered from an air raid. The Germans have a new flying bomb they have been firing at London and Antwerp, one that makes no sound as it falls. Suddenly, the house next door explodes without warning, and then, even as your ears are recovering, you hear a quick thunderclap. And the sirens. And then you are hurried toward a shelter by neighbors and old men wearing helmets and arm bands.

I am told that most of these rocket bombs fall short of the city, so maybe Germany is neither so smart nor so strong as they think.

Chapter Twenty-Seven

London, spring 1945

■ Coming out of the shelter into bright, early spring sunlight, Julianna blinked and Karl cried. With no agenda and no idea where to turn, Julianna allowed herself to be herded along with the current of the crowd emerging from the Underground. When the man in front of her stopped suddenly to turn and enter a gated courtyard, she bumped into him.

Before she could apologize, he turned back toward her. "Begging your pardon, ma'am. I really should be more careful about braking without warning right in the middle of the footpath." He glanced down at the newly disenfranchised Karl who was sucking away fiercely at his fist and whimpering softly. "Yours?"

"Yes. He's teething."

"Ah, teething. I thought maybe you had found him, abandoned, and were bringing him here. You look frightfully young to be a mother."

"Bringing him here?"

"The Bishop's Adoption Office." He pointed to the sign above the arched entrance. "It happens, you know. A young girl can get herself in a spot, especially with the young men still going off to war."

Julianna pulled herself as tall as she could manage and still had to tip her head to look him in the eye. "My husband was killed. In Lisbon. I'm looking for my in-laws. They live around here someplace."

"Around here, you say." He looked up and down the street. "And their name, your husband's family?"

"Warwick. I'm Julianna . . . Warwick."

"Julianna Warwick, eh? Recently married are we?"

"No, I mean, . . ."

"Still getting used to the name, of course, and the young man off fighting in France, and you with the baby. Oh, I'm so sorry, you did say Portugal. And how sad that you are now his widow, Mrs. Warwick. To be a widow, and you so young, and with a babe. And your husband's name was . . ."

"Otto," she blurted out, then realized it sounded all wrong. Otto Warwick. What kind of a name was that?

"Please, Mrs. Otto Warwick, come in and have a biscuit and a spot of tea. Give yourself a chance to gather your thoughts before moving on to find your husband's family." This was all said without so much of a hint of doubt or irony, yet Julianna knew that he believed not a word of her story. He was clearly not a person to be trusted nor one to be easily deceived, yet neither was he someone to be turned down. She followed him into the courtyard and then into a small storefront, with a counter and files and desks and a kettle whistling atop a gas ring.

"Mrs. Murphy, good morning. How lovely of you to have the water all ready for tea. Do you suppose you can find some biscuits for a young mother and her boy who is teething?

"Please sit, Mrs. Warwick. Warwick it shall be so long as you wish it. Or you can tell me your story. Or leave now. But not, mind you, before you have had some tea and your little boy has gummed his way through at least one biscuit."

There was something so gentle and genuine about the man that Julianna started to cry, and once she started, she couldn't stop, and then Karl was crying, and the months of terror and cold, the kaleidoscope of chaos poured out of both of them.

"I'm Thomas Ryesdale," the man said, kneeling in front of them and holding out a handkerchief for her. "And we'll sort this out. Don't you worry."

■ ■ ■

Shira looked over at Karl. "You all right? I can finish this later if you want to just rest."

"Rest? Are you kidding? They have me scheduled for physiotherapy in twenty minutes. No, please finish the letter."

The Ryesdales are some of the loveliest people I have ever known. Thomas trained to become a priest but told me that he discovered he was more interested in helping people than in saving them, a distinction that he made clear in many long discussions. Now he is a social worker arranging adoptions. His wife, Elizabeth, was a schoolteacher before she married. Now she helps Thomas at the BAO, the Bishop's Adoption Office. They have a daughter, Helen, who is about to turn 11 and who follows me around like a cocker spaniel pup, eager to please and to learn.

The Ryesdales know the whole story, the only ones on earth who do. But, of course, you do, as well. They have taken me in, given me a roof and a room and useful work to do at the BAO. And they have adopted me, so we change our names again and now are Julianna Ryesdale and Karl Ryesdale, and soon we will be able to get British passports, real ones, not just Letters of Transit. Thomas has bent some rules and filled in some extra lines on forms to make this possible, but the passports, when we get them, will be "all right and proper to the last jot and tittle," as Thomas would say.

Oh, and I must tell you the other thing that has happened. I had thought that I would, myself, somehow take your coat to Palestine and give it to the man of whom your father always spoke. I despaired that it might be many years before I could manage that, particularly as I will soon be headed in the opposite direction, to New York. But I have met another remarkable man, Israel Levitz, who is determined soon to get to Palestine despite the British government standing in the way.

Israel was an electrical engineer who left Germany in 1938 with his brother Moshe and started a business here in London, a shop that fixes radios. When I heard that they have been saving their money from their thriving wartime business to get to Palestine and start a business there, I had to tell them about your coat. I wondered if they might deliver it for me, to the Mordecai that your father mentioned. They asked me why it was so important. I told them about the magic crystals sewn into the seams, the solid valves that our fathers had invented. They got very excited. They said that they could take the valves to Palestine and find this Mordecai, who might even be a cousin, and together build better radios, like Papa did. So, I cut the seams and fished out the crystals in their rosin casings with short wire legs, like crippled insects. I gave those, along with the tiny scrolls in Yiddish that were also sewn in the seams, to the Levitz brothers to take to Palestine to study and to use to build radios. They seemed to understand how magically special these little three-legged bugs were and promised to use them to help Palestine and the Zionists there build a new country, a Jewish homeland.

In this way, a small part of my father and yours will make it to the homeland, just as a small part of you goes with me to another New World. I seal this letter now with a kiss, and with my tears. I will see you again, I know, because I see you in my dreams sometimes, not as I left you, but as you came to me, the young girl, so thin and so beautiful. I see your face, just centimeters from mine, in the dim and unsteady light of the dying embers as you whispered to me of God and love, as we touched and kissed. There have been many men, too many, and boys, too many, but there has been only you, and you will always be the only one.

My Fred, who takes me to America, knows nothing of this, nor of the men. It is meaningless to him, and without words he has told me that he needs to know nothing of my past, of the path that led me to London and to him. Of all the boys along that path, he is, in some odd way, the most naïve. He talks of our future together as if there had been no past, no war, as if we had grown up together in what he calls the Upper Midwest, in his hometown in the center of his homeland, and to him, the pivot around which the universe turns.

He teaches me about pivots and pulleys and gear ratios, even when we are in bed together. He is sweet and tender and never presses me to know why sometimes I cry at his sweetness and tenderness.

And so, I will see you again, soon, as I sleep in his arms with the memory of you, my love, my first love, deep inside. My Hannah.

Yours forever,
Julianna Nowack Ryesdale Lustig

Shira refolded the letter and sat with it in her lap, waiting for Karl to say something.

"So much I didn't know." His voice was a near whisper. "Perhaps there was good reason she spoke so little of her past. Still, I wonder if she ever told my father about any of this. Surely he must have been curious."

"Perhaps not. From what you have told me, they seemed to have had a pact, an understanding that what was past was well and truly past.

"Oh, wait, there is more. Professor Schottky says a poem, in English, was on the back of the last page of the letter, with no attribution but in your mother's handwriting. Perhaps it was written by her. The title is 'Saudade.' Professor Schottky says it is a Portuguese word that has no direct translation in English. He tried to explain what it meant, and I said there was a Hebrew word with that exact meaning: *ergah*, a yearning or longing with intense sadness for someplace or someone." She turned over the original letter to find the poem. "Okay, here it is. I'll read it."

> Like spider silk that spans the path
> From one unnoted branch to another —
>   or to nowhere—
> Gossamer steel adrift,
> Seen only when obliquely lit
>   by chance illumination.
> Yet, it remains to snare the unaware,
> Clinging: *saudade*,
> The homeland connection.
> In the lonely sighs of winds on distant sails,
> In remembered poems, repainted scenes,
> The retelling of time-distorted tales: *Saudade.*
> A homesick ache that links us to impersonal pasts,
> The hope to be at home at last,
> Whether we are here or elsewhere still unreached:
> The homeland connection.
> We travel in the faith that we are free,
> Yet it trails behind us, to teach us of
> A sticky trace as strong as love.

"So, now we know: my mother was a secret agent, even if only for a brief time. And she may have been a poet. And she played a small role in helping to kick-start Israel's electronics industry. How odd. I think I even know what happened to the 'magic crystals.' I remember passing a display in the lobby of IsTac with some tiny early transistors arrayed on black velvet as if they were gemstones. My grandfather and his friend, it seems, were doing pioneering work in semiconductors and—"

He was interrupted by a nurse and an orderly entering the room. "How are we doing this afternoon, Mr. Lustig?"

"I don't know how *we* are doing, but I'm feeling like I have been quarterbacking for the Patriots and just got sacked by half the

Giants squad. Oh, Nurse Bamberg, this is my wife, Shira; Shira meet my angel of mercy, who brings me little pills that make me feel ever so much better." He winked at the nurse.

"Well, right now we are going to make you feel ever so much worse, because it is time to get you down to physiotherapy for a workout. So, let's get you out and about, quarterback."

Chapter
Twenty-Eight

■ Anat half expected to see the man from downtown Funchal on her flight to Miami via Lisbon and Newark, but she spotted no familiar faces on any of the legs. Delayed by an unplanned overnight stay in Lisbon owing to a work stoppage by Portuguese air traffic controllers, she arrived in Newark exhausted and frustrated. She sailed through Customs and Border Protection confident that her flawlessly faked British passport would not set off any U.S. alarms, although it would immediately tell her colleagues back in Tel Aviv exactly where she was. At the airport in Miami, she picked up two fresh SIM cards, inserted one in her phone, and called Shira's cellphone.

"It's me. I made it," she announced without preliminaries. "I'll meet you at the hospital in half an hour."

"How ...? Oh, yeah. I—" Before Shira could continue, Anat disconnected and swapped out the SIM again. She located the nearest ladies' room, where she made a beeline for the last stall in the row, depositing the used SIM card in the trash as she passed. Before she sat down, she reversed her skirt, then took her time tucking her brown curls beneath a blond wig and putting on Lava Red lipstick. Before leaving, she twisted the breakaway heels off her shoes and flushed them down the toilet. The tall, mousy brunette who had entered the restroom walked out a flashy blonde two inches shorter.

Anat stood in line for a taxi outside the terminal, thinking to herself that Miami in June was at least as bad as Tel Aviv.

"Mount Sinai Medical Center, please," she told the taxi driver when it was finally her turn.

"The Main Campus? Miami Beach?"

"Ah, yes," Anat guessed. "Is that far?"

"Ten miles, straight shot out the expressway, but this hour we could hit traffic on the causeway."

A three-car pile-up on the Tuttle Causeway ended up costing them enough time to send the driver into a stream of muttered cursing. At the hospital, she told the receptionist that she was visiting her brother-in-law, Karl Lustig. "I just flew in from London. I do hope I can see him. I understand there was a terrible accident, and I caught the first flight I could."

"And what was your name?"

Realizing she might have to produce identification, Anat used the name on her passport. "Anna, Anna Deerfield."

"I am sorry, but this patient is on Restricted Visitation. I don't see your name on the list."

"Can you call up to the room? Tell him that Anna from Tel Aviv is here."

"I thought you said you were from London."

"I live in London now, but I'm from Tel Aviv."

"I am sorry, but I can't let you see him, and we are not supposed to call patients."

"Isn't there something you could do? Could I speak with your supervisor?"

The woman shook her head slowly. "My supervisor will tell you the same thing. Do you want me to call her and have her repeat what I just told you?"

"Look, Karl Lustig is a patient here, and I am family. I don't see why—"

"Are you looking for Karl Lustig? Is there something I can do?"

Anat jumped at the familiar voice behind her. She turned and threw her arms around Shira. "Hey, Sis, it's me," she said, stretching back to arm's length and locking eyes with Shira. "I just flew in from London. Lev says hello, by the way. And I've remarried; it's Anna Deerfield now." She spoke rapidly to get her coded message out before Shira could say anything. Then she leaned in again for a cheek kiss and whispered, "I heard what happened. I'm here to help." Pulling back again, she spoke loud enough for the clerk to hear. "I'm off The Hill, on my own. But these people won't let me see poor Karl. How is he? Tell these people that I just want to see my brother-in-law."

Shira smiled and said, "Of course. What was I thinking not to put you on the list. So now it's Deerfield, is it? And I do like what you've done with your hair." She grinned, then fished into her purse for her ID and handed it to the clerk. "I'm the patient's wife, as you can see on your screen. Please add Mrs. Deerfield to the list of authorized visitors."

At Karl's room, Shira went in first to stave off embarrassing exclamations from Karl. "Hi, Darling. How are you doing?"

"Mmmm, well . . ."

"That good, huh? I've brought somebody to see you. Guess who just flew in from Tel Aviv? Anna. And she brings greetings from Lev. See, they're looking out for you."

"Anna?"

Anat peeked around the corner of the door. "How's my favorite brother-in-law?" she said with a wink.

"Confused. But it's probably the meds they give me to keep me happy. How's Lev?"

"Still retired, holding down the home front for now. So what happened to put you on the orthopedic surgery ward?"

"I took a nosedive off a mountain path, not my doing." He paused as the nurse finished attending to the patient in the next bed and left the room. "Jake over there just got out of surgery. He'll be groggy for a while, but we should keep it down. You never know who you bump into in a hospital. Or on a levada walk in Madeira."

Anat slid a chair over beside the bed and motioned Shira in closer. "Are you saying you were pushed? Any idea who or why?"

"I'm almost certain the why has something to do with my design consulting. As to who, I don't have names, but I do have faces."

Shira looked surprised. "What are you talking about?"

"I told you: my camera. Did you get it back?"

"Pieces, yeah. Oh, I do have the SD card, but it's got a crack in it."

Anat reached over. "Let me see it? It might still be readable."

Shira dug down into her purse and gave the cracked SD card to Anat.

"It's worth a try." Anat unzipped her rolling case and slid out her laptop. After booting it up, she slipped the card into the slot at the side. "Nothing. 'Unrecognized USB device.' Don't you love error messages that are not only cryptic but actually wrong?" She reached for the card and wiggled it as she started to pull it out. Her computer sounded a bong-bing chime and offered to open the folder with Windows Explorer. "Okay, here we go. When something fails, try wiggling it. If that doesn't work, hit it. Right, Karl?"

"That's what we consultants always tell our clients. Okay, go down to the last photo on the card." Anat drilled down, selected the highest numbered photo file, and scrolled to the end. She double clicked on the thumbnail, bringing up a skewed shot of trees and sky with two faces in shadow visible at the bottom right of the frame. "Zoom in on those two; the one on the left pushed me over the edge."

Anat sucked air between her clenched teeth.

"You know them?" Shira asked.

"Not by name, no, but I think I recognize one of them. And I can't tell you more for reasons that I am sure you can guess." The laptop did a falling bing-bong chime signaling that the card had been ejected. Anat wiggled and twisted the card again, but the computer refused to read it. "I'm afraid we lost it."

"Wait! Don't close the viewer," Karl said. "The image is still in temporary memory. Try doing a Save-As to your desktop. Okay, did that work?"

"Like a charm. Quick thinking, Karl." She re-opened the image file with a photo editor, adjusted the gamma to bring up the shadows, and sharpened it. "That is him, all right. And I would say we probably should get you out of here. My guess is that you left a digital trail blazed in neon letters that anyone who wanted to could follow right to your bed."

"I'm supposed to be discharged in two or three days. They have these amazing surgeons here who can work through a tiny incision. I now possess a completely reconstructed hip, but they already have me up and around with a cane and it's been less than twenty-four hours."

"That's great, Karl, but I am thinking of getting you out of here now and into a safe house. Either that, or we have to somehow get police protection for you right here. Given that I am not supposed to be here and my identity could fall apart on close scrutiny, I am not sure I could arrange that."

"I have an idea," Shira said, putting her hand on Anat's arm. "What if Karl were an international fugitive? What if there were an Interpol alert? Would the feds or the Miami police step in?"

"Probably, but I don't—"

"You two wait here. I am going to find a quiet spot to call Duarte."

Anat looked more confused than ever, but Karl was smiling.

When she returned, Shira gave Karl a thumbs-up. "Okay, the wheels are in motion. We'll see how long it takes the local authorities to act."

It didn't take long. Anat and Shira were returning from the bathroom when they saw the state troopers coming down the hall toward Karl's room. Anat steered Shira into another patient's room, where the two of them smiled and apologized before leaving and turning back the way they had come.

"What about Karl?" Shira asked.

"He'll be all right for now, I guess. But what did you do?"

"We left Madeira three steps ahead of the law." Shira explained the whole story about Duarte's cousin and the arrangements for police protection in Funchal.

"How did you get action so fast here?"

"Duarte had his cousin report a possible airplane hijacking."

"My God, that is going to be a hard one to undo."

"I don't think so. Karl knows enough to keep his mouth shut for now, and once the story is checked with the air ambulance people, he's in the clear. But you have some talking to do. What are you really doing here? And what is this actually about?"

"Let's go someplace where we can talk, preferably outdoors."

▪ ▪ ▪

Pedro sat with the curtains pulled in his Funchal hotel room while he watched the BBC news.

"According to American authorities," the newsreader was saying, "the plane, an air ambulance registered in the UK and flown by an international crew, lost control of its rudder someplace over the open ocean and was forced to make a crash landing in Baltimore, Maryland." A telephoto shot of the downed plane expanded. Ground crew could be seen working around a towing vehicle being used to move the plane. "Fortunately, no one was hurt in the crash, which is under investigation. A spokesman for Macallister Air Ambulance operating out of Gatwick declined comment at this point, but in the US, an airport employee speaking off the record said that he had heard that there was evidence of sabotage. More on the story from our reporter on the scene."

He had miscalculated; the plane was not as vulnerable as his sources had suggested. Having learned the uncomfortable truth that his wounded seabird had somehow winged its way across the ocean and into port, Pedro searched out fresh instructions from his handlers, which this time arrived embedded in a less-than-viral video of a calico cat appearing to do the mambo. The deciphered message told him to "redo the repair work because the toilet is still leaking." He posted a priority query hidden in a short instructional video on Python programming for Web applications: Where? The response, hidden in a video edition of "Close-Up Magic: Exposed," arrived within an hour: Mount Sinai.

He knew that they were playing games with him by the cryptic instructions that signaled how angry they were at his failure. It took him a minute's reflection to place Mount Sinai not in the Middle east but in Miami where the plane had been heading. Another few minutes of Web surfing zeroed him in on the hospital. He faked a distraught call to confirm that his quarry was temporarily nesting at the Mount Sinai Medical Center, then switched identities to book flights through an online travel site. He cursed Madeira for no longer being the hub of international travel that it had once been.

Another day would be nearly over before he could leave to correct his own mistake.

He sorted through his toolkit. The assault rifle he had already disposed of, and there was no point trying to bring a handgun into Florida, whose notoriety for defense of personal defense meant it should be easy to obtain whatever he needed there. He opened the lid on his first-aid kit and verified that there was still a patch. Then he paid his bill at the front desk of the hotel and got rid of his mustache between the revolving doors and the taxi he hailed a block away.

On the way to a new hotel, he ran down the particulars of the current assignment. After this professor, who was left? The research assistants in Germany were clueless opportunists who had fled back to Turkey at the first hint of trouble—hints broadcast by Pedro's associates. Waldmeir in Dresden was still unsure whether he was dealing with an incident of small-scale scientific fraud or simple incompetence—or some combination. In any case, he had given no signs that he suspected diversion of samples. With the departure of his assistants, the matter seemed settled, and he had moved on. Of the others still in Madeira, only the older professor was a potential problem, but he was nowhere near the threat that this Lustig represented. Lustig was too smart and too independent, with a record of rogue action. Whether he had spread the contamination to any around him would have to be checked, but, for the moment, he was the immediate threat.

After that? What would be next? Another assignment whose importance or place in the scheme of things was not for Pedro to question, perhaps not even to know. He lay on top of the bedding in the darkened room with the lights of Funchal sneaking through the almost-closed curtains, wondering where it would end. But he didn't need to wonder for long. The answer, always there, barely hidden beneath the surface of his everyday activities, had been obvious since the day he was recruited. It would end as it had for his brothers, swiftly, after a small miscalculation, an unanticipated encounter, or simple inattention.

As he drifted into the half-sleep of anxious anticipation, he saw his brothers standing at the foot of the bed, knowing smiles on their faces. What will you die for? they asked him. What matters?

Survival. The survival of a country, a people, he told them.

Then his alarm went off and he dressed to leave for the airport.

Chapter Twenty-Nine

■ Discovering a palm-lined walkway behind a medical office building on Sullivan Drive in Miami Beach, Shira and Anat started a slow stroll along the waterfront. "If I am to help Karl, I need some help from you, Shira."

"Tell me what this is about, first. Why are they after Karl? Who are they?"

"I don't know who they are, and I will not tell you what little I know of what this is about."

"I have a right to know. He's my husband."

"Yes, perhaps you do have a right to know. And, no, I won't tell you. My sense is that anyone who knows anything is in danger. Karl seems to have stumbled onto something big, a secret that somebody is willing to kill to keep secret."

"He does have a way of stumbling into shit, doesn't he? You're doing this to protect me—and the children. Aren't you?"

Anat nodded gravely. "You have to trust me on this. You and Karl are family to me. I wouldn't be with Lev if it wasn't for you. You were our *shadkhin*, the matchmaker who showed the two of us what we had missed in each other. Now I need you to trust me, to let me work with Karl without you having to know what I am up to, without you asking Karl about what is going on."

"You are expecting a lot. Karl is my *bashert*. We're soul mates; we share everything."

"Would Karl want you to know something that could cost you your life?"

"I would give my life for Karl; he knows that."

"And what about Bini and Shoshi? What if they lost both of their parents?"

"Are you saying that I might lose Karl, that I"—she choked on the words—"I might have to let him go to save myself and my children."

Anat stopped and turned. "No woman should ever have to make such a terrible choice. I will do whatever I can so that it does not come to that. I am not the one to tell you what to do. I know what it is like to have a husband, not what it is like to have children, so I cannot advise you. What I can say is that I will not tell you more about what is going on, and I beg you, for your sake and the children's, not to try to find out more on your own.

"You are so quick, Shira, every bit as smart as Karl—and that is saying a lot—so please, don't pursue it. Let me handle it this time. Okay?"

"Okay." Shira turned to look out over the water, across to the Miami shoreline. "This is that dangerous?"

"Yes."

"Then don't say any more."

Anat wanted to say more, but not about Karl or about the mystery that now surrounded him, but about the lesson of responsibility that she had learned from Karl. She said nothing. Then she turned away as if suddenly distracted by a sound. "Give me your hat, then turn around and go into this office building here. Call Miami police and tell them that somebody is headed toward Karl's room."

"What . . .?"

"Just do it!" Anat moved away as if taking a brisk but aimless walk. She used the reflection in a door just opening to see that the man she had spotted was still heading toward Mount Sinai.

She rounded the building, crossed the street, and started running toward the hospital, cutting between buildings and dodging cars exiting a parking lot. A squad car was already pulling up outside the front when she ducked in through the emergency entrance. She walked purposefully past gurneys and interns, punched the button at a staff elevator, and just managed to get the door to close as a doctor in scrubs approached. She punched the close button and said, "Ooops!" just as he reached to put his hand between the rubber bumpers of the doors.

"Hey, wait for me!" he called, as the doors automatically rebounded.

Anat decided to risk all. She flashed an ID as she put her hand to his chest and pushed him back out. "We have a situation on orthopedics four," she announced, hoping it made sense. The doctor stumbled backwards, and the doors closed again before he could recover.

Karl was on the third floor, but Anat had no idea where she was in relation to his wing. She punched the button for three just before the number blinked onto the elevator display. She stepped off into a crowd of young women, some with nurses' uniforms, some in street clothes.

"Hip surgery?" she asked. Amidst laughter all around, one of the women pointed. Anat trotted off in that direction only to find herself facing a tee in the corridor. A small sign declared that more elevators were to her left, but nothing else gave a clue as to what else might be in either direction. She ran to the right, pushed through a set of double doors, and was stopped by a uniformed police officer.

With one hand inching subtly toward his holstered revolver and the other raised to stop her, he asked, "What's the hurry?"

Anat flashed her ID again and said, "Interpol!" as she pushed past him. She smirked to herself as she continued down the hall in long, confident strides. She knew that he was still confused over whether Interpol had any jurisdiction or role here and was not even sure about the ID she had flashed. Act like you belong somewhere, and people will assume you do; act like you know where you are going, and people will let you pass.

It was not hard to find Karl's room again, once she was on the trail of law officers. Outside the door, she pulled the same flash-and-push routine that had gotten her to the room, but the plain clothes officer blocking the way would have nothing of it.

"What the hell is this? Interpol? Where the hell do you come in?"

"Yes, we have an alert, and I was dispatched from D.C. There's been a hijacking of a British-registered aircraft bound for the continental United States. Is that reason enough?"

"I wouldn't know, but this man is in federal custody, and I am not letting you in."

"And you are who?"

"Agent-in-Charge Fields, Mizz, er, can I see that ID again?"

"Deerfield. It's Anna Deerfield. And a call to your superiors will quickly establish that I am to be granted every professional courtesy in dealing with this case."

"Are you really Interpol?"

Anat leaned forward. "Play, along, Agent Fields, and No Such Agency will look favorably on your mid-career application."

"What the . . .? Oh, yeah, of course. Sure. You want to see the perp?"

"Alleged."

"Right. Go on in."

Anat knew she had only minutes to talk, exit, and vanish before inquiries were made. Bluffing worked, but the effect tended to wear off rather quickly as small seeds of doubts germinated in fertile minds.

She caught the attention of the nurse standing beside Karl and nodded emphatically toward the door. As the nurse left, Anat knelt beside the bed.

"Karl, it's me. Tell me as quickly as you can what you know."

"Not much," he said. "Do you want the digest or the unexpurgated version?"

"Tell me what you haven't told Shira. Everything."

"Okay, it starts with these microprocessor chips showing up here, just before our trip, instead of after we get to Madeira as I had arranged. The TSA turkeys pulled me aside at the airport; they were looking for the chips, or ones like them."

"Okay, Karl. Nothing I say is likely to put you at any more risk than you are already, but I have to know first that you understand you are working with us again."

Karl stared at the ceiling. "Shira will have my hide for it, but I understand."

"Shira knows, but we need to keep her out of it. Understood?" She waited expectantly.

"Okay, Anat, I am working for you again. There, I said it."

"Then I can tell you that the Americans alerted us early in the month that military grade versions of the chipset were on offer from black-market arms traders. I started desk research looking for the source and kept getting hits with your name. The alarm bells clanged even louder when you pulled that end run to get the microprocessor x-rays from Germany. I found myself in a funny position at the Institute, working on special assignment with a wide remit, but reporting to someone who doesn't trust me. So I decided to do some field work and find out for myself what you were up to." She leaned in closer. "So, what were you up to?"

"I'm not diverting contraband, if that's what you think, but I discovered something in Madeira. The chips have been hacked. I needed the ptychograph for confirmation. Sometime, somewhere downstream of the design work at IsTac, modifications were made. I spotted anomalies in the ptychographs, then we turned loose a couple of grad students to do some reverse engineering. There is an on-board software radio that can be programmed to receive signals outside the usual military bands, there is something called a field-programmable gate array that makes possible on-the-fly reconfiguring of the processor, and there is a set of undocumented instructions that tell the chip to ignore entire classes of inputs, essentially freezing it in an unresponsive state."

"That doesn't seem possible. You're saying there is malicious code or circuitry manufactured into the very chip itself?"

"Yes. This kind of thing has happened before. A few years back, the U.S. Department of Homeland Security discovered that some commercial microchips shipping from China were arriving with embedded Trojan microcode. The backdoor access this provided could be used to remotely take control of the chip and use it for digital espionage—or sabotage."

"But we're talking about a military chipset here, not desktop CPUs or smartphone processors. The 460 series are for use in avionics, combat drones, reconnaissance robots. Hell, these things practically fly our planes. They . . ." She stopped abruptly.

"What?"

"Do you remember hearing about the crash of an F-16i just short of the Jordanian border?"

"Yeah. Never read the details, but I recall it was pilot error or something."

"That was the story for public consumption. We shot it down ourselves when the controls suddenly and mysteriously locked up. That's a fly-by-wire plane, everything under computer control, no manual backups because they are—supposedly—never needed. That plane was equipped with the enhanced Zahav avionics package based on the new chipset. If what you are saying is true, our plane was really brought down by a digital bomb built into the chipset that was supposed to help it fly."

"Not *if*. My colleague in Madeira verified that the 466 could be externally co-opted, reconfigured, disabled. In the jargon of gamers and hackers, total pwnage. Anyone with knowledge of the hidden structures and remote access—which could even be sent through radar signals—could cripple the entire air force."

They locked eyes. Anat finally looked away. "I have to tell them. Now. Is there Wi-Fi in the hospital?"

"You're not thinking of sending a message about this over unsecured Wi-Fi are you? This is the sort of thing you send by diplomatic courier, not be email."

"This is the sort of thing that you send today, not tomorrow. Besides, we have ways. Surely you remember from when you were helping us in Washington. But, you are also right, because I don't want the Americans alerted, too. So, I am going to use a coded message and a secure Web-mail server to contact our liaison at the Embassy in DC. He'll be on the next flight to Tel Aviv. Then it's out of our hands."

She took a deep breath and stood up. "I'm going to find a WC and a bench to sit on, then I am going to kick a hornets' nest."

■ ■ ■

The incoming spam, seemingly meaningless, sent Pedro searching out another online video, this time a pirated copy of a Daily Show skit that would be taken down within hours. He downloaded it and extracted the encrypted message. The emergency that the message described meant little to him except it accelerated his timetable. Others would take care of other targets. He knew where his new target was and what he needed to do.

Pedro had recognized the woman who had slipped into the hospital through the Emergency Entrance, and he already knew that she had headed toward Karl Lustig's room. Until the latest instructtions, he had been unsure what team she was on. With or without her presence, today was not the time to go after Lustig, although tomorrow could be too late. Patience was not instinctive for Pedro; it was a learned skill acquired from countless early occasions of waiting with his brothers for mistakes by drug dealers and from three long years living under deep cover in Taiwan.

There was a necessary order of events, he believed. Violate it, and events overtake you. Stick to the sequence and you are the one to walk away. First Lustig, then this desk diva from The Institute. She should have stayed on The Hill.

Chapter Thirty

■ The charges of hijacking an aircraft were dropped on a Tuesday, and Karl was to be discharged early the next day. Shira was just arriving when Karl returned from his final session of physiotherapy.

"So what did they have you doing today?"

"Jumping jacks."

"Yeah, right." She winked.

"Might as well be. That or deep knee bends. I ache, and I am tired."

"Too tired for a surprise?"

"Are you going to jump my reconstructed bones right here in the hospital?"

"No, my one-track Karl."

"You snuck in a bottle of Rockford Sparkling Black Shiraz to celebrate my impending release from the grip of physiotherapy, which translates as enhanced interrogation techniques disguised as medical practice?"

Shira smiled and let out a little laugh of exasperation. "Don't you wish. No, I got an envelope today from our redoubtable researcher in London. Filomena says hello and sent along another letter."

"Another letter? I thought we had already been through the lot of them."

"So it seemed. But this one must have slipped from the original packet or something and ended up at the back of a drawer. Helen Ryesdale delivered it to Filomena, who mailed it to us at Mother's address. When I lamented that I couldn't read German, Mother said her friend, Shmuel Berman, two doors away, probably could do it. Well, Shmuel is a 93-year-old sweetie who said yes and came by with this longhand translation just a few hours later. He had tears in his eyes. Shall I?"

"No, let me." He squinted and leaned toward the bedside lamp to read the tight script.

My dearest sister,

How it pains me to write this letter, which I know you will never read and which should have been the first. I know that you would understand why I have waited this long to put these words to paper, why the memories of that distant day are like the noonday sun in summer, which is too vivid, too intense to be looked at directly.

That day, the day I left, I could find no roots beneath the snow in the farm-field, but there was a hare in one of our snares, and as I hastened back to the cottage with its still-warm body tucked beneath my jacket, I heard the shots, just ahead but muffled. I threw myself into the soft snow and squirmed to burrow in as much as possible in the fresh cover. I heard voices, speaking German, but they were still too distant and indistinct to make out more than a few words. I dared not move. I lay there, slowing my breathing, willing my heart to silence, as the snow melted against my right cheek and poured its chill into my jaw. There was another shot, this time a rifle not far from where I hid, the sharp crack sounding like ice breaking on a thawing river, stretched into a jagged rattle as it echoed quickly from tree to tree in the wood. Then silence, then another stuttering crack.

"Another, an old Jew!" The voice was close and distinct. I was thinking that the voice was wrong, that there were already no old Jews left in Poland, and, with every day, fewer young ones. As I waited to be found and for my turn to die, I tried to shrink into nothingness. But there was nothing more, not even the sound of retreating footsteps in the snow. I was certain that a German soldier stood over me, his pistol aimed at my head, waiting for me to open my eyes or for some perversely proper moment to finish his work. I waited, also, in my certainty of death. My left hand beneath me first began to hurt from the cold and then did not, as my whole arm seemed to leave me.

Finally—it seemed hours but was no doubt far less—I stood, slowly, stiffly, the ache and the cold jabbing me as I stretched, needles prickling my skin as feeling returned to my limbs. I looked around and spotted the motion, all but invisible, a slender, snaking column of grey-white just over the ridge, moving the wrong way, rising amidst the falling snow. It should not have been there, for Papa always waited until dusk to rekindle the fire. I rounded the hillock just below the cottage and nearly stumbled over his body. I stepped around the frozen blood that haloed his head. I did not look at his face, though a part of me wanted to see him a last time. But I was afraid to see, afraid of what I would see.

The cottage door was open. It was still quite bright out, and I entered cautiously, pausing with each step for my eyes to adjust, not knowing—but knowing—what I would see. The baby was first, nearest the door, lying in a careless heap like a discarded ragdoll, his faced crushed, his beautiful, happy little-boy face gone. My stomach churned, and I struggled to keep the sour from rising and the room from spinning. I looked beyond and saw your hand, stretched out toward him, as if trying to reach and comfort him. Your face was turned to one side and your eyes were open, looking toward him and the door but seeing neither. Your mouth was not quite closed, and in the shadows, you seemed almost to be singing, crooning to him, comforting him. The other half of your face, the half beneath you, was smeared in pieces over the rug.

My mother sat in her chair, her knitting in her lap as always, her head bowed in sleep as so often it was when evening approached. The dark, irregular stain down over her jumper could have been taken for merely a shadow in the dimness of the corner.

I took in the rest of the room quickly, suddenly alert and aware that our visitors could well return at any moment. Crumbs and a greasy stain on the board at the table suggested that the soldiers had taken the loaf of bread and the last of our cheese. I checked the larder and found that it, too, had been raided and relieved of its meager contents. As I fetched the matches from the mantle and tucked them into my jacket, I first noticed the blood and few strands of downy hair on the edge, then looked down and realized what explained the smoke I had seen. There was no fresh wood in the fireplace, but coals glowed beneath the ash and the barest wisp of clean smoke drifted up the chimney. The open door must have created a draft that stoked the banked coals back into life. If the soldiers spotted the fresh smoke, they would return. I needed to hurry.

I was about to leave, when I heard it, a muted mewing like a kitten awakening from an afternoon nap. As it grew louder, I recognized it but could not locate its source. I turned and cocked my head and scanned the room. It seemed loudest when I bowed my head in concentration; then I noticed the awkward way you were lying on the floor, as if you had positioned yourself carefully. Beneath you was the small rug that added color to the rough wooden floor, and beneath that . . .

I dared not touch you then, so I apologized to you as I tugged on the corner of the rug to pull your body aside. I knew I should have lifted you gently and cradled you for a moment before kissing your face, your half face, one last time, but I could not. Instead, I pried at the loose board now exposed, hurrying, breaking a fingernail as the mewling grew louder and more distinct. I fetched a butter knife from the table and worked it into the crack at one side, bending the blade as I pried the board free.

He blinked and stopped crying for a moment as the light from the door struck his face. Then he saw me and resumed his crying with renewed force, telling all the wood of his unhappiness.

You must have just finished nursing him when you heard the soldiers approaching. He would have drifted asleep in your arms as he always did, ready for the deep rest that followed a feeding. How quickly you would have had to think and act to have laid him gently in the hollow beneath the floor, then replaced the rug and waited calmly, sitting there nonchalantly, waiting to die and to shield him with your body. If he whimpered at all at the commotion above, the soldiers must not have noticed. But he was always such a sound sleeper, sleeping in angelic repose through a thunderstorm while his half-brother screamed in protest.

I unbuttoned my jacket and lifted my jumper to put him to the breast, thankful that I, too, was still nursing. He pulled back at the unfamiliar taste and smell and looked up at me before turning back and latching on with enthusiasm. He eagerly drained my breast, so I switched him to the other. I used my free hand to assemble a pack of things that we might need, all the while talking to him quietly in that reassuring rhythm that I had learned from you. Sometimes he would turn his head aside and reach toward where you lay and let out a quiet "Mm, mm." Then he would return to nursing, which was, mercifully, his highest priority.

I used my jacket to form a makeshift sling for him and began the awkward work of removing your coat. There was some blood on the collar, but it was otherwise perfect and would be far better protection for us than my short jacket. If the soldiers returned, would they remember that you had been wearing a coat? I prayed not, but they certainly would notice the hole in the floor where before your body had been on the rug. I replaced the board, dragged the rug back, and realigned it, positioning your body as accurately as I could. Then I kissed you gently behind your ear and whispered my love for you, my dear little sister, and gave my promise to take care of your Moishele.

A part of me believes—wants to believe—that you heard me, that you hear me now, but it is only such a small part. For my larger part, I have given up on God, as he has given up on me and on us. That I am here to write these words owes nothing to the divine and everything to human strength and human frailty. I have already told you the whole story, except for this one part, so you know how I survived and what I needed to do to get here.

Because we no longer have secrets, I will tell you that the hardest thing about my departure was not that I was leaving you, or my parents, or the cold shelter of our tiny cottage for the colder shelter of the winter woods, the known for the unknowable. The hardest thing was leaving behind my baby, my beautiful son, unburied and unmourned. I could do nothing for him, and all that he could do for me would be to bring me pain and danger. So I left him to the winter and the wood—and the wolves.

Stepping back out into the snow that was growing heavier and the woods that were growing darker, I was suddenly braver and resolute. I did the unexpected but most reasonable thing and started out in the direction by which the German soldiers had left, following, mingling my tracks with theirs but risking an unexpected encounter should they double back. I continued, my heart pounding, straining to see through the snowfall and hoping to spot them before they spotted me. Then their trail swerved to avoid tramping through evergreen brush. I continued on a few meters, being careful where and how I stepped, then walked backwards in my own prints to the low bushes. There I leapt sideways as high and far as I could, cradling the baby from the shock as I came down awkwardly. He peeked up at me through the crack I had left in your coat, and giggled quietly. I did not giggle, because branches had made long scratches through my leggings. Then I laughed to myself as I looked back toward the trail I had just left. The snow was falling so heavily now that it would not be long before all our tracks would be obscured. With the snow increasing, I decided to circle back by a long detour and take shelter for the night under the old stone bridge. That night, as you already know, was shorter than expected.

I still long, even today, for the sound of your voice and the warmth of your body against mine in the loft as we whispered into the frosty air, speaking of love and fear and faith and magic crystals. I still long for your forgiveness that I was not there with you when you faced the end, even though I know that, had I been there, it would have been my end, too, the end for all of us. As it is, a part of both our families lives on. Forgive me, too, for changing Mosje's name, but I am sure you can appreciate how necessary it was.

Karl is a strong boy, with my family's eyes and your family's hair, and the intelligence that comes from both sides. Already he is learning to sing his alphabet and even does some simple sums. He speaks English like a Londoner. You would be so proud of him. And his new father, a proper father, loves him so. For their sake, I have decided to stop writing to you. We are, the three of us, starting a new life, a new story in a new country, and old tales of the old world are not part of that. Know that I loved you, dearest Chana, that I always will, and if you are right and I am wrong, we will meet again in the mind of God or in Gan Eden, and I hope you will be proud of me and approve of how I raised your son, who is become my son.

Yours always,

Julianna

Shira reached to take Karl's hand, which was shaking as he lowered it, still holding the translated letter. Both of them were crying and trying not to, but when their eyes met, the dam broke and they collapsed into deep sobs. Shira rose from the chair and leaned over the bed, hugging Karl with all her strength as his body shook.

When at last he spoke, his voice was a soft rasp. "I ... I am Mosje," he forced the words out. "I am Mosje Manczyk. I was born in Poland, in a stone cottage in the wood, not in London in February of 1945 but in December of 1944. My mother was Chana Manczyk, a young girl who gave her life to save mine."

"You are that. And you are also my Karl, Karl Lustig, adopted son of Frederick Lustig and of Julianna Nowak, another young woman who gave dearly to save you."

Karl nodded, eyes closed.

"You know what this means, beloved husband."

"What?"

"It means you are Jewish. You had a Jewish mother. I always felt you had a Jewish soul. Now we know how that is. See, it was fated that we find each other, that you end up in Israel. The connection was always there. Your soul had to bring you to the Homeland, to complete the journey that your mother had started, to reach Palestine."

Karl shook his head. "I am not such a mystic. I think things just happen, and after they do, we find reasons and explanations. We create a plot line that makes for a better story. Or maybe we do have a script we are following, a plan drafted in childhood, edited as we age. Either way, I think we are the playwrights. And actors in our own dramas."

"You think what you think, and I will know what I know. And perhaps someday we will both learn who was right. Like Julianna and Chana."

"Who knows? What I do know is that my mother, my mother who married my father—I can't bring myself to say 'adoptive mother'—was always a strong and determined woman, far more than I realized. Do you know, she earned her Bachelor of Engineering in just three years and started working with David Steinman on the Mackinac Bridge right out of college. She and my father, that was their project when I was growing up. I was twelve when the bridge finally opened, the longest suspension bridge in the world at the time. It meant nothing to me then, because this was right after Sputnik, and like every other kid in America, my eyes were on the sky.

"She made that happen. She made it to America and became an engineer, just as she had promised herself as a young girl in pre-war Poland. And she raised Chana's little boy to become well-educated and directionless, someone who goes through life with neither determination nor plan."

"You're being hard on yourself."

"No, I am being honest with myself. I take the work that comes my way, follow my nose into trouble—and out of it. The only thing I ever truly planned with passion, my unfinished first novel, sits on the hard drive of my computer, untouched for many months while I help Israel build better weapons and take speaking gigs in Madeira and blog about new technology that just feels so, so old to me. Everything that comes along is always touted as a breakthrough or a new paradigm or the leading edge. And I keep writing blah-blah blogs about the same news, the same noise. My mother, Julianna, made things happen; I let things happen. She was the author of her story; I improvise as an understudy in a walk-on part."

"Is that what you get from her story? Is that your take-away for the day? I still say that you are being hard on yourself."

"Okay, I'm being hard on myself. You win. But that doesn't mean that I don't deserve it. I'm tired, tired of following, tired of following paths that lead underground to be shot at by robots or beside still waters to be shoved off a mountain by Russian goons, to be—"

"What did you say?"

"I said I'm tired."

"No, about Russian goons."

"Well, I don't know if they were Russian, but they were speaking Russian before they shoved me over the side."

"You're saying you were pushed?"

"Pushed, helped, assisted—pick your word. It was no accident. I didn't fall from the levada, I was propelled from it. And I wasn't supposed to survive. It was supposed to look like an accident, just like with those two post-docs on their motorcycle."

"You're saying that somebody killed those kids and tried to kill you at Twenty-Five Fountains."

"Yes, and at Cabo Girão, don't forget. That's what I mean about this life I've chosen, that's chosen me. It's too bloody dangerous. Bini could have been killed in the tunnels under Jerusalem. You could have been killed at Cabo Girão. I was supposed to be killed at Twenty-Five Fountains. This is no way to live. And I don't know what to do next."

"What you are going to do next is stay another night in the hospital and then come home with me tomorrow and eat some of my mother's Jewish chicken soup and do your exercises and get better. Then we are all going to fly home to Haifa to suffer in the heat until the cool breezes finally come and Shoshi starts her first year of school and Bini his last. That is what you are going to do next."

Karl nodded in silence, but his mind was racing with the sound of voices speaking from a distant past.

Chapter
Thirty-One

■ Shira went on ahead with Anat to bring her mother's car around to the front of the hospital. The orderly who wheeled Karl to the elevator and out to the main entrance parked him beside the discharge desk while paperwork was completed. When he returned a few minutes later, the wheelchair was empty.

Anat cursed unknown forces and a face with no name even as Pedro Cabral was elsewhere cursing her. Shira was the only one who cursed Karl, but she was not cursing aloud.

■ ■ ■

With equal gratitude for the skill of surgeons, the miracle of rapid recovery, and the wonders of modern painkillers, Karl walked as quickly as he could manage down the corridor, out a side exit, and up to the waiting taxis wrapped around from the front of the medical center. He lowered himself into the seat of the taxi at the back of the line, slipped the driver a twenty to forestall a lecture about regulations, and told the grateful man to take him to the airport. Ten minutes later, he entered Miami International by one door, bought a ticket for Detroit after a long wait in line, and exited by another door after buying a new phone and an international SIM card. He had the next taxi take him to a downtown hotel, which he walked through without stopping. In the next block over, he registered with one of his credit cards, then walked back out into the hot Miami morning, bent the card back and forth until it snapped in two, and discarded the pieces in a trash receptacle. In the lobby of a third hotel, he placed a call to Tel Aviv with his new phone.

"It's me, Karl. Can you help me disappear?" The party who had answered hung up without speaking. Karl was reading a crinkled copy of *USA Today* when, fifteen minutes later, his new cell phone rang melodically. "Lev here. I'm using SkypeOut to call from an Internet café. Skype me at LevantScribe from a new account within twenty minutes." Click. Dial tone.

Karl walked back out into the heat and asked the doorman whether there was a Radio Shack nearby. "Nope, but there's an Apple store two blocks west."

"Any port in a storm," Karl mumbled as he walked slowly toward the Apple store. There, it took him nearly fifteen minutes to rid himself of the "Genius" who kept trying to help and would not believe that Karl just wanted the damned iPad and didn't need any instructions. Trying to walk as normally as possible, Karl hailed another taxi and told the driver just to head south. When he spotted a Starbucks down the block, he told the driver to pull over. In the half-empty shop he commandeered a tiny table in the corner, parked the Miami Herald he had lifted from the taxi, and lined up to order a grande latte and a croissant. Once settled, Karl logged into the Wi-Fi, downloaded the Skype app to his pristine iPad, and sent an IM to LevantScribe. The reply was almost instant: Talk to me.

Karl pushed in his newly acquired ear-buds and leaned over the iPad and his chocolate croissant. "I hate these damned ear-buds, Lev. And I actually hate croissants, particularly chocolate ones, but that is what was left at this hour. But I hate dying even more. Can you help?"

"Depends. Where are you?"

"Miami. A Starbucks on Southeast Third."

"Hmmm, let's see. Okay, it's a long shot, but I do know somebody from ITW in Fort Lauderdale."

"ITW? What agency is that?"

Lev laughed. "International Thriller Writers. We novelists have to stick together, otherwise it's too lonely. You hang loose for a bit there and let me see if I can raise Lionel. Later."

Karl was on his second grande latte when the Skype tone rang out in his ear.

"Hi, my name is Lionel Feinberg. Lev told me to call you. He said you need a place to stay. I can pick you up in about an hour. Be outside the Hyatt Regency, main entrance. It's a few blocks south of you. I'll be driving a silver Jeep Cherokee, and when I step out, I'll put on a Miami Dolphins cap."

▪ ▪ ▪

The hospital coffee shop was noisy enough to mask conversation in an aural fog of casual talk and clanking tableware. As she set down her charred espresso, Anat told Shira that there were two possibilities. "One is that Karl wanted to disappear; the other is that whoever has been after Karl has gotten to him. Either way, I think our best course is to wait to hear."

"You are saying we should just do nothing?"

"No, I am still saying to trust me."

"Why? That's what you said yesterday, and now Karl is gone. Why should I trust you?"

"I don't have an answer, but I am going to do my best to get Karl back. Go back to your mother's place and spend the time with your kids while I start some balls rolling. Here, take this cellphone. If it rings, it'll be me. If I don't start by saying 'Hey, Sis,' then just hang up, pull the battery and the SIM card from the phone, and toss everything in a dumpster."

"You are really talking cloak-and-dagger now."

"Yes. And if you don't get a hey-sis call from me in three days, you might want to do some hard thinking about where to go to keep you and the kids safe."

Shira's mouth opened but no sound came out.

"I can't make suggestions, Shira, because I do not want to know what you might do. If worse comes to worst, you'll have to think on your feet and trust your instincts. Karl and Lev have always said you're good at both.

"Now, go home to your kids. I'll call you when I have something."

Shira stood to leave. As she picked up her purse, it started to vibrate. She pawed through the contents and fished out the cellphone that Anat had just given her.

Anat looked over at the caller ID. "It's Lev. I'll take it." She opened the phone. "Yes?"

"It's me. Tell Shira he's okay. I love you. Shalom." Click.

"That was Lev. I should have told you he also has this number. He's heard from Karl. He's okay." Anat handed the phone over to Shira again. "All right. Now I've got business to take care of. I need to pick up a handgun somehow."

"Karl brought his rolling duffle bag on the trip. I may be able to help on that. I'll call you."

■ ■ ■

As soon as she could extract herself from playing with Shoshi, Shira slipped into the guest bedroom to check Karl's luggage. Although she had never actually seen Karl take it apart, she had a vague notion of how to do it. She extended the heavy telescoping handle on the duffle bag as far as it would go, then figured out how to release the ball catch to separate completely the two parts of the rectangular tubing. It took her a minute to figure out how to remove the carrier for the catch that plugged the end of the smaller, inner shaft, then some vigorous thumping to get the hidden contents of the tube to slide out onto the bed.

The break-apart Glock was a one-of-a-kind, custom-made automatic loaned to Karl years earlier by an industrial design friend with connections in Austria. Shira was not entirely surprised that Karl still traveled with it. She had once seen him take the gun apart; to her it was just a puzzle in three dimensions, like the parts of a brooch or other piece of jewelry she might design. She could do it. She started to reassemble it, then realized something was missing: no barrel. She thumped the tube on the floor to dislodge whatever might still be inside. Nothing. This was frustrating. Karl was the engineer; she was a designer. Then she noticed the heavy tee-handle at the top of the tube. The style did not match the metal extrusions and other fittings on the duffel. The crossbar seemed to be made of plastic, round, with molded plastic knobs capping the ends, and it was fastened to the tube by a strap of sheet metal held in place by recessed screws. She twisted off the end caps, revealing a precision machined hole bored through the center. Eureka. She used her pen knife to coax one of the screws loose enough to allow the barrel in its plastic sleeve to be slid free of the metal strap.

"What are you doing, Ima?" Bini stood in the doorway, scowling.

"Do you have to ask? Or do you want an explanation?"

"Explanation."

"Get used to being left in the dark, then. It's only fair. As the mother of a teenage son, I am already all too familiar with the experience."

"Fair is fair. But here, let me show you how this goes together." He took the pieces from her and quickly reassembled the Glock. "I'll show you what you need to know. And you'll have to pick up some ammunition, nine-by-nineteen millimeter. Just turn left pulling out of the back driveway, and there's a gun shop about eight blocks west. Now, this is how you release the clip."

"How do you know all this stuff?"

"From Aba. That's what fathers are for."

"I am glad to know that. I have been wondering about what they are for. Now I am wondering what else I don't know that he has been teaching you."

Bini shrugged. "Guy stuff. You know."

"Yeah, I guess I probably do."

Bini quickly ran through the basics of loading the clip and how to hold and fire the pistol. "Are you going to be all right with this?"

"It's not for me. It's for Anat."

"Oh, that's different. She'll know already. Remind her not to get caught with it. I don't imagine she has a Florida carry permit."

"She's a Mossad agent."

"Even worse." He picked at the seam of his jeans before looking back up at her. "This is about Aba, isn't it. He's not still at the hospital."

"No, but he's safe. Your Uncle Lev is watching out for him."

"Reassuring. The geezer squad."

"This is your father and uncle you are talking about. Some respect is in order."

"Don't get all bent, Ima. They're both cool, but they are both past retirement age. Aba should take a hint from Uncle Lev and hang up his holster. Don't you think?"

"Yeah, I think. And maybe your father is ready to think it's time, too. But it's not my call and not as easy as you think."

"I suppose. But you better get going and deliver this thing to Aunt Anat."

"Yeah, let me give her a call. And you go give your Bubbe a hand with Shoshi. It sounds like she could use some help."

Shira called Anat and gave her the good news in coded phrasing.

"Perfect," Anat told her. "Meet me at the mall due south of your mother's place. Main entrance, twenty minutes?"

■ ■ ■

As she made the left turn into the avenue headed for the mall, Anat began to suspect she was being followed. She slowed for a right, turning away from the mall, back toward the water, and a few blocks farther pulled into the small parking lot in front of a mini-mall housing a pharmacy, a liquor store, and Señora Marita's Tarot and Consultation Parlor. The blue Ford behind her drove past, then pulled over to the curb halfway down the block. Anat left her rental car running and trotted into the liquor store. She bought a bottle of inexpensive chardonnay, tossed the brown paper bag into the car, and left again, driving past the Ford. It was him, the man from Dror's folder and Karl's snapshot.

When the Ford pulled out and hung just three car lengths behind her, she concluded that, when it came to shadowing, the driver was an amateur. She was not. She shifted into a tactic as old as dog-fighting in bi-planes, where the chased circles back and becomes the chaser. She headed for the freeway, then used a messy interchange and a maze of city blocks to put the blue Ford that had been tailing her two cars ahead of her instead of two behind. Easy. When the driver stopped in apparent confusion, she took a sudden left across the heavy traffic, pulled into a parking lot, and ducked down. She tilted her mirror and watched him circle the block and cruise by twice before making a tire-squealing U-turn.

She pulled out of the lot and began following him north toward the airport, always keeping two or more cars between, expertly making use of traffic lights and entering traffic to sustain the illusion that she just happened to be going the same way. A few blocks short of the airport, the man made another U-turn and parked next to a big-box warehouse that was nothing more than a windowless wall of white with a single, unmarked double-door entrance on the side facing them. The man waited in his car for a few minutes, then got out and looked up and down the street before tapping away at a keypad next to the door. The moment his trailing heel cleared the doorframe, Anat was running at top speed along the wall. She spiked her Scripto pen into the narrowing gap just before the door closed completely. She counted to ten and pushed the door open just wide enough to slip through.

She was four steps inside the dark interior when she was grabbed from behind. With her right arm twisted up her back almost to her neck she was pushed across the floor toward one of a long row of supporting pillars. Before she could even consider how to fight back, her other arm was pulled behind her and she heard the cricket-chirp ratcheting of a flexi-cuff being tightened. She tried but was not fast enough to turn her wrists sideways to force some slack in the cuffs. The edges cut into her skin.

"You are out of shape," the man said dismissively, "and out of practice. You should have been more suspicious when it was so easy to lose your tail and become the hunter. But, here you are."

"What do you want?" she asked.

"Nothing. "

"What is this about? Who are you?"

There was no response.

As her eyes adjusted to the light from the narrow strip of windows on the opposite wall just below the high ceiling, she saw that the warehouse was empty except for a few scattered waist-high cartons and a forklift parked between her and the door she had just entered. The man stood in front of her, silent, as if lost in thought. Then he nodded, as if he had just reached a decision.

"I'll be right back. Don't go anywhere."

He returned a minute later carrying a messenger bag, which he set on the floor and opened. From it he extracted a square plastic box, olive green with a prominent red cross on top. He took out a small bandage, carefully tore open the sterile package along one edge, and gingerly removed the round patch, being careful not to touch the surface. He inverted the bandage on the cover of the box, then pressed his left palm down on top of it. When he turned toward her with his hands spread wide as if preparing for an embrace, Anat could see the patch adhering to his palm.

"So, it ends much as it started: a semblance of symmetry in doing what must be done," he said cryptically. "Clean, quick, and quiet, thanks to the geniuses at Nes Tziona."

Anat's heart tripped. Nes Tziona. It was the location of the super-secret center of Israel's chemical and biological weapons research. "Who are you? Are you *kidon*? You know I am Mossad, don't you?"

"Kidon?" He laughed quietly. "I know more than you do, that much remains clear."

"You're working for the Chinese."

"Or the other way around. You're guessing, grasping at straws with your last gasp." He took a step toward her, his hands held out at her eye level, as if he were a lover about to take her head gently in his hands and give her a long kiss.

Anat's knees buckled, her trapped arms sliding down the pole behind her as she slumped to the floor, ending up in a pathetically vulnerable position with her bent legs apart, knees up in front of her.

The man squatted, and stared face-to-face, smiling as his hands reached for her. Anat, her eyes fixed on the pink patch on his left hand, brought her knees up and together at the last moment, forcing his hands into a spread-fingers clap. Jerking backward in his squatting position, he was thrown off balance when she released her knees. He tried to stand, but ended up stumbling and sliding backwards into the next pillar in the row. The two sat facing each other.

"Well, that is that," he said. "You are quicker and stronger than I thought."

"This is alligator country. It doesn't take as much to force the alligator's jaws together as to pull them apart."

"You learned that in field training?"

"No, I learned that from Animal Kingdom. So, who are you?"

"The dead have no names. What does it matter now?" He paused several seconds, his eyes searching the ceiling as if trying to remember something. "Ricardo. Ricardo Mendonça. Ricardo Baruch Pereirra Mendonça. And many other names. Most recently I was Pedro Cabral. But that was the first: Ricardo Baruch." He pronounced his initial R's as deep gutturals and trilled the internal ones.

Anat recognized the accent. "You're Brazilian?"

"Was. Once. I was born in Rio de Janeiro. But Rio was a very, very long time ago; I was recruited when I was sixteen. Of course, I was tall and lied about my age. I lied about everything, but they figured that out fairly quickly and were impressed. That was part of the appeal. Plus, by then I had the scars and the experience of a grown man. So, I was recruited and trained. For this." He looked down at the tiny white spot on the palm of his right hand. The cold burning had already begun.

"Who recruited you, Ricardo Baruch?"

"Surely you have figured that little bit out. I thought you were a crack analyst on The Hill."

"Then why were you going to kill me if we are on the same team."

"We may have been recruited by the same people, but we are most definitely not on the same team." He laughed. "And that is why I am going to finish with you before this"—he flashed his right palm toward her—"finishes with me. I could have maybe half an hour, forty minutes if I stay still and put on a tourniquet. Or I can make it a little less if I keep active."

"I would have thought Nes Tziona had faster chemical agents. Why so slow?"

"It's like a sort of timed-release agent so there is time to offer the antidote if your target talks. The visible penetration and the spreading sensation add to the desired speech-inducing drama."

"Let me guess: there is no antidote."

"No. So, with the clock ticking, time for me to get back to work." He stood up, reached behind his back, and withdrew a tactical knife, its ceramic blade flashing like obsidian in the light from above. "I am sorry, but I used my last patch. It would have been far less messy. But I will make this quick and mostly painless. I learned from my father, who was a *shochet* before the neighborhood goons decided they really didn't like a Jewish butcher in their midst and slit his throat. They were clumsy. It was not quick and painless. I tried to stop the blood as my father tried to scream. We both failed. And then I ran, and my brothers and I were on our own.

"And now, we are here and it is your turn. Someone else from the team—mine, that is—will have to finish the job on your erstwhile professor. Too bad he leaves a widow and two kids." He took a step toward her.

"No!" The long scream came from behind him. He whirled to face the source, dropping into a crouch as he turned. He raised the knife, cocking his left arm to his shoulder to throw it. There was a shot. He jerked and the knife flew forward, tumbling and spinning awkwardly as he fell sideways.

Shira stepped from behind the forklift holding Karl's Glock in front of her. She was shaking. "Are you all right, Anat?"

"I'm okay. Get the knife and cut these cuffs for me. Hurry." She pulled her feet under her and pushed herself erect, still handcuffed to the pole.

Shira turned away, looking around in the dim light for the knife. Ricardo struggled to his feet and hurled himself at her. Anat watched, helpless, as they fell in a heap and rolled across the floor. Two more shots echoed in the cavernous space, then it was silent except for gasping breaths.

"God, this guy is heavy." Shira grunted as she pushed the man's body from atop her. She looked around for the knife and found it inches beyond the man's outstretched hand.

"It's not over," Anat said, as Shira cut through the plastic cuffs. "They're still after Karl."

"Who are they?"

"I don't know exactly yet. And remember, you are not supposed to know anything. Say, how the hell did you find me? And how did you get in here?"

"I was just approaching the mall when I saw you take that wrong turn, so I tailed you—and this guy tailing you, and then you tailing him. He must have been so focused on you that he didn't even think that somebody else might be in the parade. Then I saw you pull that trick with your pen, so when he came out to his car and went back in, I just did the same thing. I was waiting behind the forklift, trying to figure out what to do and when to do it, when he went for you with that knife. Then I . . ." She started shaking. "I killed him. I . . ."

"He was already dead. Poison. All you did was speed him on his way and save my life." She paused to give Shira a reassuring hug. "Now we need to save Karl's, because this guy did not work alone."

"I'll ask you again. Who are they? Tell me."

"No. All I can say is that it's worse than I thought. It's a good thing Karl has disappeared. We need to leave him that way while I try to sort out the good guys from the bad. Now, get out of here. Get back to your kids. Somebody may have heard the shots, and I need to do some quick cleanup here. So, go!"

Chapter
Thirty-Two

■ Anat checked the body. There was, as she expected, no identification, but she took an iPhone from his jacket. She removed the knife holster and slid the tactical knife back in place. At his ankle, under his sock, she found a tiny, single-shot pistol with a carbon composite body. She could only guess what the barrel might be made of, but she was quite sure it would not set off a metal detector. She pocketed it.

She hurried out to his car and did a quick once over. The rental agreement and motel bill in the center console tray both identified the man as Pedro Cabral, confirming it as merely the latest of Ricardo's many acquired identities, but it might be a starting point. His laptop was on the passenger seat and a leather athletic bag was on the floor. The confident bastard had already checked out and was ready for a quick departure. She moved the bag and laptop, then wiped her prints from the Ford before ducking around the corner to retrieve her own car.

As she drove off, heading straight for the freeway entrance, she started mulling over next steps. Some things were obvious. Stay away from Shira and her family; leave Karl in hiding and hope that Lev was as clever as ever; don't draw attention to Lev; get help.

What was not obvious was who could help. Lev, who otherwise would be her first choice, was off the list because he was undoubtedly closely monitored and might lead someone back to Karl. She really needed to get through to the Director and tell him that her last message had a postscript, that at least one conspirator was from Mossad or had been. But she still wasn't certain how much she could trust her boss, and he had made clear how little he trusted her. Who else? Who trusted her?

Yishai Barg! It was a long shot, but their friendship went way back, and over the years he had proven his loyalty more than once by bending rules to help her. She glanced at her watch; she needed to get in touch right away, and she needed to confirm that her trust was not misplaced. Suddenly she remembered something from their last conversation at the couscous place in Tel Aviv. She reversed direction at the next exit and headed back for her hotel.

In her hotel room, she used the public Wi-Fi to start browsing the Web, doing searches on "460 series avionics chipset," visiting the IsTac site, searching on maps for the location of Unit 8200. She was counting on the fact that the intercepts would be monitored and picked up by military intelligence before they could be passed on to Mossad. There might be a delay of hours, or it might wait until the daily summary was forwarded, but Barg and his people would see it first.

Twenty minutes of rattling the fences and her cellphone rang.

"Barg here."

"Yishai, thanks for the quick response."

"I'm on a secure line, you're not. Go to the Israeli Consulate and ask for Teshuva Rossi." Click.

Anat located the Consulate in the New World Tower on Biscayne Boulevard. She drove past and parked in a garage several blocks away, then walked back, rounded the block, and approached from the other direction. She was thinking how funny it was that tradecraft stayed with you even after so many years on a desk, but she suspected her efforts to avoid or identify surveillance were probably inept or unnecessary or both. At the Consulate's suite on the 18th floor, Anat used her real passport as ID and asked to see Teshuva Rossi. The guard behind the bulletproof glass in the booth said, "What? There's no . . ." Then he looked back up from his screen and said, "Oh!" He buzzed her in.

An athletic, middle-aged man in a pinstripe suit, blue tie, with an Israeli flag pin on his lapel, came out almost immediately and said, without formalities, "I'm the military attaché. Follow me." He escorted her to a tiny room with a bare desk and a black, old-style desk telephone. He motioned her to take a seat and left, closing the door behind him. Anat rose to check the door, but the phone rang, its bicycle-bell clang startling her. She let it ring several times before picking it up.

"Yes?"

"Okay, good. You made it."

"Yishai?"

"Yes, of course. That was a damn clever if dangerous way you chose to contact me. If I hadn't been on alert, it might not have worked."

"I knew you were tracking me. Us. But I didn't know how closely. If worse came to worst, the wrong people would spot me first, and I would be back where I was an hour ago. I just did not know who I could trust on The Hill. Not even the Director."

"But you trusted me?"

"Yes. Was I wrong?"

"No, you were right. In fact, the alerts you triggered at the Unit have already been deleted. I'm one of the few people who could do that. But you can also trust Avram."

"You're on a first name basis with the Director?"

"Remember, he came from our side of the highway. He still wears his fatigues. None of that is accidental, but to clear some things up, there are only four of us in the loop: you, me, Avram, and another party I can't reveal yet."

"That hardly feels like I'm in the loop. And this is the first I've heard about any loop."

"I know. But we had to do it that way. You had to go into this completely clean, on your own initiative, untainted by connection with us or biased by foreknowledge. Anyway, now you need to come back in and go directly to Avram. If I use this line too long, it could draw attention to us. Just get back."

"You know about what's been done to the 460 chipset."

"Yes, we know, thanks to your message through the Embassy. And we have operations in place to take everything down quickly and quietly—"

"Don't say that phrase, okay?"

"Okay, but we are still missing two pieces. Someone in the U.S. and someone here."

"In Israel, you mean? Or in military intelligence?"

"Or HaMossad."

"A mole?"

"A traitor. We are still trying to figure out the scope and nature of this whole thing, but we are closing in. Come back. Meet me at the usual place for lunch on Friday."

"I'd have to leave tonight."

"Do it, friend. Shalom."

The line went dead and Anat felt a chill. Damned air conditioning. Why did they always set it too high in Florida? Energy is not limitless.

▪ ▪ ▪

Anat felt guilty for not telling Shira or Lev what she was up to, but she reasoned that any contact increased the risk to them—and to Karl. She slept fitfully on the long flight out of Newark and dragged herself through procedures at Ben Gurion airport. She almost used the wrong passport when clearing immigration.

With a few hours to kill before meeting Yishai, she headed toward the beach. She was tempted to stretch out on a bench, but she had her bag with her and knew she had to keep moving. She took her time strolling along, enjoying the salty breeze off the Mediterranean. Before leaving the beach area, she bought a hat and some sunscreen at a kiosk and then set out on foot for the couscous restaurant.

Despite her meandering approach, she arrived some minutes early and took the opportunity for surveillance from across the street. She was startled by a voice behind her.

"You like Moroccan-style couscous? I hear this place is good."

She twisted at the hip to see who it was. "Director, I didn't recognize your voice. And I would hardly recognize you out of uniform. I think this is only the second time I've seen you in civilian clothes."

"It's Avram, please. Let's wait for Yishai. As soon as he gets here and signals, we'll cross over and join him as if it were a complete coincidence."

Yishai arrived promptly at noon, surveyed his surroundings, ducked briefly into the restaurant, then picked a table at the far edge of the cluster on the sidewalk, almost around the corner. He adjusted the table as if trying to find a steady placement on the uneven paving, edging it still farther from the nearest table. He nodded in their direction before seating himself facing away from them.

"You go first," Avram said. "I'll pop in after." He turned to admire his reflection in the window of a bookstore and to keep an eye on Anat as she crossed the street dodging traffic.

When he joined them a minute later, he feigned surprise, asked the next table over if he could borrow a chair, and squeezed himself in as the third at the table for two. "What have you told her?" he said as he adjusted his chair.

"Not a lot. She knows that we are the elite squad but not who the fourth player is."

"Good. Look, Dorfman—"

"Anat. If it's going to be Avram to me, then I am not Dorfman to you. Unless you insist on pulling rank."

"Okay, but it goes without saying, not on The Hill."

"Without saying."

"Okay, okay. With protocol settled, let's figure out who is the wolf in sheep's clothing. Any ideas?"

Yishai leaned in even closer. "We still have the goat."

Anat looked from Yishai to the Director and back. "Goat? Care to clue me in?"

"Someone they want, a sacrificial goat to draw the wolves out of hiding."

"I have an uneasy feeling about this," she said. "Not someone I know, I hope."

The Director looked at his hands and Yishai shifted his gaze to try and catch the eye of the waiter who was serving at the next table. "Can we order?" Yishai asked.

"*Rega, rega,*" came the answer.

Anat glared at Yishai. "If we are in this together, don't play coy with me. Just say it. Is it Karl?"

"You're the one who said it."

"That's unacceptable. He's a friend."

"And this is a matter of national security. This is what we have to do, what you have to do."

"Then we have to at least warn him, let him know what is happening."

"Not on your life. Any attempt to contact him is likely to be noticed and could compromise the whole operation. We're within centimeters of closing on this one. We have a list. We know the identity and location of everyone involved except for one field operative and our inside man. We have to move decisively while we can, before the wolves smell that the bait has been laced or else just run for the hills because they're spooked. Pun not intended."

"Is there anyone at Nez Tziona on your list? If not, then you have some more work to do."

"We've got the chemical connection on our list."

"Okay. But I have to tell Karl. He'll play along. I know him."

"No. Emphatically no. That's an order, Dorfman."

"Oh, it's Dorfman again?"

"It is when I have to be the Director. We are both professionals. We both took the same oath, and we both know the sacrifices that entails, up to and including our own lives. You have your orders, Dorfman. You are not to contact him. Understood?"

Anat locked eyes with him. "Understood. I am not to contact him."

"Excellent, Anat. Now, let's order some couscous." He signaled again to the waiter, who this time crossed over to their table.

"What can I get for you?" he said, an impatient half-smile pasted across his lips.

Yishai gave Anat an inquiring look before smiling up at the young man. "I think we'll both have our usual."

The Director said, "Yes, I'll have my usual, too." That set Anat to thinking about just how this alliance that she was now part of had been operating thus far.

When their couscous arrived, she waited until the server left again before speaking. "I think I know a way to find out who our disguised wolf is, but it will take a little preparation and some precise timing. And we will all have to be careful to keep our stories straight." She outlined what she had in mind.

"Okay, that's a plan," the Director said and Yishai nodded in agreement. "The details of the taps and traces fall on TechServ, Anat. Do you have someone exceptionally good you can trust with the details?"

"Dafna Barg, your niece, Yishai. She's brilliant, she's family."

"Great. Take care of it. And I'll do everything I can to make sure your asset is safe." The Director took another forkful of couscous.

"He's not my asset; he's our ally and my friend." She stood up. "Look, I need a long shower and a short nap. I'm going to head out to the apartment for both, then I'll meet you back on The Hill." She looked down at her untouched food. "I just don't have the appetite today. It's yours, Yishai. Your turn to pay, anyway.

▪ ▪ ▪

The apartment was graveyard quiet when she let herself in. In the sitting room, she smiled down at Lev napping on the couch. He opened both eyes, then winked at her. "I heard you turn the key," he said. "I only half sleep when you are away."

"Good thing I don't do that too often. Look, I need a little sleep myself, but first a quick shower." She leaned over, gave him a warm kiss, and whispered, "Follow me into the bathroom."

"I'd follow you anywhere," he whispered back.

In the bathroom, she turned on the shower as hard as it would go.

"Aren't you going to get undressed? I was looking forward to this."

"First we have to talk. After washing up, I have to get a nap. Anything else will have to wait." An exaggerated look of disappointment spread from his eyebrows to his chin. "Cut that out," she said. "You'll make me feel guilty. Or you'll get me thinking. Right now we need some action, but not that kind. Do you know where Karl is? Do you have some way of contacting him without setting off alarm bells?"

"Yes, and yes. Karl is—"

"Don't tell me. Just take care of it while I take a shower. Warn Karl. Let him know he is being set up by Mossad as bait for an encounter tomorrow morning. And remember your tradecraft. You're a katsa again."

"And passing on this message is okay with your bosses? I'm just asking."

"I had explicit and specific orders not to contact Karl; I am following orders to the letter." She winked at Lev as she started to undress. "Now, get out of here, my geriatric voyeur."

When she entered the bedroom fifteen minutes later there was a note on her pillow: "Out shopping. Lev."

▪ ▪ ▪

Karl pursued his host out onto the deck of the small faux-Mission house in Fort Lauderdale. "What do you mean, you don't know anything about guns? What kind of a thriller writer are you?"

"I write supernatural and occult thrillers. Guns are useless against ghosts and invading spirits. You want to know thirty-seven exorcism techniques, and I'm your man. I don't do firearms."

"And people actually read that stuff? I mean, you make a living off of ghosts and ghouls?"

"Well, not as much as those riding the zombie apocalypse wave, but I pay the rent and utilities that way. Like our mutual friend in Tel Aviv, I'm retired. Say, how old are you, anyway? Isn't it time you moved on from doing cloak-and-dagger stuff for real and settle into a life of margaritas and manuscripts. Lev says you're a writer, too."

"Wannabe writer. Science fiction. My first novel is sitting nearly finished on my hard drive where it's been for a decade. Nearly finished."

"Well, sit right down now and finish that sucker. Nobody's gonna read it sitting on your hard drive."

"It's not that easy."

"Sure it ain't, but if I can do it, you can. Now Lev, he is a scary dude. I've written seven books in twelve years and consider myself pretty productive. Lev has written seven books since he retired four years ago."

"Yeah, well, that's true, but he's also only sold about seven copies each."

"That's because, not offending anyone of the tribe, but the things are written in Hebrew. Where's the market? He speaks English; he can learn to write in English. I keep telling him, his stuff is tailor-made for the American market."

"You're probably right. But look, I still have a problem. Can I at least get you to play postman for me? Go and tell my wife I'm looking for something from my duffle bag. She'll know what I mean. My son Bini can help her with it if she has any trouble. Just bring whatever she gives you back here. Okay?"

"Okay. For a friend of Lev's, I'll risk jail time. I can tell by the look on your face you don't understand Florida. This is not Israel where everyone carries. It's complicated here. We have this contro-versial stand-your-ground law that essentially lets you kill some-body if they scare you, but it takes three months to get a carry per-mit, and they throw you in the cooler if you carry without it."

"You've been clever so far in how you handled retrieving me and communicating with Lev. Just think like a writer, create a scenario."

"Good idea. I think I know how Lev would write this scene, so I'll try it. Now where is your wife staying?"

Chapter Thirty-Three

■ Anat skipped her nap. As soon as she reached her office at the Institute, she summoned Dafna Barg. The family resemblance to her uncle stopped at the dark skin. Where Yishai had the perfectly proportioned classic face of a Michelangelo model, Dafna's eyes were too small, her forehead too high, and her chin too broad. The overall effect was to make her look fiercely intelligent and somewhat intimidating; at twenty-eight and a rising star at the Institute, she was both.

Anat held a slip of paper out toward her. "I have two special assignments for you. First, here's a list of people I want you to set up total communications monitoring on: phone, email, cellphones, Web surfing, the works. Record everything automatically and route it to an encrypted log file. No one but you is to have the credentials to access the file, and you are not to touch it. These are all our people, so we automatically have the authority as part of their terms of employment and on national security grounds. I hope you can read my hand writing."

Dafna scanned down the list. "Wow! Top guns. The Director, too?"

"Yes."

"Your name's on here, and my uncle's. You really want me to tap you, too?"

"Absolutely. I want an incontrovertible record for all these people. Oh, and add yourself to the list. All media, all channels. And if we find out anybody has tried to access that file or there is evidence of tampering, your butt is on the line, so don't be tempted to peek before I give the order."

"How soon do you want this?"

"Now. I have a meeting scheduled for 16:00. It's all got to be in place by then."

"I don't know how I can do it that fast."

"Then figure out a way. You're the best. Keep up the work you are doing, and you can take over my office when I retire."

"You're not planning to retire, are you?"

"Of course, I am. Do you think I want to die at my desk? But not for a long time. Besides nobody in our group is ready yet to fill my shoes, so I have to stick around." She reached under her desk and pulled out a laptop. "Secondly, give this to your choice of who is best with disk forensics and can work independently. Tell them to scour the hard drive for whatever they can find and bring the results to me ASAP, anything they can recover between now and 15:30. Clear? Now go. You have work to do. And the list I gave you goes into a burn-bag. I assume you will cover your tracks. And—"

"I know how to do it. Let me get going." She started tearing the list into shreds as she stood to leave. "For your burn-bag. I've got it memorized."

■ ■ ■

Anat was rehearsing her coming performance when Dafna returned. "How did you do?" Anat asked.

"Everything's set and checked out. Do you want the forensics on the laptop?"

"Yes, tell the analyst to come here."

"She's here. I did the work. Well, Seth helped with some of the code analysis; he's a better code jockey."

"You did that and the tap-and-trace?"

"Yeah. The inside jobs were a cinch. I cheated and used my connections through my uncle to set all the external intercepts. And we lucked out on the laptop. The user must have been in a hurry and had closed the cover, sending it into sleep mode before the Windows shutdown had completed. Sometime later, as the battery ran low, the system woke up again and went into hibernation, which writes the memory state to the disk. We have ways around Windows passwords and the built-in encryption. Easy."

"What did you find?"

"The computer was being used by a pro who covered his tracks well, erasing history files, cookies, recent-files list. He was good. But his browser was open when he shut down. It would have automatically cleared its history if the exit had been completed. The last site he visited was YouTube. He has a channel, maybe more than one. He was still logged in when he shut the case."

"And?"

"Now here's the interesting part. The videos are totally lame: reposts of old videos, pointless shots of rain falling, an iPhone record of walking down a village street. That one is somewhere in Portugal from the signs. And the number of views are all in the single digits; recent posts have only a single view."

"Let's get somebody to work on those video files."

"Already sent them over to crypto. And we found something else that we sent to the crypto boys. There was very little software installed, and Microsoft Office had never even been activated, but we found some executables that were not standard. Seth didn't have time to do any deep study, but he spotted something obvious in one of the decompiles. According to him, this one EXE does all kinds of direct stuff with the GPUs in the graphics card."

"Which means?"

"Either something funky in the way of video games or some really intense math processing. The GPUs are—"

"I know, they're actually little mathematical supercomputers. You're thinking cryptography, aren't you."

"Or image processing or both. The guys in crypto have been alerted to the possibility of a new variant of steganography. They have a leg up because of their work with the system used by that group who launched the plot against the Dome of the Rock. They've been told to ping you when they find something."

"Impressive work, Dafna. So, you can go for now. I have a meeting in ten minutes."

▪ ▪ ▪

The Director waited for the last of the inner circle to arrive in the conference room before shutting the door himself. He looked around the room as he prepared to speak, hoping to catch a glimpse of any sign of apprehension. Of course, everyone in the room, including his quarry, was a professional with long practice on maintaining a poker face under pressure. Dror Magen's downturned mouth blinked upward as the Director's eyes swept past him; David Bulofsky showed his dour disapproval of having to break his routine; and Julian Savoy stared into the distance, lost in some inner puzzle. Except for Anat, who was also scanning the room in search of suspects, no one's demeanor stood out.

"Okay, everyone. This is about the chipset caper." Before the Director could continue, there was a rattle at the door, and Yishai Barg poked his head in. "Ah, please come in, Colonel, we are just getting started." The Director gestured toward the chair next to his, one that none of the local team ever had the chutzpah to take. "Because of the subject and the seriousness of the matter, I've asked Colonel Barg to sit in this once." Everyone nodded in greeting, but there were also several expressions of surprise at such an unprecedented violation of protocol.

"I want to thank you all for working so hard and keeping me updated on developments. No reflection on the rest of you, but the only one to hit pay dirt was our own Chief of Technical Services, Anat Dorfman, who has been working on special assignment for me. And, she has proven that she could have been a first-class katsa if she had wanted to become a field agent instead of driving a desk. So, tell us what you have, Anat."

She stood and flicked on the palm-sized LED projector at the end of the table. "On the screen you see a kind of x-ray picture of the 466 microprocessor, like the one Dror Magen showed us at our recent meeting, part of the chipset that our own Israel Tactical Systems designed to power the next generation of avionics and military electronics. And this next slide is a simulated x-ray of the same chip as originally designed by IsTac."

There was a stir of uncomfortable shifting around the table. "Somebody changed it. Is that what you're saying?"

"Yes, Julian. For reasons known only to generals and pencil pushers, the decision was made to outsource the manufacture of the chips to a company called Tenido Industries."

"The Chinese." Bulofsky said, sending his wooly-bear eyebrows toward his receding hairline.

"The Taiwanese," the Director corrected, "at least by geography and legal incorporation. At any rate, we now know what the changes were about."

"Hang on a minute," Julian Savoy said, raising a pudgy finger in protest. "I thought this whole chipset brouhaha was about the chips being diverted and appearing on the black market."

Anat studied his boyish face as she explained. "A diversion, nothing more than a distraction from the real agenda." She paused, looking for a reaction of some kind. Nothing.

"So, what do these modifications do? Do you have any idea?"

"No, not yet. Nothing certain, that is. Possibly the mods lead to early failure in the field." She glanced around again for signs of disbelief. "But we are closing in on somebody who knows the whole story: an American named Karl Lustig. Does the name ring bells?"

"The Secunia Security worm?" offered Savoy.

Bulofsky shook his head. "No, that attempt on HaKotel."

"No," Savoy came back, still quiet but more assertive. "It wasn't the Wailing Wall. He was involved over the attack on the U.S. electric grid."

Anat held up her hands in a gesture of peace. "It was both: the Dome of the Rock incident and the Web-games investigation. What is significant is that he has worked with us before with good results. Unfortunately, he's gone into hiding, but we've tracked him to the Miami-Fort Lauderdale area in the U.S., contacted him through discreet channels, and arranged for him to be brought in from the cold. He's got the technical specs as well as names and photos of those involved. We have a rendezvous set for the Admirals Club at Miami International at 5 o'clock tonight, midnight our time."

The Director stood again. "So, we wanted you all to be in the loop on developments, but, needless to say, this is absolutely only for you in the room."

"Needless to say," Julian said quietly.

"Right. Then not a word to anyone inside or outside the Institute. No messages, calls, emails or any mention of any kind to anyone."

▪ ▪ ▪

Except for the guards and the overnight IT staff, they were the last in the building. Anat was scrolling through the accumulated log file while struggling to keep her eyes open and her brain engaged as the Director and Yishai Barg looked over her shoulder. "Listen, fellows, we have less than two hours left. It's late. There's nothing here. No one seems to have tried anything; no one has made a move. It doesn't make sense, unless the person we are after was not in that room."

"Or, they already knew before we started monitoring." The Director's voice was hoarse from fatigue. "Let's push the timeline back. We can start with Lev's call to his writer friend to warn Karl shortly after you abandoned us at lunch."

"What? You knew?"

"Of course, we knew. I told you, that's my job not to miss anything. You think I wouldn't keep tabs on you and Lev and Karl?"

Anat hesitated. "Is Lev involved other than as a conduit?"

"We don't know for certain, which is why we have kept such close tabs on him."

"You really don't trust anyone, do you?"

"No," he said softly, looking her in the eyes. "No."

"What's next? Let's look at the early entries in the log."

"Okay," Yishai said, pointing. "There's one right after Avram summoned everyone for the big pow-wow, about a half an hour before the meeting, a YouTube upload. It didn't pass through the switchboard and it's from a mobile that is not registered to anyone on our watch list. How did that get in here?"

Anat thought for a second. "It must be the result of Dafna's shortcut. She used Unit 8200 intercepts. She must have defined the filter parameters too broadly. But wait, YouTube video. Can we take a look?"

Yishai clicked on a link in the annotation field of the log and ended up at a jittery handheld video of cars at a highway interchange. The camera was aimed too low, and only the tires were visible.

"Look at the number of views: one."

"Well, it's been posted less than half a day."

"Yes, but click through to the channel. There, see? This channel has dozens of videos and none of them have more than a handful of views."

"What do you expect with such non-descript titles. If they are anything like our 'Passing Cars' video, they will be as interesting as dripping water. Hey, there is one labeled 'Dripping Water.'"

Anat was impatient. "We have to track the subscriber of the cellphone."

"Why is this so important."

"Because this is the other end of a conversation: the mole end. Dafna found that our rogue kidon was using his laptop to traffic in short, pointless videos. We're guessing it's video steganography, which is brand new, although crypto says it seems to build on some work we were already familiar with. So, we need to get the cellular service to release their subscriber data."

Yishai shrugged. "Why bother. It has to be somehow connected to someone on our list, or it wouldn't be logged. I can go back to the intercepts to extract the triggers and suss out the connection."

"Do it, for God's sake."

Yishai frowned at the Director but reached past Anat to do some quick typing on her keyboard.

"I'm sorry, Yishai. I know you're observant." The Director sounded genuinely contrite but continued. "I should have said for HaShem's damn sake."

Yishai stopped typing, his hands hovering over the keyboard.

"Okay, I am sorry. I'm tired and I was kidding, which I shouldn't. Let's just do this."

Yishai typed another command, then tapped the Enter key dramatically. "The phone belongs to Eugenia Turkle, who got tracked because another number on the same account belongs to David Bulofsky."

The Director slapped his hand on the desk. "We got him!"

"Wait, there's another entry in the log *before* the meeting. What's this?" Anat pointed.

"That's mine, from my office, obviously, my secure message directing our man in Miami, late of Madeira, to take up a position watching out for Karl."

"I know I may sound clueless, but what man? Who are we talking about?"

"The katsa we had in Madeira, who we moved to Miami when we found out you and Karl were headed back there. I told you, we had a man in Madeira when we started this operation."

"Not Ricardo Baruch Mendonça."

"No. Who's that?"

"The real name of the Brazilian kidon, the traitor passing as Pedro Cabral when I last saw him dead in a warehouse in Miami."

"No, not him, obviously. I'm talking about our man, whom we sent to Madeira in anticipation of Karl's visit."

"You knew about that, too."

"How many times do I have to repeat it? That. Is. My. Job. Vlad was in East Africa; it was easy to move him through the Canary Islands to Madeira. He's a Russian Jew of Spanish descent. He's been on several extremely sensitive field—"

"What did you say? Russian Jew? In Madeira?"

"Yeah, he's our—"

"Would you recognize his picture?"

"I think so?"

Anat located her filed copy of Karl's levada snapshot and enlarged it.

"Yes, I think that's him. Not a very good photo. I don't recognize the other man."

"It's not very good because it was taken as Karl was falling off a cliff, and the other man is our rogue kidon, the man who pushed Karl off that cliff. Karl told us that they were speaking Russian as they approached."

No one said anything as the implications sunk in. Yishai shook his head gravely. "There's not much we can do now. We have to authorize Operation Herzl immediately, so that there's time to get everyone in place to move at the same time."

"We have to get word to Karl. He's being guarded by one of them."

"There's no way we can do that without risking tipping our hand. This is too important to take that chance. It's all split-second, last-minute timing so no one can warn anyone else. We're using military police and crack paratroopers as the strike teams because we can't trust our own people. We can't, any of us, contact Karl. And we certainly couldn't send paratroopers into Florida. We're talking about the sovereign territory of the United Fucking States."

Yishai scowled at him.

"How the hell did you ever get through the IDF, Barg, without swearing?"

"Oh, I swore. I also drank and fucked and offended HaShem in many ways. But I learned."

"Okay, but just don't expect me to learn. Look, you two, we have nearly a hundred people on standby in five countries, and Yishai and I have to give the go ahead order jointly. I am sorry about Karl, I really am, but he is on his own. You are under strict and specific orders to make no attempt to contact him, directly or indirectly. Do you understand? Disobeying my orders could be the basis for charges of treason."

"I understand. I will make no attempt. May I go home now?" she said stiffly.

"Go. We'll brief you in the morning. It will all be settled by then."

Chapter
Thirty-Four

■ Lionel wanted to go along, but Karl convinced him to do a drop off in front of the terminal and leave before the final rendezvous. "Are all thriller writers adrenaline junkies?" Karl asked as he said goodbye.

Lionel smiled. "Probably. We just get our highs from different things. For me, my heart starts pounding over creaking floorboards late at night and shadows that move in impossible ways. This stuff doesn't do it for me. You take care, Karl. I'm sorry your wife wasn't around when I checked in. You sure you're going to be all right without any heat?"

"I'm sure. I probably wouldn't have been able to get it past security anyway. The Admirals Club lounge is past the checkpoint. This is proving to be a very expensive vacation. Do you realize, I will have to buy a plane ticket for today just to get into a damn airline lounge. What is this country coming to?"

"That's why I live in my world, where the spirits and demons are everywhere, but the good guys always win. Take care, buddy. And finish that novel." He gave Karl a high-five, then pulled the Jeep away from the curb just as a trooper approached from behind.

Karl looked at the long lines at the American Airlines ticket counters, then at his watch. There was plenty of time. If he waited a bit, the lines would go down, and he would have to spend less time standing with his new hip. He spotted a bench and walked over to sit down. As he turned to brush the seat, he noticed someone entering the terminal. The man was a stranger, but the face was burned into his mind. It was the Russian from the levada.

Karl turned away and tried to melt into the crowd. Think fast, he told himself. He looked back outside through the glass wall and spotted the trooper who had been about to shoo Lionel away. Suddenly inspired, Karl walked back out of the terminal. After making sure he was followed, Karl walked past the officer. With the Russian playing nonchalant to the hilt, Karl rushed the officer from behind, unsnapped the man's holster, and grabbed at the service revolver while shouting, "Look out, he has a gun." The Russian pulled a pistol from his jacket as Karl and the trooper wrestled over who actually had the handgun. Karl managed for just a moment to get the pistol pointed toward the Russian, who obediently played his part by preemptively firing at the two of them. Confident that the officer could handle it, Karl let go and bolted toward the parking garage.

He had overestimated Florida's finest almost as much as the Russian had underestimated Karl. Two shots were fired, and when Karl caught a glimpse over his shoulder, the police officer was down and the Russian was making a broken-field run through the crowd toward Karl. Karl, who could not yet run, walked as fast as he could into the car park.

Straight ahead, two cars were parked askew from the marked rows. One of them was Lionel's Jeep. Karl wasn't sure about the other car, but he recognized the driver, who stamped on the accelerator and headed straight for him. Karl panicked and dove out of the way, then heard gunshots behind him. He picked himself up awkwardly and looked back just in time to see Shira drive squarely into the Russian, throwing him backwards and then pinning him against a white Florida Cabletech van. She stepped out of the car holding Karl's Glock in front of her, pointed at the Russian, who was now slumped down against the side of the van.

Lionel squealed his tires, then slammed on his brakes as he stopped beside them. "Get in. I'll tell you the next scene as we get out of here."

"What about my mother's car."

"It will be reported stolen—very clever of me to think of that—and it will be recovered. Let the local police sort it out. But now, we are going to do the last thing they expect. We are going to head right back into the terminal and get you on the next flight to

London. By the time you land, I'll be back in touch with Lev, and we will have this whole piss-pot sorted out."

Karl nodded and said, "Thanks, Lionel, you're a good man, even if you write ghost stories." He grinned.

Shira was shaking her head. "Karl, aren't you forgetting something? We can't just leave Shoshi and Bini."

"Well, we sure as hell can't take them with us on the run."

Shira looked to be on the edge of tears, when suddenly the Jeep was surrounded by men in riot gear with "FBI" in white block letters on their jackets.

"Okay, everyone keep your hands in sight and exit the vehicle slowly."

Lionel raised his hands and fluttered his fingers. "Hey, you guys," he shouted. "Any one of you know how to open a damn car door from the inside while keeping your hands in sight?"

The nearest agent jerked the driver-side door open with his left hand while holding his assault rifle in the other. "All right, smart ass, out. On the ground, face down, hands behind your head." He looked into the Jeep. "Are you Lustig?"

"Yes, I'm Karl Lustig. These two had nothing to do with it."

"I don't know what the hell you are talking about. I have orders to evacuate you and your family."

"What about him?" Karl flicked his still raised hands toward Lionel, who was lying prone with his fat cheek against the stained concrete and his hands locked behind his head. "He didn't do anything. He just offered us a ride."

"We don't give a fuck about him, sir. Our orders cover only you and your wife. And him." He turned toward the Russian, who was just coming around. The agent shifted his assault rifle to his left hand, withdrew a pistol with a suppressor from a pouch, and shot the man twice in the head."

"What the fuck?" shouted Lionel.

The agent looked down at him, smiled at Karl and Shira, and said, "Shalom. Let's all get out of here." He hurried Karl and Shira toward the ramp to the next parking level while two of his partners helped Lionel back into his Jeep.

"Where to?" Karl asked their escort.

"Home." He handed them two passports and a ticket wallet. "Maybe we'll see you there sometime."

"We have to pick up our kids."

"They're already here, waiting for you in the Admirals Club."

"This was the plan all along?" Karl asked.

"I wouldn't know, sir. We're just doing our job. And now our job is to take care of the car and then disappear quickly. You just have to walk out the side entrance, back into the terminal, and go meet your kids. Have a nice flight." He saluted them, turned, and took off at a trot.

Karl's jaw dropped. "Holy shit. Do you realize who that was and what just happened here?"

"Yes, but I just want to go hug our kids."

Chapter
Thirty-Five

■ The Director hung up his secure telephone. "That's it. Yishai reports that the last of the teams under him have reported in. Everyone is down."

Anat looked up from her notepad. "Down?"

"Dead or in custody."

"Percentages?"

"A lot of them put up a fight. Some committed suicide. It was tough, but the news is not all bad. Karl's bodyguard was taken out by one of our teams doing some risky role playing, and Karl and his family were extracted. They should be on their way home,"—he glanced at his watch—"soon."

"You sent in a team after all."

"We remember our friends and our obligations. McCauliffe and the Americans conveniently looked the other way. As for the rest, we have a few in custody."

"I see. You weren't trying for prisoners. This is going to be one hell of a mess when it comes out, not just the whole chip compromise, but also this operation. And the compromise of Mossad and Aman with moles working deep inside. Anything else?"

The Director coughed. "It's not going to come out."

"It will, eventually. Count on it. There will be leaks and rumors."

"Trust me, by the time any of this story comes out, all of us will have been dead for decades."

"I don't think so. As soon as we start a recall on the chips or switch manufacturers or swap out systems in our jets—"

"You don't get it, Anat. Nothing is going to change. This was an inside job. It didn't start out that way, but that's how it went down. These were Israelis, not Chinese or Iranians. Think, Anat, how could something like this operate, how could it get so far? Yes, it was originally a small, rogue effort, but how exactly was it initiated? Where did they get the resources, the expertise?"

Anat tried to read his face. "You are saying this was an official program, that it was sanctioned."

"I haven't said anything. You are the one who is conjecturing. In any case, nothing changes, really. We will continue to make the best avionics and military electronics systems in the world, and the *goyim* will continue to do what they can to obtain them by whatever means they can. Some will sign deals with us at the front counter and others will bid behind the store for what has been siphoned off."

"But the chipsets will continue to flow and continue to have secret backdoor access."

"Look, no one has to remind us that we have many enemies in the region, Anat. For the moment, we have some military advantages on most of them. We are rumored to have a large and growing nuclear arsenal, never officially acknowledged, of course; we have the reputation of having the best air force in the region; and experience shows that Iron Dome is an effective anti-missile system, at least for short-range rockets. And we have us. With time, we may be able to drop their planes and missiles from the skies and stop their tanks and cripple their communications without firing a shot. That's how high the stakes are on this one."

"What about the Americans?"

"What about them? They sell arms, too. Everywhere and to everyone. And they are our friends as long as the right people are in Washington. The Americans do not need to know anything, will not know anything. If ever any of this leaks, there are plenty of avenues of plausible deniability, an entire herd of scapegoats to tie to a post in the desert if need be. In the meantime, nothing out of the ordinary has happened and nothing changes. The chipsets are produced, and they get spread around through channels and tunnels"

"This was all just a charade. You knew all along and you used us. We were just means to an end. What exactly was that end?"

"To sweep away the tracks of the caravan, to leave a pristine desert of featureless sand."

"No loose ends, right? Even if loyal patriots have to die. Or innocent and ignorant riders on the caravan." She stopped, thinking of Karl. "There are still people who know about the embedded backdoor."

"Yes, but they think it was a rogue operation now quelled. So, as I said, the tracks are covered." When Anat said nothing, he continued. "Look, I did not know from the beginning. I was used, too, told only what I needed to know to do a job: uncovering and neutralizing a rogue operation. It wasn't until I was ordered to stand down and take no further action that I knew the whole story. Or what I now understand as the whole story. None of us ever knows for certain; in this business none of us is ever fully trusted."

Anat stood and held herself with an air of formality. "That's it, then. I can't do this anymore. I resign, effective immediately."

"Are you sure you want to do that? There is so much that you can still do. You are privy to inner workings in ways that few are. You have become a trusted member of an inner, inner circle. There are only four of us."

"Dror?"

The Director laughed. "Dror Magen is just Dror Magen. Competent, but more ambitious than capable."

"What about his briefing folder, with a picture of Ricardo Baruch Mendonça, the guy who tried to kill me?"

"Who? Oh, you must be talking about that Monchu character, someone Dror's East Asia people were watching."

"So not Dror. I still know only three. How much trust is that?"

"You know all of us. You see the fourth member of our little cadre frequently, even if not in person, at least on television. He's the one holding the defense portfolio. Now do you understand?"

"Oh, yes. I understand. And I resign."

"As a civilian, you know you will be extremely dangerous to us. The last grain of trust is blown away."

"I'll have to live with that. Others have. An old friend of Lev's, Shira's first husband, showed the way. Maybe this was all fated when I married Lev."

"Nonsense. Fate is just another name for developments we haven't yet deciphered. I still advise you not to quit, and I remind you that you are bound to absolute secrecy whatever you do, wherever you go"

"It goes without saying, sir. Good luck in dealing with our fourth co-conspirator. And with whoever happens to hold that portfolio in the future." She turned sharply, somehow driven to savor the drama of the moment with a decisive exit but also already thinking of Lev and a future life in bright light and deep shadow.

Chapter
Thirty-Six

■ With the cabin lights still dimmed in the Israel-bound plane and Shoshi asleep beside her, Shira leaned out across the aisle and took Karl's hand. She nodded toward Bini who had just drifted off again next to Karl, his head cocked back, mouth open. "He's not a little boy anymore, except when he sleeps."

Karl turned to look. "He reminds me so much of his father."

She glanced at Bini, then Karl. "He does take after you."

"No, I meant his father. He looks so much like that quirky, cocky college kid I knew a few centuries ago, a young man standing on the edge of adventure."

"You're his father. It's you Bini talks about all the time, you he emulates. He so looks up to you. You're the reason he wants to go into intelligence work. He doesn't remember Migdal—he was six then—and he doesn't even know many of the stories."

Karl searched her face as if looking for confirmation of what she was telling him. "I thought Bini was embarrassed by me. He's always ragging on me about not having a 'real' job, making cracks about my white hair and wrinkles and—"

"He rags on me, too, but you're the one who is his hero. You always have been."

"Well, maybe he needs to expand his definition of hero. You pulled off some amazing escapades on this trip."

"Maybe. But if escapades are what taking holidays without the kids entails," she said, "I think I will take a pass next time."

"What? You don't like traveling on adrenaline?"

"No. It' scary."

"Educational. That's what I would say: more enlightening than frightening."

"Ha, ha. And what did you learn, my intrepid, well-tutored traveler?"

"That it's truly time to retire. That friends and family are more important than all the rest of life summed together, that sometimes we do not really know even our own family."

He lifted the packet of letters, once more neatly tied up with the same faded satin ribbon. "For me, this has been the biggest education of all: reading my mother's story. It's like reading a novel where you know the last page before you begin the prologue. I mean, here I am, living testimony to the fact that she made it. She saved herself—and me. I knew how it all came out, but I didn't know how it happened. What kept me turning the pages, reading the letters, was wanting to know how. How did she make it? How is it that she survived and that I am here, today, to live my life with you and Bini and Shoshi?"

"She never looked back."

"And neither have I."

"Not so, dear love."

"What do you mean? I am just like my mother. Julianna, I mean, of course. I never knew Chana."

Shira leaned closer to catch his eye. "And what have you been doing? What are you doing now? Looking back."

"I never thought of it quite like that. How odd. I'm only now, so late in my own story, breaking with a long family tradition, a tradition on both sides of the family to separate from our past. Strange how that came about."

"Strange? Inevitable."

Karl looked down at the packet of letters resting in his lap. "She was a mystery, a puzzle."

"And she raised a son to thrive on mysteries and puzzles. And left behind a packet of mysteries and puzzles waiting for him to solve. Surprise!"

"It's that Fate business again, isn't it. Predestined, everything all written out in advance. The moving finger writes and having writ . . . *Bashert*. All of it: fated. You truly believe that."

"I do. She left those letters for you, Karl. She primed you with her life as a blank screen. Tell me—tell yourself—that this is merely an accident."

"You are the mystic, Shira."

"And you the rationalist, the realist. And here we are, together, united by our pasts, bound by the choices of people long dead. And now, today, you are a Jew, returning with me to the Jewish homeland. For the first time. Do you realize that, Mosje Manczyk? Do you now understand, Karl Lustig? You are, for the very first time, returning to Israel as a Jew, completing a circuitous journey across continents and generations, started by your mother when she was only a young girl in Poland."

"So now I am a Jew and before I was not? Why? Because now we know I had a Jewish mother? Did my friend, Mitchell Rossing, who brought us together in the first place, did he have a Jewish mother? Was he a Jew after he changed his name to Migdal but not before? Or was it because he gave his life for a Jewish country? To your mother, it was not until after he was gone and I came into your life that she acknowledged him as a Jew.

"And what kind of a Jew was he? A devout non-believer who was a Jew by virtue of a year of study that was part of his cover for a Mossad operation and by virtue of a conversion ritual in which he himself did not believe. Now I am a Jew because of ancestry that could never be proved and a rule of descent that I decline to legitimize. How easy and how hard it is to become a Jew."

"You are, Karl Lustig, the most infuriatingly rational man I have ever loved. Doesn't it mean something to you to find out you are Jewish? Doesn't it feel different now that you know? Do you understand?"

"Yes. It is different, and no, I don't understand."

Somehow this seemed to please Shira, who suddenly beamed. "You know, Lev and Anat are meeting us at the airport."

"Yeah, I know."

"We shall have to all say *Shehechiyanu* together. A blessing for a first: your return as a Jew."

"All right, already. Shehechiyanu it is. And you can call me a Jew now. But no surgery."

Shira laughed quietly. "No, no more surgery required. I love you just as you are, my love, bits of flesh intact and masses of metal and ceramic embedded."

"Speaking of carving, there is something I want to show you and something else we must do when we get back up to Haifa."

"What is that?"

He reached into his jacket pocket. "We have to put up this." He handed her a small, irregular piece of wood, carved and polished to bring out the grain.

"It's lovely, but what is it?"

"A mezuzah, see the *shin*. I made it from the 4,000-year-old piece I retrieved from the bogs in England. While I was hiding out with Lionel I had time on my hands, so he lent me his Dremel tools. I—"

He was interrupted by the seatbelt sign coming on, announcements in Hebrew and English, and the ordered chaos of flight attendants completing preparations for landing. All the activity awakened Shoshi, who was fairly bouncing with excitement in her seat. Beside Karl, Bini, exhausted by late nights with his new American friends, stirred only briefly when Karl pushed the button to bring the seat back upright. Within minutes Bini was back asleep, head bowed.

Karl reached carefully past his sleeping son to raise the window shade partway. The plane banked for the approach into Ben Gurion airport, giving Karl a glimpse of the sunlit coast of Israel: the Homeland, his home.

Epilogue

■ Shawn McCauliffe took the exit off the George Washington Parkway a bit too fast as always, braking smartly and lowering his window as he rolled up to the gate at Langley. He had his identification out and ready before the marine guard even asked.

The guard took his badge, made a telephone call from the booth, and returned. "Could I ask you to pull over there, sir, and wait in your car for an escort."

It was a game. McCauliffe smiled to himself. It was always a game. The DCI was expecting him, and his authority came directly from the top, but there were these little ceremonial niceties that had to be observed—the double-checks, the escort, the extra pat-down—the pretenses that he was not fully an insider. Even here—especially here with the Director of Central Intelligence—the masquarade was maintained.

Outside the Director's office, he was told the DCI was unavailable at the moment but he could wait. He smiled and acted the part of a privileged but undistinguished visitor until the DCI, by reputation a punctilious clockwatcher, arrived a few pointed minutes late. Another part of the pantomime.

McCauliffe was ushered into the office, offered coffee, which he declined, and the door was shut.

The Director leaned back in his Aeron chair, opened his hands, and said, "And?"

"And nothing." McCauliffe spoke quietly, with an emphatic resonance that gave weight to his words, but his eyes never stopped their slow, furtive scanning as if he were on alert—which he always was. "The Israelis did the work for us, just as I said they would, without asking and without ever knowing precisely what they were doing."

"But, of course, and they were playing us every bit as much as they were being played. Any tracks left in the sand?"

"Not a trace. And nothing to tie back to our own independents. It was a textbook operation, just what I would expect from Aman and Mossad."

"You have more faith in them than I do."

"I have no faith, not in anyone or anything, for that matter. But I understand and respect professionalism and predictability."

"So, the pipelines are still flowing and the shutoff valves are well oiled?"

McCauliffe smiled again. Even here, the allusions, the coded references. It was a job to McCauliffe, but the DCI seemed to enjoy this sort of thing. "Yes, everything works, as we confirmed with the flight over the Negev." Something ambiguous flashed over his face. "We had to test it under operational conditions."

"Yes, of course. And, the Israelis? What do they know?"

"That depends on who is asking and who is being asked. At the very top some know that we collaborated in Operation Inholding. As to our having the codes and the additional functionality of our own design? No."

"All in all, an excellent plan, brilliantly executed, McCauliffe."

"It was not my plan, merely my accident. Sure, it was my idea in the first place, and my suggestion we collaborate with the Israelis on the technology, as we did with Operation Olympic Games and Stuxnet. But I didn't expect they would be quite so resourceful and efficient putting the backdoor in place. Typically they are as burdened by political anxiety and bureaucratic inertia as we are."

"In the end it was costly, though, and I am not talking about dollars or shekels. Do you think it was worth it?"

"That's not my call, sir. I think it serves as a kind of technological detente that is sorely needed in the modern world, but I'm neither a military strategist nor a political analyst. I think it's one more arrow in our quiver—and the Israelis'. At least until it is exposed, at which point it's entirely their arrow. It will be obvious that it was their baby, their off-the-reservation ops that pulled it off, and their decision not to kill production once they knew."

"Well, wherever credit belongs, you did good work, McCauliffe. So what is next for you? Ready for another special assignment?"

"With all due respect, sir, I'm thinking of packing it in, taking early retirement."

"Had enough, have you?"

"It's not that, sir. I'd like to have more time with my boys. Theo is already in high school; he's going to be gone in a few years. And I'd like to write a book."

"You and every other agent. Don't forget, any manuscript has to be vetted."

"Oh, I know the drill, sir. But I'm not thinking of writing a spy story. The real money these days is in zombie apocalypse and end-times thrillers."

■ ■ ■ ■ ■ ■

If you liked this novel, don't miss the rest of the books in The Homeland Connection

Bashert ▪ *The Dome* ▪ *Web Games*